With a Kiss I Die

With a Kiss I Die

A Novel of the Massacre at Mountain Meadows

Rod Miller

FIVE STAR
A part of Gale, a Cengage Company

Five Star Publishing, a part of Gale, a Cengage Company

LIBRARY OF CONGRESS CATALOGING-IN-PUBLICATION DATA

Names: Miller, Rod, 1952– author.
Title: With a kiss I die : a novel of the Massacre at Mountain Meadows / Rod Miller.
Description: First edition. | Waterville, Maine : Five Star, a part of Gale, a Cengage Company 2022. | Series: FIVE STAR Western | Identifiers: LCCN 2022007885 | ISBN 9781432895808 (hardcover)
Classification: LCC PS3613.I55264 W58 2022 | DDC 813/.6—dc23
LC record available at https://lccn.loc.gov/2022007885

First Edition. First Printing: October 2022
Find us on Facebook—https://www.facebook.com/FiveStarCengage
Visit our website—http://www.gale.cengage.com/fivestar
Contact Five Star Publishing at FiveStar@cengage.com

Printed in Mexico
Print Number : 1 Print Year : 2023

Dedicated to my friends Richard Turley
and the late Will Bagley,
who know, and knew, the facts of the matter.

ROMEO. Under love's heavy burden do I sink.

—William Shakespeare,
Romeo and Juliet, act 1, scene 4

JULIET. Prodigious birth of love it is to me,
That I must love a loathed enemy.

—William Shakespeare,
Romeo and Juliet, act 1, scene 5

ROMEO. Thus with a kiss I die.

—William Shakespeare,
Romeo and Juliet, act 5, scene 3

Prologue

Like an irregular, ridged, pitted bowl, the Great Basin dropped into the heart of the Intermountain West as if cast off, discarded as imperfect, by its potter. The shallow dish fills the land between the Sierra Nevada range on the west and the Wasatch mountains and plateaus in the east; from the rim of the Snake River drainage in the north where streams make their way to the Columbia and the Pacific Ocean, and south to the desert divide beyond which the waters that feed the Colorado River seek the Sea of Cortez.

But the Great Basin has no outlet. The liquids that fall within it are left to darken the soil, then soak and seep into the earth below or evaporate into the harsh, dry skies above, unseen and unknown to the world beyond.

It is, then, perhaps fortuitous that the place known as Mountain Meadows on the Old Spanish Trail, the southern road to California, lies just beyond the rim of the Great Basin. If not, a matter of mere rods, a few footsteps, may have meant the blood spilled there on 11 September 1857 would drown in the dirt of the Great Basin; forever hidden away, covered up in the soils of the secretive, sacred sinkhole of the Latter-day Saints who claimed the Basin as a homeland, protected within its confines from the persecution—and wickedness—of the United States they had fled.

Rather than contained, the blood, like the scant waters of Magotsu Creek, would dribble away from the killing field to slowly, ever so slowly, reach the consciousness of the nation. Following a different, but likewise reluctant, route than that of the sluggish stream, word of the horrific slaughter there would make its way out of Mountain Meadows. And, just as Magotsu Creek finds the Santa Clara River, the Rio Virgin, the Colorado River, and *Mar Pacifico,* the peaceful ocean, reports of the massacre would reach the *Los Angeles Star,* the *San Francisco Bulletin,* the U.S. Army, the Congress, and, in time, the United States District Court.

But, like shallow waters in the dry climate of the territory of Utah, the truth of the matter dispersed and dissipated and evaporated before fully told. The whole story of the Massacre at Mountain Meadows is forever lost to the ages.

Chapter One

Beller's Stand, Arkansas, April 1857

Campfires and cook fires burned low around the meadow and into the verge of the woods, reflected light glowing warm on the canvas covers of wagons parked in clusters. The brightest light flickered and danced from a bonfire across the meadow. Sparks rose in a stream, defying gravity to seek a place among the stars that salted an otherwise dark sky. Knots of men stood and sat and squatted and sprawled, silhouetted against the pyre. Jugs stoppered with cobs passed from hand to hand and mouth to mouth. Shared stories and ribald jokes raised laughter here and there. Somewhere, a fiddle bow sawed mournful tunes, accompanied by the twang of a jaw harp. Elsewhere, banjo strings plinked and plucked out the melodies and harmonies of deep woods ditties. Rings of men cheered on arm wrestlers and grapplers and others testing their strength. Raised voices and arguments boiled up more and more often as night deepened and liquor went shallow in the jugs.

Polly Alden watched from afar, the distance across the park lengthened by darkness. She sat, sound sleep eluding her, wrapped in a shawl and propped against the rear wheel of a wagon, a diary and stub of a pencil in her lap. The blank book was a gift from her schoolteacher, given in parting with a wish for Polly, her erstwhile star student, to "jot down the feelings of your heart, your thoughts, your memories, as well as the happenings of your days." But the diary held only two entries in

Polly's careful script—a tear-blotched note recording the death of her family, and another on being taken in by the Baker family for the pending journey to the far-off land of California.

For the next months—five of them, she was told—the wagon she lazed against would be her home as it made its way west. Wagons gathered at this place in springtime, forming trains for the trip west as families flowed toward opportunity, as relentless as water seeking the sea. But Polly, orphaned and left homeless by a fever that scoured her household of all save her, had no family and no prospects, and so sought deliverance from Captain John Baker, an acquaintance of her late father and an important man in Crooked Creek Township.

Baker offered her passage and a chance at a new life in exchange for labor—a situation not much different from the slaves the family held in servitude. Along with family and household, Baker would be taking a herd of cattle to populate a hoped-for ranch in California. His herd, joined on the trail with the stock of other emigrants, required drovers and Captain Baker had employed five young men for the crew, one of which was his son and another a slave he owned. It would be Polly's job to cook for those herders, launder and repair their garments, tend camp, and treat their illnesses and injuries. The hired hands and the girl would, for all practical purposes, form something of a family for the duration. It was that pending responsibility, a heavy burden for a young woman looking ahead to her fifteenth birthday, that robbed her of sleep.

Tonight, her charges, like most men in the camps most nights, relieved the monotony and boredom of waiting with festivities at the bonfire.

The patchwork of noise from around the distant fire faded as Polly drowsed, but she snapped back to wakefulness when her chin dropped to her chest. She squirmed to a more comfortable position against the wagon wheel and tightened the woolen wrap around her shoulders. A scream interrupted her next fade toward oblivion. She looked toward the bonfire but could see only the shapes and shadows of men moving against the flames, all darting across the light in the same direction.

In the dancing light of the fire, the screaming man cupped a hand to capture the blood that poured from a knife wound slashed deep across his forearm, nearly severing the member. Swaying on wavering legs unhinged by shock and alcohol, he watched the viscous crimson liquid overspill to the ground. He screamed again as he watched his own knife fall from its grip at the end of the wounded arm, then abandoned the attempt to capture his life as it drained away, shaking off the handful of blood and swiping at his shirtfront to clean the hand of the residue. Dropping to his knees, his all-but-amputated fighting arm weak and useless at his side, he reached across his body with the off hand, still slippery with blood, and pulled a pistol from his waistband.

"Fritz!" someone shouted. "Don't do it! Fritz!"

The man named Fritz did not hear, or did not listen. He raised the pistol toward the stars, its wobbling muzzle tracing constellations among them as he struggled to draw back the hammer.

"Fritz!"

The stained and dripping knife still in his white-knuckled grip, the man who had bloodied Fritz stared wide-eyed at his kneeling opponent.

"Fritz! No!"

The shout had no effect on Fritz as he struggled with the gun, but it jolted the winning knife fighter out of his stupor. He looked anew at the gun barrel now coming to bear, glanced at the bloody blade in his hand, and rushed forward.

Charged with buck and ball, the Prussian percussion pistol stopped his advance when the hammer snapped down to pop the cap and ignite the powder, lead erupting from the explosion to pulverize flesh, shatter ribs, and shred heart and lung before obscuring its victim in a cloud of pungent white smoke.

Haze dissipated to reveal the shooter lying on his side, all life drained away through the arm cut to the bone. The winner of the knife fight lay on his back, arms spread to his sides, the weapon still in his hand, his chest a mire of gore. Unseeing eyes reflected pinpoints of light from the sky and the flicker of the bonfire, his life blown away in a powder flash the instant the gun turned his victory to loss.

The unexpected violence paralyzed the emigrants for days. There had been fights aplenty, for certain, what with hot-blooded men fueled by whiskey and boredom. But no one anticipated that the brawling and mauling would lead to death. And to lose two lives to senseless savagery at once lowered a pall over the camps. The bonfire still burned at night, but it illuminated fewer men, and they were subdued and solemn. Arriving travelers wondered at the somber mood in the meadow, and were themselves dumbfounded by whispered reports of the grotesque deaths.

Still, preparations for the road went on apace. Men exchanged ideas and philosophies, shared information, and listened to reports from the experienced travelers among them. Almost to a man, they believed themselves able and equipped to make the trip with less difficulty than those who went before; sure to arrive in California with the wherewithal to settle into the new land and grow rich from its bounty.

They formed and abandoned alliances, elected and rejected leaders, organized and disorganized trains, and waited for the appointed day—an appointment turned disappointment again and again as grass inched towards its ability to sustain traveling cattle, horses, and mules. Frustration grew and tempers sometimes flared as the emigrants waited on the collective wisdom to finally determine the time to be right, when, one by one, the wagons would find their places in the chosen companies and roll away from the past and toward the future.

Polly relieved the tedium of the tiresome days of waiting by visiting the camp circles, seeking advice and wisdom from older women, and companionship and diversion from the younger women and older girls. She came to know Huffs and Mitchells, Dunlapps and Prewitts, Poteets and Tackitts and Joneses, Camerons and Millers, and other families leaving Marion, Crawford, Carroll, Benton, and Johnson Counties.

The women held no sway in the making of plans, but talked of what they heard from their men. Polly took comfort—and pride—in knowing that her benefactor, Captain John Baker, had gained the respect of many and was emerging as a leader. Another man, called Colonel Alexander Fancher, likewise gained stature and attracted followers. He carried with him the benefit of experience, having twice traveled to California, driving cattle there to feed the booming population of miners, and he and his kin had already established ranching operations there and registered a brand in Tulare County to identify their herds.

"The Fanchers now, they know whereof they speak," one woman said. "The colonel has been out there to Californy already."

"It's true," another woman said. "Made hisself a packet off from beef. Them Fanchers has money to burn—only that you can't burn gold."

And another, "I'm told them wagons of theirs has false bottoms, underneath of which is hid that gold."

And yet another, "Only it ain't 'Fancher' like you-all are a-sayin'. Out of their mouths, it's '*Fawn-sheer*.' Right uppity, if'n you ask me."

Then, "Still and all, if he knows the trail, which he does, there's no reason on God's green earth not to follow the colonel's tracks."

And, "I ain't sayin' it ain't so—but I also say, like as it says in the Good Book, 'Pride goeth before destruction, and an haughty spirit before a fall.' Them Fanchers and Bakers ain't the end-all and be-all, no matter if them and some others might think so. My man will be keepin' his own counsel, and you-all—all you-all's menfolks, that is—would be wise to do the same."

"Your man would do well to follow the lead of Colonel Fancher—"

"—Or *Fawnsheer,* if you please—"

"—he got all what he's got by bein' a step ahead of most."

"The same can be said of Captain Baker."

"Them two didn't get where they got by bein' thick headed and spiteful."

The road the Arkansas emigrants would follow west, such as it was, was called the Cherokee Trail, so named for having been blazed by people of that tribe lusting after California gold in days gone by. The path went north by northwest out of Arkansas to reach Hickory Bluffs and cross the Verdigris—*Verdigree*—River, then cross the bottom of Kansas to join up with the Santa Fe Trail. That well-worn road along the Arkansas River pointed the way west to Bent's Fort. There, the Arkansawyers would leave the trade route to continue west along the river to the abandoned *El Pueblo* trading post, then make a hard right turn to the north and follow an old trapper's trail along the face of the Rocky Mountains. These emigrants would leave the track of the Cherokee Trail on the Laramie Plains. Rather than turn west toward reported shortages of grass and water on the Red Desert, they would continue north until joining the main overland trails to cross the Continental Divide at South Pass. After passing Fort Bridger and on to the relatively settled environs of Salt Lake City, the road crossed yet another desert to follow the Humboldt—what passed for a river in the deserts of the Great Basin—then over the Sierra and on to California.

At least that was how the trip mapped out in the minds of Captain Baker and Colonel Fancher. Polly Alden and the rest of the ensemble of emigrants awaiting departure at Beller's Stand—save a few other experienced sojourners—lacked any real alternative to following their lead. Fate would intervene at Salt Lake City and Captain Baker and Colonel Fancher and their followers would find themselves on a late-season detour that would lead to an altogether different place.

But that was far away in the future and unknown, even uncontemplated. So the trains pulled out when the grass allowed. For days, then weeks, Polly walked beside her wagon, following wherever the trail led. The unaccustomed long walking, bookended and interrupted by camp duties, wearied her so that she gave nary a thought to the diary tucked into her folded bedding. But she grew accustomed to the travel and her chores became routine, and one evening after washing up the supper dishes, she took the book to hand, opened its pages, and rolled the stub of pencil across her tongue.

I do not know where I am. Somewhere in Indian Territory I think, or maybe Kansas. Since the Cherokee settlement, there has been no trace of people here except those in our train and the ones sometimes before and sometimes after us. I guess by now I am getting used to what life has become and can now end the days able to do more than roll into my blankets and sleep. The weariness has pushed aside thoughts of my lost family and the sorrow has faded some.

I feel to write something of my station. Since losing mother and father I have been taken in by father's friend Captain Baker and that is why I am here, wherever that is. Which does not matter only to say somewhere on the way to

California. With the wagons are a hundred, maybe a thousand of all manner of cows, some of which belong to Captain Baker. My boys—I call them my boys but all but one are older than me—help herd the cows and have been given to my care while on the trail. We arise before the sun and I boil a mess of porridge or mush and cook a skillet of bacon, then send them on their way to see to their cows. They are quiet in the mornings, tired out I guess from the sleep missed when taking turns herding at night. They are always on the lookout for Indians but we have seen none for some time and those friendly enough.

A word about my boys as I call them. They are five in my care. One is the son of Captain Baker and sometimes eats with his family. He is aged 17 and given his name is Baker he fancies himself first among the boys. His given name is Abel and he goes by Abe. Also of the Bakers is a darky called Trajan. He is a good boy of 13 years and he misses his mammy who was left behind in Carroll County with some of the Baker kin. Howard is 16. He is sweet on me but I shun his advances. He shies away from wash water and I suspect he would refuse a bath if one were offered. His lips and chin are stained with the tobacco he chews at all times and it has likewise discolored his remaining teeth of which there are but a few. At last I come to Billy of which there are two. Billy Red and Billy Brown as I call them, on account of their hair color. Those names have been taken up by others and the boys do not seem to mind. Billy Red is 14 years old as am I and a pleasant young man with always a smile on his freckled face and a ready laugh. Billy Brown is as quiet as Billy Red is not. He is the oldest, aged 18 years, and is impatient to reach Calif where he intends to find riches in the goldfields if there is any more money to be made there, he says.

Chapter Two

Kansas Plains, three weeks later

Polly Alden awakened in fits and starts, roused repeatedly from slumber by the clink and rattle of trace chains, the chunk and split of ax blades slicing kindling wood, the nicker of horses, and the clank and clatter of pots and pans. Throwing off the blanket, she slid her dress over her head, hands and arms seeking sleeve holes, then pulled the fabric down over her chemise to bunch at the waist. She performed much the same motion with feet and legs, pulling a limp petticoat up her legs and over her pantalets. She lifted her backside to pull the petticoat above her waist and the dress below. Tugging on socks and dusty shoes, she folded her legs under and rose to her knees and crawled to the back of the wagon, reaching over to free the latches and lower the end gate. Sliding out and dropping to the ground, she took a moment to straighten her dress, freeing it from the friction of the undergarments, then tied on an apron and tucked her unruly hair beneath a sunbonnet.

By the time she stoked the coals in the fire and fed it kindling to raise a flame, Trajan came carrying in one hand a wooden pail holding the paltry amount of milk he had been able to coax out of the milk cow, and a bucket of water in the other.

"Thank you, Trajan."

The boy nodded. "Jus' doin' my job, Miss Polly."

She smiled, and Trajan ducked his head, wondered what to do with his empty hands, then turned and walked away. Polly poured water into a coffeepot and hung it from the pothook on the frame over the fire where the flames licked its bottom. She fitted the lid onto the milk pail, and carried it to the wagon. She folded her bedding and stowed it and put the milk pail in its place in the corner, and shifted things around in the wagon to leave room for the kitchen boxes, camp equipment, and the boys' bedrolls.

Back at the fire, steam shot out the spout on the coffeepot. Polly wrapped her hand in a rag and pulled it away from the flames, then lifted the lid, dropped in a measure of grounds, replaced the cover, and set the pot near enough the fire to stay hot as it steeped. When it was time to pour, she would splash in a bit of cold water to settle the grounds.

Coffee, and corn pone left over from the night before, would be the only sustenance for now for Polly and the boys. Similar fare would refresh the emigrants in other wagons. After a few hours of travel, the wagons would stop to allow the draft animals to rest and relieve themselves. Then, the cooks would fix a more substantial breakfast.

But, for now, it was hot coffee. And the boys were eager to get it. As they came in—the two Billys from the last shift on night herd, Howard from saddling mounts for the day, Trajan from yoking the oxen and hitching them to the wagon, and Abe from meeting with his father for the day's marching orders—Polly filled an enamel mug for each, and passed out pones to gnaw on.

Howard fingered the cud of tobacco out of his cheek and flung it away as Polly poured his coffee. Wiping the slime from his hand on a pant leg, he took the cup and the corn pone she offered and sat down on a kitchen box. He dipped the stiff bread into the steaming cup and let it soak, then sucked the liquid from the pone before biting off the softened bit. He worked his cheeks and tongue, moving the mush around, the wad visible more often than not in his open mouth. Satisfied he had got all the flavor out of it, he swallowed the mass and washed it down with a slurp of coffee.

"Darn good coffee this morning."

Polly looked up when he spoke, but said nothing.

"A man could get used to bein' waited on by you."

Again, Polly did not reply.

"Fact is, I'm of a mind to take you on permanent. You could see to my needs every day—and night." Howard punctuated the talk with a smile that revealed his brown and yellow teeth, as well as the gaps left by those that had abandoned his mouth.

Polly snapped to attention, her face showing its blush in the firelight, wide eyes staring at Howard.

"Well, whaddya say, Polly? You wanna be my woman?" The snaggly smile grew even wider as Howard reveled in his cleverness.

"No, Howard. I don't," came the reply, so soft it barely covered the distance.

"Aw, c'mon. I'd fit right fine in that wagon beside you."

"Leave her alone."

"Well, now! Who died and made you king, Abe Baker?"

"Just leave her alone."

"Or what?"

Billy Red and Billy Brown rose as one.

"You heard what he said," Billy Brown said.

"And you had best pay attention, or you'll be sorry," said Billy Red.

Howard's smile, now a tight-lipped sneer, looked from one to the other. His gaze settled on Trajan, sitting off to the side, coffee mug cradled in interlaced fingers. "How 'bout you, boy? You gonna take up ag'in me too?"

Trajan took a deep breath, but said nothing, his eyes fixed on the coffee in his cup.

"Well, boy, what you got to say?"

Now, Polly spoke. "Howard, leave him alone! There is no cause for you to bother Trajan." She looked from one of her boys to the other. "My job is to cook for you-all and launder your clothes. Nothing more." She looked at Howard. "*Nothing* more."

Howard tossed what was left of his corn pone into the fire, stirring up a shower of sparks. He tossed out the coffee in his cup and, as he stood, threw the mug to the ground in the general direction of the washtub. By the time it stopped bouncing and rolling, he was on his way.

Polly and the others watched him walk away, arms stiff at his sides, fists clenched. After a time, Abe Baker spoke. "Polly, Pa says firewood is near used up and there'll be little to find from here on. He says as you walk along, fetch up as many chips as you can. We'll sling a canvas under the wagon to hold them."

"Chips? What's that?"

Abe's weight shifted from one foot to the other. He hooked his thumbs into his braces, then pulled them out and let his hands fall free. His jaws clenched and he pursed his lips and a flush crept up his neck, then face. He plucked off his hat and swiped at his hair, then plopped the hat back onto his head. "It's . . . well, I . . . what it is, is . . ."

Billy Red giggled. "Chips ain't nothin' but, well, y'know, poop! From buffalos or maybe cattle."

Polly's brow furrowed like a tobacco patch and her blush rivaled Abe's. "You mean like we've been seeing on the ground? And I . . . I am supposed to pick it up?"

Again, Billy Red laughed. "Aw, it ain't a-goin' to hurt you none. Ain't never been nothin' to it but grass and water. 'Sides, it's all dried out—leastways I wouldn't advise you to pick up any that ain't."

"But what's it for?"

Abe stepped in, clearing his throat and removing his hat and cradling it against his chest. "The kid's right about what it is, Polly. Chips is what they call it—buffalo chips. Pa says some call it 'prairie wood' or maybe 'buffalo wood.' It makes a fire when you haven't any wood."

Polly thought it over as she went about stowing the camp equipment and dousing the fire. The woods were long since behind them, and even the isolated clumps of trees as the forests gave way to grassy plains had become scarce. The only trees of any account out here were along streams or streambeds, and even then only sometimes. But dung was plentiful in places, marking the paths of migrating or feeding herds of buffalo—although she had yet to see any of the animals.

As she walked beside the wagon that morning, she soon grew accustomed to picking up the clumps of buffalo dung and carrying them in the loop of her upheld apron skirt, then emptying it into the sling under the wagon. When the train hove to for breakfast and to rest the animals, she dumped an apron load of chips onto the ground and determined to give the new fuel a try, so as to grow accustomed to its use and not find herself caught short when all the wood was gone.

She took a spade and shoveled out a hole in the sod. A few handfuls of twisted dried grass made the tinder for the fire, and she set it alight with a phosphorous match. Imagining you would make a fire with chips much as you would with wood, she broke a clump apart, revealing the darker, dried dung beneath the sun-bleached surface. She crumbled it further, feeding small bits onto the flaming tinder. The chips smoked, but did not flare up. Polly coaxed the fire to life, leaning in and blowing. She huffed and puffed until lightheaded, then fanned the smoldering heap with her apron as she added fuel. Now and then tendrils of flame flared, but soon retreated back into the smoldering chips.

With a shrug, Polly realized the chips would not burn like wood, but their smoldering heat was intense. The time spent kindling the fire forced her to hurry with preparations for breakfast. She stabbed the iron stakes of the cooking rack into the ground and propped the rod with its pothooks over the fire. She filled the coffeepot and a kettle with water and hung them from the hooks, then set a short-legged metal grate at the edge of the fire and put a frying pan on to heat. While she waited for the water to boil, she unwrapped a flitch of bacon, sliced off thick slabs and laid them in the skillet, then went about setting out the other food and utensils.

While waiting for the bacon to sizzle, the water in the kettle boiled. She tossed in a few handfuls of rice and gave it a stir. She rummaged through a kitchen box and found raisins. When the rice was almost cooked, Polly added the raisins and stirred them in to plump and soften. After removing the rice from the fire and draining off most of the water, she used the blunt edge of a knife to scrape sugar off a cone into the pot and gave it a stir. She spooned up a bit and blew it cool, tasted it, and scratched off more sugar—every one of the boys had a sweet tooth, and she indulged their tastes whenever possible. To top off the dish, she splashed in some milk, then hung the kettle near enough the fire to stay warm.

Polly measured cornmeal into a bowl, added salt, then mixed a stiff dough with boiling water from the coffeepot. Setting aside the bowl, she added coffee grounds to the remaining water in the coffeepot and set it to steep, forked the crisp bacon onto a plate, then spooned the cornmeal dough into the hot grease to fry up a batch of pones. As she fiddled with the little cakes, the boys drifted in. Each accepted the plate she offered—rashers of bacon, a heap of corn pones, and a big dollop of the rice pudding. The boys who remembered their manners gave Polly a polite "thank you"; beyond that, they said nothing except to request more coffee and ask for seconds and thirds until the food was gone. Between tending to the boys, Polly ate the same fare, finding it plain but filling, and judged it as good as the breakfasts served up at other wagons.

Howard, who said not a word throughout the meal, dropped his empty plate, cup, and fork to the ground with a clatter and huffed away. The other boys sought out a box or wagon wheel to lean against and sat, or lay down on the ground to rest until Captain Baker called out orders to ready the train and the herd to again take up the trail. Only Polly and Howard were active—she cleaning up after breakfast, he off away from the fire making some small repair to his saddle with awl, knife, and whang leather.

"It might do to keep a sharp eye on Howard," Abe said in a voice so soft Polly strained to hear.

"I do not think he will give me any trouble."

"Still and all, I think it best not to find yourself alone with him. He has his eye on you, and I do not think his upbringing is such that he will show you the respect you deserve."

Polly blushed, and went back to her work.

"He gives you any trouble, I'll clean his plow," said a muffled voice from beneath the hat over Billy Red's face.

Abe laughed. "Billy, you best be careful. Howard's got a few years and several pounds on you. Don't bite off more than you can chew."

Billy Red sat upright and tipped his hat back with a forefinger. "Aw, hell—'scuse my language, Miss Alden—he don't scare me none."

From the shade of the wagon, Billy Brown pitched in. "If he lays a finger on Red or gives Polly any trouble, he'll have me to deal with."

Trajan, perched atop the stacked yokes from his ox teams,

followed the conversation. He had his own thoughts on the subject, but chose to keep them to himself.

Chapter Three

As the trains wended their way across the plains, Polly came to know that while they were in a wild, isolated country, it was far from a wilderness and they were far from alone. The other wagon trains that left Arkansas when they had were still in the vicinity—the wagons led by Alexander Fancher, as well as other trains—sometimes behind them on the trail and other times ahead. Other wagons that had set out from Missouri and other points east also followed the same trail. Now and then wagons would leave the Baker circle to join others, and new families and wagons would join up with their train—membership in one camp or another was ever-changing as the wagons rolled.

And there was ample evidence of other travelers on the Cherokee Trail. Wagon ruts braided the prairie, stretching the road wide. Skeletons of broken and abandoned wagons, pilfered for any useful parts and pieces, hunkered along the trailside. Discarded furniture and household goods littered the plain, some weathered and rusted, some cast aside this season.

Polly stopped one afternoon to study a recently jettisoned iron cookstove, well used but serviceable—at least it had been before others had relieved it of its burner lids, regulator knobs, ash grate, and even the oven door. She forced open a stuck broiler drawer and found a bellows and two kitchen knives stowed inside. She pumped the bellows handles and felt air gush from the nozzle. *That will save my breath come fire-lighting time.* She quick-stepped back to the wagon and tossed the bellows and knives over the end gate, prodded the oxen into motion, and rejoined the train.

When the wagons circled up for the night, Polly tested her theory, and, as she imagined, the bellows had the buffalo chip fire sizzling hot in no time.

"These biscuits is mighty tasty, Miss Alden," Billy Brown said as he stepped up for a second helping of beans seasoned with bacon, and biscuits slathered with milk gravy.

"Why, thank you," Polly said as she ladled up fresh helpings until the beans and gravy nearly overflowed the plate.

Howard elbowed Brown aside. "Don't be feedin' all that grub to him. I want some of it, too. I been ridin' all day."

"Don't worry, Howard. There is plenty to go around. There is no need to be impolite."

Howard watched as she refilled his plate, then stood shoveling beans into his mouth as Trajan walked up and held out his plate.

"More beans, if you please, Miss Polly."

"Of course, Trajan."

He smiled and turned away with the full plate. He had not taken more than one step when Howard extended a foot and tripped him. Trajan broke the fall landing on his elbows, and the steaming hot beans splashed his face as the plate fell from his grip. He rolled over in an instant and sat up, swiping and wiping away the burning food.

"Howard!"

He smiled. "Sorry, Polly. It were an accident." Howard walked away and plopped down on the box he used for a chair. He smiled at Polly as she mopped Trajan's face and neck and hands with a wet rag, then glanced at the other herdsmen busy at their suppers.

"There was no call for that."

Howard grimaced. "Shut up, Abe. Like I said, it was an accident."

Billy Brown said, "It seems like your 'accidents' only bother that boy Trajan. How come that to be? You don't never seem to bump into me, or knock Abe down. Hell, even Billy Red seems to be safe around you most of the time. It's only Trajan that has any trouble with your 'accidents,' seems like."

Howard shrugged and smiled, but said nothing.

The boys were quiet as Polly finished cleaning up Trajan and filled him a new plate with beans. Billy Red walked to the fire and asked for more biscuits and gravy.

"I sure like your biscuits, ma'am. Your corn dodgers is mighty good, too. But I sure do like me a biscuit—'specially hot, with butter."

"I will tell you what, Billy. If we lay over Sunday long enough for the cream to rise on the milk, I will skim it off and churn up a batch of butter. I will see if Mother Baker will give me the cream from her cow, and ask at other wagons as well, so there will be enough cream to bother with. Then we shall have butter for our biscuits, at least for a day or so."

The boy's freckles wrinkled in a smile that covered his face. "That will be right fine, ma'am."

"Please, Billy—do not call me ma'am—it makes me feel like an old—well, older—woman."

"Sure thing, ma'am—er, Miss Polly."

This afternoon Capt Baker hurried back to the wagons, his horse spent and lathered. He ordered us to halt the wagons and to mind the teams as there was a buffalo herd coming. He then whipped his horse out to the boys and the cow herd and they raised a dust hurrying the cows and horses and mules back down the trail—I guess it was to get them away from the buffalos. I never imagined my first sight of those

> animals would be thousands of them at once. The most of the herd passed ahead of the wagons but some of them on the edge passed right among us as if we were not there, bumping the wagons and giving the oxen a fright. The dogs raised an awful fuss barking and running in circles, nipping at the buffalos and sometimes getting knocked aside for their trouble by a kick or a jab from a horn. Children were shooed into or under the wagons. I was jostled aplenty and had my feet trodden upon as I stood amongst my teams trying to calm them as was the case at other wagons. The buffalos are large beasts, bigger than all but our largest oxen, especially the males with their wooly humps and big heads. They grunt and groan as they march and smell to high heaven. There were many babies among them who plodded along much like the others. It took no time to realize while watching the herd pass for the better part of two hours why buffalo chips are so plentiful on these prairies.

The encounter with the buffalo paved the way for the train's first brush with wandering Indians. The sun had yet to rise when the band rode toward the circled wagons. At first sight of their approach, men saw to their firearms and, again, mothers hustled children into the wagons. Baker studied the Indians and talked the situation over with Colonel Fancher, visiting that morning to deliberate over disposition of cattle herds, order of travel, and trail conditions.

Spread out in a line an arrowshot from the wagons, the Indians waited. The men sat horseback, the women and children stood scattered behind them and watched, holding horses laden with packs and trailing travois heaped with loads secured under buffalo robes or canvas sheets.

"Stay calm, boys," Colonel Fancher said. "This here is a hunting party. They mean us no harm."

"How do you know that?" someone said.

"Look at 'em. They got women and children with 'em. If they was a war party, they would've left the women behind. It's plain they're followin' them buffalo we saw yesterday."

"Plain to you, maybe. I say we give 'em a taste of powder and lead."

John Baker walked up and stood beside Fancher. "The colonel is right. Those Indians are not looking for a fight."

"I say we give 'em one anyway!"

"Stop it! The first man to fire a shot will have me to answer to!" Baker said in a voice that left no doubt he meant it.

The men shuffled about, murmuring. One said, "Well, what we goin' to do then? You-all got any idee?"

Fancher looked at Baker. Baker sensed the question and nodded in reply.

"Captain Baker and I will walk out and talk to them. You-all just stay here and stay calm."

Baker told Abe to gather the other drovers and saddle up and ride out to the herd to reinforce the last shift of night herders, but to do nothing but keep the animals bunched and watch that none of the Indians drove off any stragglers.

"Like I said, you-all stay calm and don't do anything stupid," Fancher said.

"Don't you-all worry none, Colonel Fancher, Cap'n Baker. But the boys an' me'll be ready if there looks to be trouble."

"There won't be any trouble," Baker said. He and Fancher shouldered their rifles and walked toward the waiting Indians, altering their course when one of the men rode out of the line, flanked by two others, and reined up, meeting the wagon masters with unblinking eyes and expressionless faces. One of the Indians stayed mounted, the leader and the other swung to the ground.

A quarter of an hour passed while the four men talked, during which the emigrants inside the circle of wagons fussed and fretted. Then Baker and Fancher walked back to the wagons. The head Indian stayed put, while the other two passed through the line of mounted men to the cluster of women and children and horses with their pole drags.

"Well?" one of the Arkansawyers said. "What do they want, Fancher?"

"Just as we thought. They're on a buffalo hunt. Kiowa. A little outside their usual hunting grounds, but they go where the buffalo take them."

"Fine. But what do they want with us? Soon as our backs is turned, we'll likely find an arrow in it."

Baker chuckled. "Naw. They'll likely save their arrows for buffalo."

"How d'you-all know that? You talk Kiowa?"

Again Baker chuckled. "That one Kiowa boy speaks English better'n you do, son. I don't know for sure about their head man—he never said a word in English, but I got the feelin' he didn't miss much."

Baker called the women together and told them to put together packages of tobacco, coffee, and sugar.

"You-all aim to give away our supplies to them heathens?"

"Not give them away," Fancher said. "Trade. Barter—and don't worry about the supplies. I will replenish a share from our wagons."

"All well and good," one of the men said. "But, trade? What the hell—pardon my tongue—has them red savages got that's fit for white folks?"

Baker smiled. "That we shall see."

"Well, they ain't gettin' none of mine."

Baker's smile disappeared and he glared at the woman

through slitted eyes. "You—all of you-all," he said with a nod to the circled women, "will put something in the pot. Everyone." He turned to his wife and told her to see to the organizing of the packages, and to make sure everyone pitched in.

Within minutes, Baker and Fancher and two other men walked back out to where the Kiowa leader and the young one who spoke English waited. They all sat on the ground around a tanned buffalo hide the Kiowas had spread on the grass while Fancher and the two Kiowas negotiated the exchange of goods.

The emigrant men came back to the wagons laden with fresh buffalo meat and packs of smoked-and-dried slabs of jerked meat. When they returned, the wagons had been loaded, the oxen yoked, and the train rolled out within minutes. The Kiowa stayed put, and only the slow turning of their heads as they watched the wagons and cow herd pass by let on that they were not sculpted from stone.

That evening, like most after a long day plodding along beside her teams, found Polly leg weary and bone tired as she went about her evening chores. The boys, however, having spent the day in the saddle, had stamina to spare. With supper in their stomachs, they saw to their gear, joshing one another with idle boasts and backhanded compliments.

Trajan sat cross-legged on the ground, replacing the cracker on the end of the whip he—as did other drovers—used to control the cattle. He opened an eye in the end of the cracker, a thin strand of braided leather, and slipped the fall of the whip through, then half-hitched the cracker around the fall and pulled it snug. Giving it a few extra tugs to ensure its tightness, he rose to his feet, and, in a motion smooth and steady, lifted his arm overhead and felt the whip thong reach behind. He paused for an instant, then, just before the cracker touched the ground, lowered and extended his arm, throwing the whip forward. The whip stretched ahead of him, the new cracker emitting a satisfying pop.

"Sounds pretty good, Trajan," Billy Brown said.

Trajan nodded, and popped the whip again.

Abe said, "That'll keep them cattle on the move. Wake 'em right up should they get to dozin' off."

"Aw, hell," Howard said from his perch on a kitchen box. He leaned over and spat out a syrupy glob of tobacco juice. "That ain't nothin'." He walked to his saddle and retrieved his whip. With more speed and jerk than Trajan, he snapped out his whip with a stroke that ended with a louder crack. "That's how it's done, boys."

"Well," Abe said, "that's all fine and good, Howard. But there's more to it than makin' a lot of racket. You got to pop it where it'll do some good—close enough to a critter's ear to where it can feel the breeze, but without touchin' it."

Howard snorted. "Aw, hell, don't matter none. Them cows ain't bothered by a little smack now an' then."

"Still, your better herdsman don't bother the cattle any more'n he has to. Like ol'Trajan there. I been watchin', Howard, and that boy uses his whip lots better'n you do."

"Bullshit. I can wipe a horsefly's ass with this here whip, and not ruffle a hair."

"I say the boy's better," Abe said.

"And I say he ain't."

Billy Red piped up. "What say we set up a contest?"

"How would we do that, Red?"

"Hell, I don't know. Got to be some way."

"I got an idea," Billy Brown said in a voice so soft the others had to strain to hear him.

"Oh? What's that?" Howard said.

"Drag that box you been sittin' on over here and I'll show you."

Billy Brown scooted the box back and forth on the ground to get it level. He dusted off a discarded Dr. Hartshorn's patent medicine bottle and stood it atop the box. Fetching a leftover biscuit from a basket by the fire, he broke it into quarters and perched one of the pieces on the lip of the bottle.

"There," he said. "You-all boys see if you can knock that biscuit off from there 'thout tippin' over that bottle."

"Aw, hell, that ain't nothin'. Watch this." Howard unfurled his whip, stepped off the distance, and stood for a moment staring at the target, the hand holding the whip twitching. With a jerk, he struck. The whip snapped but bottle and biscuit stood, untouched.

Billy Red sniggered; Abe and Billy Brown smiled. Polly looked on from a distance, her eyes on Trajan, whose eyes were on the grass at his feet.

"Gimme another shot," Howard said. He shifted his feet and struck again. This time, when the whip cracked the bit of biscuit disintegrated, and the bottle spun away, whistling through the air. "Sonofabitch," Howard said to himself.

Billy Red hooted and applauded. "Way to go, Howard!"

"It can't be done," Howard said.

"Hold on a minute," Abe said. "Trajan gets his chance."

"I say it can't be done!"

"We'll see," Billy Brown said. He retrieved the bottle and rebuilt the target atop the box with another bit of biscuit.

Trajan had not moved, still standing, head down.

"C'mon, Trajan. Your turn."

He raised his eyes to look at Abe. "Oh, I don't know, Mister Baker, sir. Could be Howard's right."

"Well, we won't never know unless you try."

Trajan shifted his weight from foot to foot, tapping the coiled whip in his hand against his thigh.

"Go on, Trajan," Polly said. "You can do it. I know you can."

The boy looked at Polly, looked down again, then stepped slowly toward the box. He stopped at what he guessed to be a good distance, let the coils of his whip fall, and, with a flick of his wrist laid the thong out ahead of him on the grass. Then, with a slow, smooth motion he raised his arm and waited as the thong floated up and back, looping behind him. When he felt the balance reach the right point, he extended his arm toward the biscuit on the bottle on the box. The whip snaked forward. The cracker popped. The biscuit disappeared. The bottle did not move.

Chapter Four

Crawford County, Arkansas, 13 May 1857

The horseman rode out of the shade of overhanging trees into the sunlight. Ahead in the small clearing, three riders blocked the road.

God help me, the lone rider thought, recognizing the man on the middle horse as Hector McLean. Sensing no escape, he rode on and reined up a few yards from the trio.

"Well I'll be damned if it ain't Parley Pratt," McLean said with a sneer.

Pratt squirmed in the saddle. "I would be obliged if you would let me pass."

McLean laughed. "Just because that worthless judge let you go ain't no sign I will."

"Mister McLean, I am unarmed."

McLean smiled. "That's your own damn fault, Parley. I heard tell the judge offered you a pistol and a knife when he snuck you out of jail back there in Van Buren."

"Like I told his honor, gentlemen," Pratt swallowed hard, "I do not rely on weapons."

"For that, you are a fool. Me, I find that weapons come in handy, times like this."

McLean pulled a revolver from a holster strapped to the pommel of his saddle and emptied all six rounds in the cylinder into Pratt's chest and belly. The bullets rocked Pratt, but he stayed upright aboard the horse as it skittered and shied, tossing its head and snorting. McLean holstered the smoking pistol and drew a Bowie knife from a scabbard on his belt. He urged his horse forward a few steps and stopped beside Pratt and thrust the knife into his belly.

Pratt still sat in the saddle, his eyes watching McLean with a fading look of disbelief. Withdrawing the blade, McLean stabbed the dying man again, using the force of the thrust to shove Pratt off his horse. Pratt hit the ground with a groan, his body quivering. His mount sidestepped away from the fallen rider and set out through the clearing at a gallop.

"Dumb bastard." McLean wiped the blood from his blade across his thigh and returned it to its sheath. He looked down at Pratt bleeding on the ground, shook his head, and spurred his horse into motion. His companions followed, riding away in the direction from which Pratt had come.

They rode for a few minutes, then one of the men expressed concern that Pratt might live.

"Bullshit," McLean said. "He's leakin' blood out of so many holes there ain't no way in hell he'll survive."

"He was still breathin'."

"He's likely quit it by now."

"I don't know, Hec. He was still watchin' you as we rode off."

McLean jerked his horse to a stop and glared at his friend. He exhaled long and slow. "Oh, for God's sake!" He wheeled his horse around and spurred it into a trot back down the road.

When the riders reached the fallen man, he lay still in the road.

"See there," McLean said. "He's deader'n hell."

Pratt stirred, forced his eyes open, and tried to raise himself on his elbows.

"Sonofabitch," McLean said under his breath. He turned to one of the other riders. "Give me your pistol." He took the old single-shot caplock, drew back the hammer, and in a blast of powder smoke sent a ball into Parley Pratt's neck, knocking his head back to the ground with a hollow thump. "Now let's get the hell out of here."

Before the dust of their departure settled, a farmer drove his wagon into the clearing. He pulled out of the ruts to avoid the body in the road, stopped the team of mules, and stepped down from the wagon and knelt beside the bleeding man.

"Mister—you still in there?" the farmer said, grasping Pratt's shoulder and giving it a shake.

Pratt's eyes blinked, and he managed to keep them half open.

"I heard a shot," the farmer said, studying the bloody holes in Pratt's coat. "Looks like I missed the most of the shootin'. Who done this to you?"

Pratt tried to swallow, clenching his eyes shut in the effort. He abandoned the effort to open them again. "Hector McLean," he whispered.

The farmer shook his head. "What must've you done to make him do you this way?"

Drawing a ragged breath, Pratt said, in a voice so weak the farmer had to lean close to hear, "He accused me of taking his wife and children. I did not do it. They were oppressed, and I did for them what I would do for the oppressed anywhere."

The man thought for a moment. "That's a mighty fancy speech. I guess I heard about you in town. Can't recollect your name, though."

"Pratt. Parley Pratt."

Pratt said no more. The farmer stayed with him for the two more hours it took for him to finally bleed out and die.

"You're one tough sonofabitch, I'll give you that," the farmer said. He lifted the body and laid it out in the back of the wagon and hauled the load into town.

Back in Van Buren, McLean made the rounds of the local

saloons and billiard parlors, making big talk about dispatching the man who had made off with his wife—a woman McLean would never see again.

And then Hector McLean left town, never to be tried or even arrested for the murder of Parley Parker Pratt.

Parley Parker Pratt was among the guiding lights of the Mormons, the Church of Jesus Christ of Latter-day Saints. He threw in his lot with Joseph Smith in upstate New York in 1830, mere months after the birth of the church. Five years later, when Smith organized his Quorum of the Twelve Apostles, Pratt was among its members and would be for the rest of his life.

World-traveling preacher and missionary, soldier and prisoner in defense of his church, frontiersman and explorer, Pratt was also a publisher and writer. Over the years he penned some thirty books and pamphlets, ranging from theology to missionary tracts to poetry to history.

It was while doing missionary work in San Francisco that Pratt met Eleanor McLean. She was a zealous convert to Mormonism—much to the dismay of her drunkard of a husband, Hector. He beat her, threw her out of the house, and threatened to have her committed. Fearing she would run off to live with the Mormons in Utah Territory and take their children, Hector shipped the two boys off to Eleanor's parents in New Orleans.

Eleanor did, in fact, go to Salt Lake City, where she and Pratt married in a religious ceremony—never mind that Eleanor was still married to Hector, and Parley already had eleven wives.

When Pratt left for the East on yet another missionary journey, Eleanor saw it as an opportunity to rescue her children. She accompanied Pratt as far as Missouri, then went south on her own. In New Orleans, she spirited the children away from her uncooperative parents and traveled to Texas, meaning to meet up with Pratt somewhere, sometime, and return to Utah Territory.

Hector was on her trail, tracking her through Texas and Indian Territory. Assisted by a posse of fellow Masons, he ran her to ground and had her arrested and jailed in Arkansas. He set the United States marshals after Pratt, having intercepted a letter from him to Eleanor arranging a meeting in Indian Territory.

The two appeared before the judge in a crowded courtroom to answer Hector's charge of kidnapping and hear his tale of woe. Since there was no provision in the law allowing Eleanor to be tried for kidnapping her own children, Hector charged the pair with theft for stealing the clothes the boys wore. A mob numbering some five hundred angry souls packed the courtroom, hostile toward Pratt for wife-stealing.

Sympathizing with the abused woman and finding the case against Pratt weak, the judge dismissed the charges, turned them loose, and advised Parley to get out of town.

He made it twelve miles.

"Went to see the dead body of my beloved Parley," Eleanor wrote to Pratt's friend and fellow apostle, Erastus Snow. "I saw his wounds—saw his blood dripping from his heart making a puddle on the floor and spattering a vessel put to catch it. Saw his coat full of holes where the balls passed through, and two rents made by the knife which gave him the death wound on his left breast."

In reporting the murder of the Mormon apostle, a California newspaper feared repercussions, wondering "whether the hot blood which now must be seething and boiling in the veins of Brigham Young and his satellites, at Salt Lake, is to be cooled by the murder of Gentiles who pass through their territory."

The writer asked "whether the 'destroying angels' of Mormondom are to be brought into requisition to make reprisals upon travelers, or, whether, as has been done before, 'Saints' disguised as Indians are to constitute themselves the supposed ministers of God's vengeance in this case. No doubt that such thoughts, such intentions as these, are prevalent among those saintly villains, adulterers and seducers, of Salt Lake."

Chapter Five

Polly Alden stumbled in the rut and barely kept her feet. But she could not help watching the freight train passing in the opposite direction, the first she had seen. Captain Baker said they would encounter freighters on the Santa Fe Road along the Arkansas River. But the wagons exceeded her expectations; bigger, even, than her imagination. Her wagon—teams and all—would easily fit inside the high-sided freight wagons with room to spare for a load of cargo.

The rear wheels on the wagons stood taller than she did—taller, in fact, than any man of her acquaintance. The wheels, besides being tall, were wide, and rimmed with a double thickness of iron tires. Some trailed a second wagon, hitched to the rear. Drawn by eight or ten or even twelve teams, the parade of draft cattle pulling the freight wagons made the two teams she prodded along the trail seem insignificant.

Then there were the bullwhackers. Unlike the goad she used to control her oxen, the freighters used stock whips. But it looked to Polly that the crack of their whips only got the attention of the oxen, and that the bullwhackers controlled them with voice commands seasoned with a good deal of profanity. And their whips differed from the bullwhips the drovers she cooked for carried—the bullwhackers' whips were longer throughout, from the stock to the thong to the fall.

"They're coming back from Santa Fe," Abe said that evening at supper. "Leastways that's what Pa says." He picked a strand of bacon rind too tough to chew from his mouth and tossed it aside.

"What d'you-all reckon they had in all 'em wagons?" Billy Red wondered around a mouthful of beans.

"Most likely whatever they can get out of them Mexicans," Howard said, whittling a cud of tobacco off a lint-covered plug pulled from his pocket. "Can't imagine what any Mex'd have that a white man would want."

"You've heard of the Mexican War ain't you, Howard?" Billy Brown said. "Ever since, Santa Fe and all that country out there has been American. All the way to California and the ocean."

Howard shrugged and spit. "Even so, a Mex's still a Mex. They ain't reg'lar 'Mericans like me and you."

After a time, Abe picked up the conversation. "Pa says there's a lot of wool comes out of Santa Fe—raw fleeces, and wove into blankets and such. Furs, too. Mexican silver dollars; silver and gold bars, too."

Howard spit. "I guess I could do with some of that—the silver and gold, that is."

"You saw they was trailin' a right smart of mules," Billy Red said.

"They sell them mules, too, back in Missouri. That worries Pa some," Abe said. "All them mules and all the spare cattle they got eat a whole lot of grass. Could be we'll have to move our herd off the trail a good distance to keep their bellies full."

"I don't guess them freighters' stock could eat up all that much."

"Well, hell, Howard—you don't think there's but the one train, do you? Pa says we'll be seeing them all along this road, coming and going. All them, along with wagon outfits like ours, will sure use up a lot of graze."

The emigrants would encounter more freighters along the Santa Fe Road, but none would impress Polly Alden like the first, with their high-sided, tall-wheeled wagons and big hitches of oxen. Most trains used wagons of the Murphy and Conestoga type—larger than the emigrant wagons, but less impressive in scale than the lumbering giants.

A few days down the trail, as the emigrants parked their wagons and unyoked the teams to take a nooning, a detail of cavalry troopers led by a young officer trotted into camp. Colonel Fancher from the nearby wagon train rode with them.

Polly went about her business, but kept one eye on the mounted soldiers who sat swatting at flies and squirming in their saddles as their lieutenant and Colonel Fancher squatted in a circle with Captain Baker and a few other men.

"What do you suppose that's all about?"

"Couldn't say, Trajan," Billy Brown said, both boys wolfing their food in order to get back to the herd and relieve the other drovers so they could eat.

Army uniforms were as strange a sight to Polly as the big freight wagons had been. "My, but don't their uniforms look smart," she said. "A mite dusty, but you can tell they're handsome underneath."

Howard, too busy eating to talk until then, said they looked like a bunch of damn Yankees to him. The boys snugged up their cinches, mounted and spurred their horses into an easy lope toward the grazing herd, and within minutes Abe Baker and Billy Red rode into the circle for their dinner. Abe sat horseback for a time, watching his father and Fancher talking with the army officer, and studying the mounted troopers biding their time on hipshot horses.

Polly stirred up the fire and tossed on a chunk of firewood. With the trail following the sizeable river along its tree-lined course, wood was again readily available and that meant—much to Polly's pleasure—that buffalo chips were left to lie where they had fallen on the prairie. Abe dismounted and eased the cinch on his saddle, and asked Polly about the soldiers.

"I do not know. They have been talking with your father and the others nearly as long as we have been here." She nodded toward the mounted troopers. "Those men are falling asleep in the saddle. Their horses look to be just as weary of waiting."

By the time Polly handed Abe a plate, Billy Red was back at the cook fire, smiling and holding out his already emptied plate for a refill.

"Well," Abe said as he chewed, "I reckon Pa will let us know."

"I sure hope so," Polly said. "I confess curiosity has gotten the better of me. I have no experience whatsoever with soldiers. These are the first I have seen. It does not look to be an exciting life."

"I 'spect it's a hell of a lot less dull when somebody starts shootin' at you," Billy Red said.

The soldiers left, riding away at a trot as they had ridden in. Fancher rode out in the opposite direction, back toward his wagons. Captain Baker offered no explanation, giving, instead, orders to move out. The women struck the temporary camp, the oxen were yoked and hitched, and the train took up the trail, leaving Polly to wonder through the long afternoon as she plodded along beside her teams.

After supper, with the camp winding down for the evening, Captain Baker carried a brand from his wagon's cooking fire and used it to set alight a heap of wood in the center of the circle. Once the bonfire was blazing, and more wood heaped on the flames, he called the company together.

"I reckon you-all are wondering about the soldiers who paid us a visit today," Baker said. "Those troopers are on patrol out of Fort Riley. Their job is to guard the road, for the protection of travelers like us and for the freighters. Some of those wagons carry government freight to supply forts out west."

Baker held his peace for the moment, letting his introduction take root before continuing. “The lieutenant said we should be able to reach Santa Fe without danger. But when he learned our journey would not take us there, that we were bound for California on the Cherokee Trail, he advised us to reconsider, warning of troubles ahead.”

Again, he paused. A voice came from somewhere in the crowd. “When the Indians show up, I hope you-all take a firmer hand than last time.”

“He’s right,” another man said. “You can’t trust ’em! They’ll shake your hand one minute and stick a knife in your gizzard the next!”

Others in the crowd voiced similar sentiments, urging offensive action at the first sight of Indians. Baker allowed the talk for a time, then raised both hands overhead for quiet.

“While there is always the possibility of an encounter with Indians, they are not the danger the officer warned against.”

The assembled men and women were quiet for a moment, then whispered conversations and muttered questions rippled through the crowd. Then a woman stepped out to confront the captain.

“Who, then? If’n it ain’t Indians, then what?”

This time, Baker did not have to entreat for silence. He looked from face to face, meeting the eyes of many in the company. He cleared his throat. “Mormons.”

The revelation created another quiet stir. Baker let it continue for a time, then raised a hand for quiet. “Some of you-all have had dealings with Mormons. Missionaries passed through our communities back in Arkansas from time to time.”

“Other’n tryin’ to talk you to death, they never seemed so dangerous to me,” someone said.

“I would agree,” Baker said. “We passed through their country on my earlier trip out to California, and I never had any cause for complaint against them. And, as you-all know, a good many of us intend to resupply in Salt Lake City."

"So what's the trouble?"

Baker's mind worked as he drew in a long breath and let it out slowly. He cleared his throat. "It seems there have been disagreements of a political nature between the Mormons and the government in Washington. I do not know the exact nature of their quarrels, but President Buchanan has declared Utah Territory to be in a state of rebellion."

When the muttering and murmuring dissipated, Baker continued. "At this very moment, the Secretary of War in Washington and the Commanding General of the Army, Winfield Scott, are assembling an expedition of more than two thousand soldiers, under the command of General William S. Harney, to march on Utah and regain control over the territory."

"What do you-all reckon we ought to do?"

"Colonel Fancher and me, and some of you others, have talked it over." Baker paused. Then, "We intend to proceed as planned."

"Good hell!" came a voice. "We could be walkin' into a buzz saw!" Others expressed similar sentiments.

Baker raised his voice. "Maybe so! But we figure it will take a good long time for the army to assemble. Supplies must be gathered. As anyone who has served in the army knows, nothing gets done the easy way, or quickly. It is our contention that we will arrive in Utah Territory well in advance of the troops, and, in fact, be long gone before they get there.

"That is what we intend to do. Of course, any of you-all who disagree are welcome to take your families and join up with another company. Or, when we reach Utah Territory, you are free to leave us and take the trail to Fort Hall and bypass Salt Lake City and most of the Mormons altogether. It is up to you-all to make your way as you wish."

The talk continued with plenty of questions and answers—most speculative. With the subject well chewed over and talk winding down, Baker asked for attention.

"One more thing, concerning all you-all young men who don't have families depending on them. The army needs soldiers. That shavetail lieutenant believes the recruiters will be delighted to enlist as many of you-all that's willing. Those troopers will be coming back this way, and will escort you to Fort Riley if any of you-all wish to enlist. Or you can make your own way there or to Fort Leavenworth to sign up."

Back at the wagon, the drovers—all of whom, save Trajan because of his color, and Billy Red, owing to his age, would qualify for military service—lay in their bedrolls and talked over what they had heard.

"What d'you think, Billy Brown—you of a mind to join the army?"

"Hell, no. I'm on my way to Californy to fill my pockets with gold. I sure as hell don't intend to put on no army uniform." Brown rolled over in his bed and wormed into the blankets. "Or get shot dead by a Mormon."

Chapter Six

Salt Lake City, 29 May 1857

Not since coming west with a wagon train four years ago had Tom Langford seen so many draft animals drawing so many wheeled vehicles. But these were not covered wagons bearing emigrants across barren plains. Here, there were freight wagons, delivery wagons, carriages, farm wagons, white-top buggies, buckboards, water wagons, surreys, coaches, and conveyances of kinds he could not name maneuvering the streets of Salt Lake City. Horses, mules, ponies, and oxen in harness and under yoke navigated the wide streets leaving steaming piles of evidence of their presence, which were periodically shoveled up and hauled away in handcarts.

Tom sat stiff on the seat of the wagon, knuckles white on taut lines as he guided the team around and through vehicle traffic and pedestrians. He had been in the city before, but never on his own and never saddled with such responsibility. At age seventeen, confidence wrestled with doubt as he made his way to the General Tithing Office at the intersection of Main Street and Brigham Street in the heart of the city. Stacked in the wagon box were sacks of wheat and barley from the tithing office back home—surplus stored through the winter and now bound for donation to and exchange for other goods from the general stores of the Mormon church.

Turning into the yard behind the multistory building, Tom reined up the team, heaved a long sigh, and felt his shoulders sag. He watched the workers bustling around the yard, loading and unloading goods into and from wagons parked at loading docks framing the angle of the *L*-shaped building. Beyond the ell, a network of pens held livestock, mostly cattle but also sheep, horses, and mules.

"Hey! Yokel! Get out of the way!"

Tom heard the yell, but paid it no attention.

"Move it!" came the voice again. "Get that wagon the hell out of the way, you damn hayseed!"

Turning to find the source of the anger, Tom saw a four-horse team hitched to a Murphy wagon, laden with hogsheads and barrels, trapped in the yard entrance, blocked by his wagon. A flush crept up his face as he fluffed the lines and told the team to step up. Once clear, the Murphy wagon rolled past, missing Tom's wagon by mere inches.

The driver spat a long stream of tobacco juice in Tom's direction as he passed. "Stupid hayseed," he said, then smeared stray spittle off his lips and into his beard and mustache with a shirtsleeve. The sleeve and beard carried evidence it was not the first time he had performed the maneuver.

Another voice, this one kindly, came from the opposite side of the wagon. "Can I help you, son?"

Tom turned to see a gray-haired man as clean-shaven as the angry driver had been bearded. He wore spectacles, protective cuffs over his shirtsleeves, and a bibbed canvas apron.

"Yessir. I brung this grain up from Springville."

"Springville, eh? How are things down on Hobble Creek?"

"Just fine, I reckon." Tom reached inside his shirt and pulled out a folded paper and handed it to the man. "I'm supposed to pick up the stuff on this here list—leastways whatever of it I can—to take back home with me."

The man studied the paper, then directed Tom to drive the wagon to the proper place on the dock. He questioned Tom to get the necessary details to record on his paperwork, then told him it would take some time to unload the wagon and fill the order, suggesting he might want to have a look around the town, but not to stray too far.

"Thanks. I'll do that. I'm obliged for your help."

"Think nothing of it, Brother. Our job here is to serve the Lord's children. Now, mind yourself, and we'll see you back here in a little while."

Tom left the yard and walked around the street corner the tithing office occupied. At the opposite end of the same block was the Beehive House, where the leader of all the Mormons, Brigham Young, lived and worked. Tom had seen the place before, but before reaching it he passed another building equally impressive in style, and so new its paint still looked fresh. A passerby informed him that it was called the Lion House—named for Brother Brigham, the "Lion of the Lord"—built to house more of the church leader's ever-growing and overflowing family of dozens of wives and scores of children.

Crossing the street and angling back to Main Street, Tom started down the wide thoroughfare, eyeing the shops and stores lining the street, deciding there were more businesses on one side of this one city block than in all of his hometown. His stomach, seldom filled in all his seventeen years, growled at him. In sending him on the errand, his stepfather had given him a bit of money to spend on food, handed over with a stern warning to be frugal. Rather than seeking sustenance at any of the eating houses he passed, Tom continued along until reaching "Whiskey Street," the blocks of Main Street where saloons and grog shops congregated. He intended to fill his stomach from the free lunch counters the drinking establishments offered, and add most of the money his stepfather had given him to his meager savings.

He veered off into the first saloon he encountered, stopping inside the door while his eyes grew accustomed to the indoor dim. The room was narrow, but deep. The bar lined half of one wall, starting near the front door. Standing room filled the space behind those whose heels hooked over the brass rail and elbows polished the bar. Beyond the end of the bar, a row of tables—all empty at this early hour—lined both walls, separated by a narrow aisle leading to the back. The saloon offered no amusements beyond the beverages it served—there were no card tables, no pool tables, no piano.

But there was a lunch counter—Tom could see it on the back wall. He stopped at the far end of the bar and slid enough coins across to purchase a rare bottle of fizzy lemonade. He deposited the bottle at one of the first tables, from which he could listen in on the talk of the patrons clustered around the bar. But before taking a seat, he studied the offerings of cold cuts of roast beef and dried ham, shriveled sausages, boiled and pickled eggs, a dill pickle, baked potatoes gone cold despite the wrinkled jackets they wore, and slices of crusty dry bread. He swished away the flies and heaped some of everything on his plate, pocketed a tarnished fork, and balanced the load in both hands back to the table.

Washing the food down with slow sips of the lemonade, Tom listened to talk of a kind as rare in his hometown as pinfeathers on the pickle he held in his hand.

He heard tell of a herd of seven hundred cattle Brother Brigham had sent to California a few months back—inspired by thousands of head passing through the territory from points east in the hope of turning a tidy profit when the drovers sold them as provender for gold miners.

Last year's presidential election was still a subject of debate. The winner, Democrat James Buchanan, was reviled by most of the men, who had favored the candidate of the Know-Nothing Party, Millard Fillmore They decried the influence of John C.

Frémont in the election, his presence on the ballot peeling off enough votes from Fillmore to give Buchanan the victory. While many admired Frémont as frontiersman, his newly minted Republican party, with its promise to eliminate the nation's "twin relics of barbarism"—slavery and polygamy—made the party's platform anathema to Mormons and their practice of wedding multiple women.

The practice of slavery, of little interest to the men in principle, came up for discussion for its practice, particularly the violent arguments for and against it in Bleeding Kansas, as reported in the newspapers.

"Popular sovereignty," one man said. "That's how it ought to be settled. Let the people of Kansas determine the question by their votes." Many voices in the crowd voiced approval.

"The hell you say!" said a booming voice from a man Tom could not see. "Missouri Pukes is pouring into Kansas Territory like piss out of a milk cow. Who wants them bastards deciding what goes and what don't?" That, too, earned a round of acclamation.

"But!" came another voice when the noise allowed. "But! Abolitionists are sending in their own in numbers as well! The vote would not be that of the citizens of Kansas—their voices will be drowned out by Missouri Pukes and Yankee abolitionists. Popular sovereignty is not the answer there, or anywhere! Such questions should—and must!—be decided by the Congress in Washington!"

The assemblage, in voices muttered and raised, broke into multiple conversations concerning that notion. Tom thought he sensed a growing tide of approval for federal control, when the tap, tap, tap of a beer glass on the bar interrupted. As the glass tapper gained attention and the talk died down, he reminded his companions that their very own territorial legislature—as decreed by the true government which operated in the shadows, the General Assembly of the Independent State of Deseret—had sent a memorial to Congress in March. The memorial declared that the citizens of Utah would not abide by any federal laws they disagreed with, would reject any officers appointed by the federal government they found unsuitable, and would demand self-determination in, among other things, the practice of what they called "plural" or "celestial" marriage, and the rest of the nation called polygamy.

"In a word, brethren," the speaker concluded, "popular sovereignty."

"That's two words," someone said, sparking laughter that soon died away, replaced after a time with muted conversations among members of small groups.

A man crashed through the door, breaking the relative quiet. "News!" he hollered. "News from the East! George Albert Smith and John Bernhisel pulled in not an hour ago with the spring mail—first to make it through the mountains this year."

"Well, what's the news?"

"They say Buchanan plans to replace Brother Brigham as territorial governor!"

One man laughed. "Hell, that oughtn't surprise no one! His term expired back in '54. Only thing to wonder about is why it took 'em so long to get around to it."

"But that ain't the half of it, my friend. Buchanan, ol' Ten Cent Jimmy, has declared the people of Utah defiant to federal authority and rebellious, and intends to have the army escort whoever it is he has crowned to rule over us, and see him seated in the governor's office. At gunpoint, if needs be!"

Silence held sway for a long minute that seemed like ten.

"The army, you say? Soldiers? Coming here?"

"So it is said. 'Hostile' they say we are to the government! Even as we speak, General Harney has been ordered to assemble a force of more than two thousand troops to act as a posse comitatus to bring us to heel. Mind you, there has been no official word. But Elder Smith and Brother Bernhisel heard it with their own ears on what they say is good authority."

His plate empty and stomach full, Tom swallowed the last of his fizzy lemonade, then shook a few last droplets out of the bottle onto his extended tongue. He slithered and shouldered his way through the stirred-up crowd and out the door and made his way up the street to the tithing office. He found the man who had advised him earlier and learned the wagon was ready to go, parked out of the way beyond the livestock corrals.

"Your mules were given a bait of grain while we loaded the wagon, and watered not long ago."

"I don't know how to thank you, mister."

"Oh, no! No, no, no! No thanks necessary, Brother. We are doing the Lord's work here, and that is thanks enough. Now, you travel safely on your way back to Springville. Our prayers are with you." He handed Tom a paper sealed in an envelope, saying it was an accounting of the day's transactions to be delivered to the bishop in Springville. "Will you be seeing him soon?"

"I reckon so. He's my pa—leastways he's Ma's husband." Tom removed his cloth cap and raked his fingers through his hair. "My own pa, he took sick and died on the trail out here, along with my two baby sisters and little brother. Only Ma and me made it. Somehow Bishop Mendenhall from down in Springville took us in and married Ma."

"I know Aaron Mendenhall," the tithing worker said. "He seems a fine man, loyal to the Church and a faithful servant of the Lord."

Tom said nothing. He shoved the paperwork into his shirtfront, shook hands, and walked to the wagon. Along the road south, he wondered about what the man at the tithing office said about his stepfather. He supposed it was right, as far as it went. Tom knew the people of Springville thought highly of their bishop—but they did not know what went on behind closed doors.

Tom's mother, Mary, was Mendenhall's third wife. As such, she was at the bottom of the pile, expected to be subservient not only to her husband, but to the wishes of her "sister wives" as well. Jane, his first wife, was well along in years, and her children were grown and gone. Given her advanced age and superior position, she did little in the way of keeping house beyond ordering Mary around. The second wife, Grace, though much younger than Mary, still held a preferential position. Lazy by nature, Grace contributed little to the household other than children—she was fertile and prolific, giving birth regularly. Her oldest, a son named Hiram, at eight years old, was the only child mature enough to lend a hand. He was eager, and worked the fields and did chores with Tom as much as he was able, which was not much, truth be told. Hiram had two younger sisters, a brother yet a toddler, and his mother Grace was again in a family way.

Upon reaching home, Tom expected he and Hiram would be sent out to the cornfield in the fertile bottomland along Hobble Creek, hoes in hand, to continue the endless and hopeless assault on invasive weeds. If past experience was any indicator, the boys would be rousted out of bed in the dimmest gray light of dawn to eat breakfast and see to the barnyard chores as the sky paled. Afterward, at the back door, Mother—Tom's mother—would hand him a package of wrapped food that would serve as dinner to be eaten in the field.

Bishop Mendenhall would repeat his usual instruction to the boys to start work when their shadows appeared on the ground, keep at it until they could step on the heads of their shadows, then stop long enough to eat their dinner—and not a minute more—then get back to work and stay at it as long as they cast shadows.

But for today, Tom would enjoy his leisure. He would plod along on the wagon until reaching Murray, some ten miles up the road. There, he would drive to the town's tithing office and pen the mules after parking the wagon, whose running gear would serve as the ceiling he would spread his blankets under for the night.

Come first light he would set out again, passing the Point of the Mountain that separated the Salt Lake Valley from Utah Valley, then on to the burg called Lehi and repeat the process, which would put him, upon awakening, one long day's drive to Springville and a short night's sleep. His father would want a report of goings-on in the capital city and Tom mulled over the discussion and debate overheard in the saloon, and rehearsed how best to report the news—particularly the rumored approach of soldiers.

He could only guess at the bishop's reaction. But one thing was for sure. No matter how the old man reacted, there would still be weeds in the corn rows.

Chapter Seven

Thin columns of smoke striped the still air, rising until spreading into a hazy ceiling. From the talk these past few days, Polly knew the smoke signaled their pending arrival at Bent's Fort. The place would be the first sign of settlement the travelers had seen since passing through the Choctaw and Cherokee communities in Indian Territory, now more than six hundred miles distant.

As the wagons rolled across the floor of a wide swale, Captain Baker and his son Abe sat watching them from horseback atop a low rise that concealed the fort that lay beyond. The captain, with much pointing and sweeping of arm, indicated where to put the cattle herd and horses on grass. Abe urged his mount into an easy lope toward the drovers. His father waited for the wagons, then turned and rode at the head of the parade.

Polly's eyes widened when she topped the gentle ridge. The fort sat on a bluff above a bow of the river, its high walls shining in the sun. Clusters of tipis dotted the surrounding plains, along with groups of parked freight wagons and the circled wagons of other travelers. Grazing herds of horses, mules, and cattle scattered beyond into the distance, and loose hogs rooted around.

People were on the move everywhere, walking and riding hither and yon, here to there among the dispersed campsites, and to and from the fort. As the train drew nearer, sounds reached Polly's ears—shouts, laughter, ax blows, gunshots, and the ring of a hammer striking an anvil. Then smells—woodsmoke, cooking meat, rotting garbage, animal manure, human waste; odors familiar, yet more intense, than she had encountered in weeks.

Baker led the train on beyond the fort, past the bend of the river, and ordered the wagons to circle up there, near the watercourse but distant enough from other campsites to avoid encroachment. They would lay over here for a few days, repairing and refitting wagons, replenishing supplies, and recruiting the animals.

And, Polly thought with a long sigh as she lifted the yoke off her lead team, a chance to rest herself.

Bent's Fort

We have arrived at a place unlike any other in my experience. It is called Bent's New Fort. I am given to understand there was an earlier Bent's Fort on this same river and trail but some miles west of this one that was abandoned years ago. The Bents are traders of long standing in this country I am told. I have yet to visit the Fort itself as this afternoon and evening have been taken up with getting camp here situated for our stay. My Billys have laid in a good supply of wood for cooking but they tell me the trees along the river are thin, and there is no sign of game. We suppose it is from the presence of the Fort and all those who stop here as we have.

Some in our camp will be laying in supplies for the road ahead. Mrs Baker says we will replenish our flour somewhat and see about some bacon. But with Capt Baker having the means our wagons were well stocked before setting out and are yet well supplied. Mrs Baker says we are fitted out for Salt Lake City and that goods will be available at better prices there.

I look forward to spending a day without the endless walking. My clothing will get its first thorough cleaning in some time and if circumstances permit I myself will benefit from a good wash.

Howard and Trajan are coming in from guarding the herd to get their supper.

The next morning, Baker returned from the fort and ordered Trajan to empty Polly's wagon of all it held, even removing the cover and bows. Men from the camp loaded wagon wheels in need of fixing into the bed. The captain yoked up an ox from another team to Polly's off leader, then hitched them with another mismatched pair to the wagon, tying a fifth and sixth animal to the rear.

"Take Trajan and drive right on into the stockade," he told Polly. "You-all will find a smith and wheelwright there to refit the tires and see to other repairs as needed on those wheels. These cattle need shod, and I've organized that, as well. You should not encounter any troubles, but be mindful—the men here are a rough bunch."

Howard, watching and listening, stepped forward. "Say, Cap'n, don't you think I oughta go along? Make sure Polly's safe? That boy Trajan, he ain't no good if trouble comes."

Billy Brown laughed. "You ain't foolin' nobody, Howard. You're just a-wantin' to get at one of them Injun women they say hangs around the Fort sellin' their wares. You ain't talked about nothin' else for days."

Howard spun toward Brown, screwed up his face, and squirted out a string of tobacco juice in his direction, but no words escaped.

The captain spoke up before the boy could find the right words. "Mister Brown, mind your manners. There's a lady present, if I must remind you!"

Billy reddened. "Sorry, Captain Baker. You too, Miss Polly."

Baker turned to Howard, still staring at Brown, his face florid. "And you, Howard—don't you be worryin' 'bout Trajan. Like I said, I don't expect trouble, but if there is I'd sooner trust Trajan and Miss Alden to sort it out than I would you. Your mind always seems to be somewheres besides where it ought to be."

Howard spat again, not in the captain's direction but the insult was implied. He had better sense than to speak. But no sooner was Captain Baker out of earshot than he turned loose a tirade directed at both Trajan and Billy Brown, with a few hateful glances cast Polly's way thrown in for good measure, before stomping off through the camp with no apparent destination in mind.

Polly goaded the oxen toward the stockade, and her eyes did not sit still for more than a few seconds at a stretch. Trajan's eyes were just as busy. They watched the Indian women and children among the lodges they passed, noting how thin and bony the little ones looked, even as their stomachs looked full. Their clothing, what of it they wore, consisted of odd mixtures of ragged and stained hides and cloth.

White men stood outside tumbledown tents and shelters, draped in furs and hides and fabrics as shabby as those the Indians wore. There were freighters lazing about, some in exotic clothing she assumed to be Mexican in origin.

She saw shooting and knife-throwing contests, much passing of liquor bottles and jugs, horse races on the flats, flayed and partially butchered cattle, sheep, hog, and deer carcasses hanging from tree limbs, and hides stretched and pegged to the ground, a few from buffalo.

The pounding of hammer on anvil grew louder as they neared the walls of the fort. They rolled through the open doors of the stockade wall and Polly prodded the teams toward a corner of the enclosure where the blacksmith's forge smoked. An Indian boy worked a lever that pumped a large set of bellows to feed the fire. A farrier rasped and cleaned hooves and nailed shoes on a big ox hanging in a sling, alternating his work there with the same job on a smaller ox thrown and tied and lying on the ground, passing shoes back and forth for fit and shape to the blacksmith at the forge and anvil.

The smith was a big man, sweat forming a sheen on his bare black back, chest, and arms. A band of cloth wrapped around his head kept the sweat from his eyes, but, still, he swiped his forehead and scalp now and then with the arm that held the hammer. Trajan stepped close to the blacksmith, eyes wide as he watched the man work and listened to him giving orders to others on the work crew.

When the shoes were fitted for the ox in the sling and the one on the ground, the smith stepped away from the forge to squat in the shade of the stockade wall. An Indian boy carried over a wooden pail and dipper. The smith drank, then laved a dipperful of water over his head, letting the liquid run and drip down his face and neck, and dribble on down his chest and back.

Trajan followed the man's every move.

"C'mon over here, boy," the smith said.

Trajan took a small step, stopped, took another, hesitated, then walked over and stood before the man, head down and hands clasped behind his back.

"What's your name, boy?"

"Trajan."

"Aah, Trajan—named for a Roman emperor. You know that, boy?"

Trajan shook his head.

"You know what a Roman is?"

"No, sir."

The smith shook his head and drank another dipper of water from the pail. "What are you doin' here, Trajan?"

The boy nodded toward the wagon with its load of wheels and tethered cattle. "We brung these wheels to be fixed, and them oxen to be shod. Cap'n Baker, he sent us."

"Captain Baker, eh? Yes, we talked earlier. What's Captain Baker got to do with you?"

Trajan's brow furrowed, and he cocked his head. "Don't know what you mean, mister—I's his, I guess. The Cap'n, he owns me. Takin' me with him out to Californy."

The man nodded. "I see. And this girl—she belong to the captain too?"

"Oh, no—she works for him, but she don't belong to him. Miss Polly, she takes care of our camp—I and the others that herd the cattle."

Again, the smith nodded.

No one spoke for a spell. Trajan stood staring at the big blacksmith, then said, "Mind if I ask your name, mister?"

"Not at all, Trajan. My name is James—Jim—Beckwourth."

Trajan swallowed hard. "D'you belong to them that owns this place?"

Beckwourth chuckled. "No, son. Not me. I don't belong to nobody but myself." He watched the boy watching him. "Time was, years back, I belonged to a man away back in Virginia—I was a slave, just like you, but that man was my father as well as my master. He apprenticed me out to a blacksmith so's I'd have a trade and be useful. That's how I come to know this work," he said, gesturing toward the forge and anvil.

"But that smithy treated me ill and we fought and I quit him. I taken off for the West and joined up with a fur trapping outfit run by a man named Ashley. Become a mountain man, I did—and a free trapper."

Trajan asked if he was still a trapper.

"No, Trajan. The fur business, it's gone under. Ain't been no profit in it now for years. Now I do whatever I need to do to get by. I've set my hand to a good many things out in this country."

The boy stood spellbound, with Polly just as intrigued, as Beckwourth spun stories of his time as a fur trapper, his years living with the Crow tribe to the north, where he claimed to have been a chief among them. He told of trading on the Old Spanish Trail, from California down into Old Mexico, of scouting for the Army, and of his time in the California gold country.

"You been to Californy?"

"Yes, Trajan—I have been durn near everywhere. You say you-all are goin' to California. Could be you'll cross them Sierra Nevada mountains through a gap they call 'Beckwourth Pass.' You know why they call it that? They call it that because I found the place—I blazed the trail through there. Beckwourth Pass."

The big smith stood and flexed his back. "But you ain't never goin' to get to Beckwourth Pass or anywhere else if we don't get slippers on them oxen and re-set the tires on them wagon wheels."

Beckwourth went at the work hammer and tongs, shaping and re-shaping shoes as fast as the farriers could nail them on. Trajan watched the big man work, but Polly soon wandered off to explore the stockade. Next to the blacksmith shop in front of which Beckwourth plied his trade was a shop littered with wood shavings and sawdust, parts and pieces of wheel spokes and felloes, axles and bolsters, hounds and hardware—enough, she thought to assemble an entire wagon from scratch.

She studied a fur press sitting empty in the yard, and peeked in the door of a dusty storeroom holding bundles of buffalo hides and other pelts, along with traps hanging from the rafters by their chains, and other of what she assumed to be tools of the trapping trade. Other warehouse-like rooms held barrels and boxes and bundles and bags and bales and bolts of all manner of goods, with a small adjacent room set up with desks and counters and tables to conduct trade.

Steam and smoke and noise spilled out the door of a big kitchen. Inside, a black woman and a Mexican woman ordered and instructed cooks in the preparation of large quantities of foods. The next room held rows of long tables lined with a mixed mess of benches, stools, and chairs. Polly looked into, but did not enter, yet another dim room where billiard balls clattered around a table and men stood drinking at a bar and sat around card tables.

Polly studied the row of rooms sitting atop the ones she had visited, assuming them to be sleeping rooms. Bedding and items of clothing draped over the railing lining the second-story walkway. Again, she made note of the mix of people—many of the workers appeared to be Mexican, along with some younger Indians, and there were whites and blacks and many revealing mixed parentage. She heard familiar accents, others tinged with French and Spanish, dialects she knew to be Yankee, and Indian languages she could neither identify nor understand.

Back with the wagons and animals, Polly found the work well in hand and could see she would be back at camp soon—too soon to satisfy her curiosity about the place and people. A man and a boy from another emigrant train stood by waiting their turn, the man in conversation with a hanger-on dressed in hides and furs, squatted down and hunched against the wall. The emigrant asked the man about the mountains.

"Oh there'll be plenty of mountains," the grizzled old trapper said through thick beard and mustache. "Don't you worry none 'bout that. Time'll come when you'll be wishin' you never heard the word."

"So I have been told. But I have yet to see any sign of them."

The mountain man waved to the west. "Well, pilgrim, you keep yer eyes peeled as you go yonderway. Three, four days, maybe, you'll start to feel 'em out there. First off, it'll look like a cloud bank layin' on the horizon. Then it'll look like them hills they likely got back where you come from. Soon enough, they'll be standin' up there starin' down at you, darin' you to come on. Them'll be the Rockies you'll see first. But they won't be the last of 'em."

Shifting his weight from one foot to the other, the traveler stared at the raconteur with a blank look.

"There be ranges of mountains everywhere out here." The trapper gestured widely toward the southwest. "There's the Sangre de Cristos and San Juans and Sandias." He pointed westward, then swept to the north. "The La Sals, the Tushars, the Wasatch. Rubies and Owyhees. There's the Unitas, the Medicine Bows, the Wind Rivers, and the Tetons. Bitterroots and Bears Paw. Absarokas. You got your Black Hills and Blue Mountains. Sawtooths. And, of course, yer Sierra Nevadas—them'll make you wish you never left home. That ain't the half of 'em, neither. And all them mountains, ever'one, can whiten yer bones."

The old man stood from his squat. "Like I said, you'll see plenty enough mountains 'fore you get where you're goin' to, wherever that is." The old man smiled. "Unless you figger to go back where you come from," he said, and walked away.

Polly let the oxen plod along at their own pace back to the wagon camp. She and Trajan did not speak, absorbed in thoughts of their own about what they had seen and heard and learned. Some new, unwitting threat gnawed at the girl. Something so deep down she barely felt its presence—and yet she trembled at the thought of the mountains that lie ahead.

Chapter Eight

Tom stepped out of the dim barn into the still-hazy dawn, milk pail brimming with white foam in hand. While Hiram slopped the hogs, scattered scratch for the chickens, and gathered the eggs, Tom had milked the cows and then turned in the calves for their share. The two boys shuffled back to the house for breakfast, Tom ruffling Hiram's hair and poking him in the shoulder, the boy grinning and squirming out of the way then stepping back in stride for more. After breakfast, while Hiram saw to his studies, Tom would move the family's bunch of beef cattle out into the communal pastures in the meadows. Then the two of them would once again challenge the weeds in the cornfield.

Passing the kitchen garden in the growing light, Tom saw that it was overgrown with weeds. He thought to spend the day there rather than in the fields. But his stepfather believed gardening to be women's work—and that meant a further burden on his mother, as neither Jane nor Grace, her sister wives, would be of much help. So, Tom lent a hand whenever possible. This morning, he stopped in the cellar under the back porch and strained the milk out of the bucket through a dish towel into the cooling pans on the shelf before going in for breakfast. It was a small thing, he knew, but his mother would appreciate the help.

In most ways, these summer days were much the same for Tom, and much like those of the other summers since Bishop

Mendenhall took his mother to wife. In other ways, this summer was like no other.

Since hearing of the assembling armies readying to march on Utah Territory, Mormon leaders in every town—under direction from their superiors in Salt Lake City—were launching preparations of their own to meet the rumored troubles. Feed grains, for animals as well as people, were rationed and stored. Brigham Young wanted a biblical seven-year supply laid by. New land was plowed and planted to grain and to row crops. Meat animals destined for slaughter were saved for consumption at a later time when the need for sustenance might be greater. Frontier scouts explored deeper into the mountains and valleys and deserts seeking places of refuge. Others looked farther afield.

Fleeing was but one possibility. Tom, along with every able-bodied man from his tender age to those gone gray, was enrolled in a local unit of the Mormon militia—the Nauvoo Legion, it was called—and drilled in the streets of the towns. Workers were assigned to gunsmiths, and firearms were assembled factory fashion. Bullet molds were busy, and miners prospected hill and valley in search of galena ore from which more lead for more bullets could be smelted. Brigham Young, in a letter to Aaron Mendenhall, ordered the bishop to put a crew to work harvesting saltpeter from white salt deposits in the cliffs and ledges of Hobble Creek Canyon for the manufacture of gunpowder. Missionaries sought out leaders among Shoshoni, Ute, and Paiute bands to negotiate alliances and assistance in fending off the soldiers, with promises of plunder from the army and from travelers on the trails as recompense.

Through it all, federal officials assigned to the territory continued to leave town, as they had done over the years. Unwelcome and usually ignored, judges, secretaries, marshals, surveyors, Indian agents, and other officers sent out from

Washington fled for more welcoming environs, sometimes with encouragement and prodding, and often with scathing reports about their treatment at the hands of the recalcitrant and rebellious Mormons.

And all the present recalcitrance and rebellion, burning hotter by the day, stemmed from nothing more than rumor. No official word from Washington had yet reached Utah Territory about armies, governors, administrators, civil servants, mail contracts, or anything else concerning relations between the Saints and the United States.

Shaded up against the wall of the church building to avoid the heat and glare of the low-hanging sun, Tom sat with his friend Eli Price. Their rifles, old muzzle-loading caplock muskets that had survived the long trip West from the States, stood propped against the adobe bricks.

Eli pulled off his hat and hung it on an upraised knee and heaved a long sigh. "What d'you think of all this playin' at soldier?"

Tom thought for a time. "I don't know. I guess we've got it to do."

"Me, I'm damn tired of trampin' around the streets. If there is to be a fight, I can't see how all this marchin' will help us shoot any straighter."

Tom shrugged. "Bishop Mendenhall says it's important—and he gets his orders from Salt Lake City."

Eli stared at his friend. "How come you call him Bishop Mendenhall? Why don't you call him 'Pa' or 'Dad' or 'Father' or somethin'?"

"You know good and well he ain't none of them things. He's married to my ma, but that's all. He ain't my pa."

"Still . . ."

"Still nothin'! I got to live in his house, and I got to do what he says on account of he's the bishop. But I don't got to act like he's kin, 'cause he ain't."

Eli stood and dusted off the seat of his pants. "Reckon I best be gettin' on home. Them chores won't do themselves."

Tom stood and picked up his rifle. "Me too. If I don't see you out on the meadow in the mornin' I guess I'll see you tomorrow afternoon for some more drill."

With a snort, Eli allowed that he would not be looking forward to it.

Tom laughed. "Don't know why you're so contrary. You ought to see Hiram. That boy can't wait to make a soldier. Spends ever' free minute he's got marchin' around the place with a stick propped on his shoulder for a rifle."

"Dumb kid. Or maybe it's us that's dumb. Hell, that stick he's carryin' is likely as good a weapon as these antiques they give us."

"Maybe so," Tom said as he walked away, the long rifle swinging from his fist. "Maybe so."

Back at home, Tom stepped into the kitchen, stopped and took off his hat, and bowed his head. At the table, Bishop Mendenhall carried on, uninterrupted by Tom's entrance, with his prayer of thanks and blessing on the food. Tom paid little attention to the words. He had heard it all before, at least once a day and usually more often. The Bishop's exhortations to the Lord were long and loud, often rendering the food cold before anyone had a chance to take a bite. At least officially. Through the veil of his eyelashes, Tom watched Hiram break a chunk off a biscuit hidden in his lap and pop it into his mouth. From the look of the biscuit, it was not the first bite.

". . . in the name of our everlasting Lord and Savior, even Jesus Christ, Son of our Eternal Father, Amen," the bishop said.

"Amen," came the accustomed agreement from around the table.

Hiram's hand shot out and he grabbed a serving bowl filled with creamed peas fresh from the garden.

"Hiram! Mind your manners! Put that bowl down and wait for Mother Mary to serve you."

The boy ducked his head and mumbled, "Yessir."

Tom's mother served the bishop first, heaping his plate. She then rounded the table as many times as there were dishes to be served, ladling and spooning and forking food onto the family's plates. Most, save the bishop, waited until she was finished to start eating. But each time she came around to Hiram's plate, it was almost empty.

"I swear, young Hiram, you must have a hollow leg," Mary said as she drenched yet another biscuit with milk gravy. "I cannot fathom where you put it all."

Hiram blushed, but his fork kept working.

"He's a growin' boy, Ma," Tom said.

The bishop cleared his throat. "That he is, Tom. But tell me—does young Hiram do enough work around here to make all the food he eats profitable?"

Tom looked at the bishop, then at Hiram. "Well . . ."

Hiram's widened eyes locked on Tom and he sat upright, spoon heavy with food hovering in midair.

Tom let the boy suffer for a bit. "Well, sir, I guess I'd have to say he does a right smart of work."

Hiram let loose a long-held breath, shoved the spoon in his mouth and smiled at Tom as he chewed.

"I am glad to hear it." The Bishop turned to Mary, who was at last eating at her place at the table. "I declare, Mary, these peas are as tender as can be. You have outdone yourself."

Mary ducked her head and blushed. "Thank you, Father."

"I see the garden is somewhat overgrown."

Mary's blush deepened. "Yes, Father. I have let it get ahead of me, I fear."

"You are not overburdened, I trust."

Head still bowed, Mary glanced at her sister wives. "No, Father."

"Jane—Grace—you are not shirking your duties at Mary's expense are you?"

Jane harrumphed. "Aaron Mendenhall, I have raised one family in this household. It is not my responsibility to raise another."

The Bishop nodded. "Grace?"

Hands out of sight beneath the table, the young wife twisted the skirt of her apron. "Oh, Father . . . I am so tired all the time . . . and this heat . . ."

With a snort, Jane said, "*This* heat? Come July and August, you'll know what heat is."

"But in my condition . . ."

"Your condition! I walked a thousand miles from Winter Quarters in that 'condition.' And in heat the like of which you shall never know!"

"Now, Jane," the bishop said.

"Don't you 'now Jane' me, Aaron. I lost that baby, you will recall. My last, buried in an unmarked grave on the Sweetwater. Wolves probably dug up her bones. And her too tiny to make even a snack for those infernal beasts. Tired! Through all that, I never missed a step." She looked at Grace and sniffed, then turned her attention back to her supper.

Grace, pale and downcast, moved the greens around on her plate with the tines of her fork.

The silence, interrupted only by the slow scratching of the fork, stretched on until Mary spoke. "It is all right, Father. The work gets done, one way or another. We will get by."

Sunday morning started as any other Sunday for the people of Springville, crowded into the meetinghouse for Sabbath services. Following the hymn singing, the ritual of the sacrament, scripture readings, and sermons by men chosen from the congregation, Bishop Aaron Mendenhall stood at the pulpit.

"Brothers and sisters, we have truly been spiritually fed this morning. It is a comfort to know our Savior Jesus Christ is watching over us in these trying and uncertain times. We, as a people, have suffered before and shall surely feel the lash of persecution again before our time here on Earth is finished. But buck up, and know the Lord is with you.

"And now, brothers and sisters, I have sad news. Many of you are aware of a visit I received two days ago from an emissary sent by the brethren in Salt Lake City. On this Tuesday past, the twenty-third day of June, a mail coach arrived in Salt Lake City. It carried news that will break the heart of every Saint—news of the death of our beloved Apostle Parley P. Pratt."

Gasps and gulps and exclamations rippled through the congregation. Men rose to their feet, unsteady, grasping the backs of the pews before them for support. The Bishop allowed the news to settle before raising a hand and gesturing for quiet, and for those upstanding to be seated.

"Some of you know Elder Pratt only by reputation. Many of us know—knew—him personally. We have served the Lord with him, fought our enemies beside him. There are men in this room who fulfilled missions with him to spread the Gospel, here among the Indians, back in the States, or across the oceans. I, myself, followed Parley as we explored this country shortly after our arrival here, seeking suitable locations prepared by the Lord for the settlement of His people. Elder Pratt was truly a giant among men, and a faithful and valiant servant of the Lord's church."

The worshipers sat in silence until one man rose and cleared his throat. "Bishop Mendenhall . . . you have told of the death of Elder Pratt. What do you know of the circumstances?"

"It is a tale too sad to tell. But you—all of you—deserve to know. Parley Parker Pratt died at the hand of an assassin."

Again, the shock radiating through the congregants was audible.

"As I understand it, Elder Pratt was traveling in the state of Arkansas when set upon by one Hector McLean—a name familiar to some of you—and shot down like a dog, and, for good measure, penetrated by McLean's blade. He died as bravely as he lived, I am told, his faith in our Savior strong."

Another voice sounded from the crowd. "And this man McLean? What of him?"

The Bishop shrugged and shook his head. "So far as I know, nothing. There was no word of his arrest, trial, or conviction. As I said, little is known. It may well be he has not been, and will not be, held accountable in the state of Arkansas for this foul deed."

No one spoke for a time. "Rest assured, brethren, that the Lord took note of Parley's demise," the bishop said. "As the Bible teaches, not one sparrow shall fall on the ground without our Father's knowledge. 'Fear ye not therefore, ye are of more value than many sparrows,' it says. The Lord knows all. We can rest assured that those responsible for this outrage—*all* those responsible—will be held to account. If not in our time, then in the Lord's; if not in this world, then in the next."

"Like hell!" raised a voice. "If ever I cross paths with any sonofabitch from Arkansas, there won't be no waitin' on the Lord!"

Chapter Nine

Northern Colorado, June, 1857

The sun was gone, but the light would last much longer. Polly stacked the ox yokes on the wagon tongue, stood upright and, with a forearm, wiped the sweat from her forehead. She looked to the west, her gaze climbing the broken foothills to the mountains beyond. Sunstruck snowfields on the high slopes glowed in the rays of the sun, beaming out from behind the craggy peak silhouetted against its glow.

"Girl, quit that day-dreamin' and get to fixin' us some supper. I'm hungry."

Polly started from her reverie. "You are always hungry, Howard."

The drover spat. "Durn right I am, honey. And I got a hunger you've yet to satisfy."

Despite hearing the same kind of patter from Howard for weeks and now months, Polly still chafed at his rude behavior. With clenched jaw, she walked to the back of the wagon and lowered the end gate, then slid a kitchen box over the lip of the wagon bed and lowered it to the ground, then reached for another.

Billy Red walked up behind her. "Whyn't you get a fire goin' and let me do that."

"Why thank you." Polly looked to Howard, sitting cross-legged on the ground, a bridle rein from his still-saddled horse in hand. "Billy Red, it is a pleasure to have a gentleman in the camp."

Billy's already ruddy complexion flushed brighter behind its freckles. "Yes, ma'am."

"Please—do not call me ma'am, as it ages me beyond my years. 'Polly' will be fine, as I have told you many times. If you find that too familiar—which you should not, by now—then 'miss' will do."

Billy Red smiled and nodded and stuck his head into the wagon box to see to the unloading of the camp equipment. Polly lifted the spade from its slings on the side of the wagon, found a suitable spot, and broke ground to carve out a fire hole. Trajan, back from seeing to the ox teams, fetched a bucket from the wagon, carried it to the stream beyond the camp circle and returned, water sloshing over the rim as he walked.

"You-all boys is mighty handy at doin' women's work," Howard called out, punctuating the insult with a string of tobacco spit.

"Well, Howard, near as I can see, you ain't much good for any kind of work."

Howard sprung to his feet. "Best watch that mouth of yours, Red."

Polly stopped digging and watched as Billy Red walked toward Howard, stopping a few yards away. Howard stepped forward. The rein drew taut and his horse snorted and jerked its head. He turned around and lashed the horse across the snout with the rein and the horse scurried backward, again tossing its head. Howard took a firm grip on the rein, taking a wrap around one hand, set his feet, and laid back, fighting the horse. He pulled and jerked and cussed and the horse stood.

"You oughtn't mistreat that horse so."

Howard spun around. "You ought to mind your own damn business, Red. I'll kick your ass six ways to Sunday."

"I wouldn't try it if I was you," came a voice so soft Howard barely heard it. He shifted his glare to Trajan, who stood just behind and to the side of Billy Red.

"What did you say, boy?"

Trajan ducked his head and mumbled, "I don't think you can take the both of us."

Howard spat, then wiped his mouth with his shirtsleeve. "Boy, you had best be careful how you speak to your betters. I'll tie you to the wagon wheel and have at you with my whip."

Billy Red cleared his throat. "Like he said, Howard—you try anything and you'll have the two of us to deal with."

Howard stared, shifting his glower from one to the other. "You-all had best watch your backs." Again, he ejected a string of tobacco juice. He turned and walked away, jerking the horse around to follow.

The boys watched him go. Billy Red let loose the breath he held. "I thank you, Trajan."

"Ain't no need. We gots to stick together with a body like Howard."

"You're right. But he's right too—we had best watch him. He gets one of us alone, there'll likely be hell to pay."

They said no more, but watched Howard going until the sound of the shovel slicing through the sod interrupted the quiet.

Billy Red turned to where Polly was back at her work digging the fire pit. "I'm awful sorry you had to see that, ma'a—miss."

Polly again stopped digging, balancing the spade upright with one hand. "I am sorry you boys have to put up with him."

"Well, he don't treat us no worse than what he treats you."

"Do not worry about me. Where I am concerned, I believe Howard is all talk. I doubt he will try anything, not with you and Trajan—and Billy Brown and Abe—and Captain Baker, if need be—looking out for me."

Polly went back to work. Supper would not fix itself.

The Cherokee Trail, following the tracks of the old Trappers' Trail, skirted the verge of the plains and the foothills of the Front Range of the Rocky Mountains. Riding point one morning as the train neared the place the trail would bear west toward Fort Bridger, Captain John Baker sat horseback on the trail and watched the approach of two riders from the north, one with a pack animal in tow and the other leading two. Both clad in buckskin, one of the men looked to be a white man behind a bushy gray beard, the other an Indian of an indeterminate tribe. Halting a rod or so from Baker, the bearded one raised a hand in greeting.

Baker nodded in reply. "Good morning, gentlemen."

The man with the beard laughed, his bellowing bray turning Baker's thoughts to the pair of mules on the man's lead. The racket did not seem to affect the mules, who stood quiet with twitching ears, eyeing Baker and his horse. Nor did the Indian seem to notice his companion's laugh, instead watching Baker as intently as the mules.

The laughter died in a snort and chuckle. "Don't know who you are, mister, but you're mistaken in thinkin' us gentlemen."

Baker squirmed in the saddle. "Oh? Why is that?"

Another peal of laughter, this one less explosive. "No partic'lar reason—only that bein' outside of society these long years has shed me of any notion of manners I ever had." He nodded toward the Indian. "That, and that ol' Pohague here, he ain't never got comfortable bein' 'round more'n two or three white folks at a sittin'."

Baker smiled. "I see. I would ask what you-all are doing in these parts, but I can see that is a question you-all should be asking me." He nodded toward the Indian, said, "Pohague," then asked the white man what he was called.

"I have been given all manner of names, dependin' on who's givin' 'em out at the time. Most folks calls me Crooked Leg, on account of a thievin' Arikara left one of his arrows in m'knee years back, and it ain't worked proper never since. But in my younger days, thirty years and gone, when I first come up from down there," he said with a nod to the east, "I was known as David Girard. It ain't likely anybody knows that but me, these days. So, I reckon Crooked Leg will serve, if it's all the same to you."

The men talked for a time. When Crooked Leg dismounted, Baker could see the reason for the nickname. His right leg, which looked fine when mounted, kept the same bend standing on the ground as it did when in the stirrup. Horses tied, the men sat on the ground and talked—rather the white men talked and Crooked Leg laughed while Pohague listened. Crooked Leg asked about news from the States. After passing on what he knew and what he had heard, Baker told of the wagon trains coming behind him. Crooked Leg asked about their origin and destination. Baker asked about the trail ahead. Crooked Leg told of his present journey with Pohague since traveling east from Fort Bridger.

"It's dry as the Mojave River in summertime out there on the Cherokee. Them herds of cattle you say you got won't find a mouthful of grass anywheres around that country these days. Weren't hardly no winter snow and there ain't been no rain since God knows when. Just the two of us, me and Pohague, stirred up enough dust with our animals you could grow corn in it—if you could get it watered, which you couldn't on account of there bein' no water."

After another bout of braying laughter, Crooked Leg said, "You folks might could make it across, but you'll lose critters doin' it. Likely lose some people, too. If you want my advice, which I reckon you do since you're askin', you'd do well to stay away from that country—Pohague, here, he'd tell you the same if he was inclined to talk. You'd best follow the North Platte on up to the Sweetwater and take that wagon road on over South Pass and down to Fort Bridger. I believe you'll find plenty of grass thataway. It'll take a longer time—but dead is a hell of a lot longer."

The old man and the Indian mounted up. Pohague said his goodbyes with a solemn nod followed by an unexpected smile; Crooked Leg hollered, "Watch yer topknot," and let loose a braying laugh that faded away as they rode off to the south.

When the wagons came up, Baker directed them to a fitting place to stop for nooning, then rode on down the back trail until finding the Fancher train.

"Colonel," he said to Alexander Fancher, "I do believe there's a change of plans in the offing. . . ."

It has been some time since I set down my thoughts on these pages. There is less wagon traffic on the trail now. A few days after leaving Bent's Fort we passed the burned out ruins of the old fort. We kept to the Arkansas River but the road to Santa Fe went another way and all the freighters with their big wagons and teams departed with it. Now there are only our train and Col Fanchers and another one from Arkansas and one from Missouri that I know of. They keep their distance but we see their fires at night. We followed the River to the foothills of the mountains that are now a constant presence looming over us. I well understand the caution the old gentleman at the fort conveyed concerning them. For reasons I cannot explain I find them frightening and cannot imagine a wagon road could ever penetrate them.

On the Fourth of July Capt Baker called us all together

before ordering the wagons to pull out. He had asked me the evening before if I recalled anything of the Declaration of Independence from my schooling. It was not without a touch of pride that I informed him I had learned the preamble by heart and could remember it yet. He asked if I would be willing to recite it before the company in celebration of the day and of course I agreed. We gathered with the morning sun lying low on the horizon and Capt Baker called the company to order and reminded them of the calendar day. Some were unaware and the knowledge excited them. I was then asked by the Capt to step up on a box and render the preamble to the Declaration of Independence, as I record it here.

We hold these truths to be self-evident that all men are created equal that they are endowed by their Creator with certain unalienable Rights that among these are Life Liberty and the pursuit of Happiness. That to secure these rights Governments are instituted among Men deriving their just powers from the consent of the governed. That whenever any Form of Government becomes destructive of these ends it is the Right of the People to alter or to abolish it, and to institute new Government, laying its foundation on such principles and organizing its powers in such form, as to them shall seem most likely to effect their Safety and Happiness. Prudence indeed will dictate that Governments long established should not be changed for light and transient causes and accordingly all experience ~~has~~ hath shown that mankind are more disposed to suffer while evils are sufferable than to right themselves by abolishing the forms to which they are accustomed. But when a long train of abuses and usurpations pursuing invariably the same Object evinces a design to reduce them under absolute Despotism it is their right it is their duty to throw off such Government and to provide new Guards for their future security.

Memory served me well and I recited the preamble word perfect and am pleased to say that there were but few dry eyes among the company upon completion. To close out the observance of Independence Day the men all fired their guns into the air which caused quite a stir.

There are Indians in this country—I am told they are of the Shyan Tribe and perhaps some Arapahos and Utes and Shoshonee. One night a lone man came to our circle. Capt Baker and he exchanged hand signs and the Capt assured us the Indian meant us no harm but some of the men did not believe it and kept their rifles at their sides thinking the Indian up to no good and likely backed by others of his kind. At dark their fears grew with the sight of many campfires around us. But nothing untoward happened and the Indian left in the morning.

Chapter Ten

Trudging along beside her ox teams, her prod serving more as walking stick than goad, Polly crossed South Pass unaware. What she noticed most about the place was the wind. Stiff and incessant, it tugged at her clothes, scoured her skin, and the dust and dirt stirred up by the wagons peppered her like buckshot.

Off to the right, the Wind River Mountains showed blue against a paler blue sky, the peaks still frosted with patches of white. Southward, the Oregon Buttes subsided into the sagebrush. The pass itself passed without notice, spread as it is along a wide, shallow saddle across the Continental Divide. The physical insignificance of South Pass, despite its geographic prominence, offered some degree of respite for the emigrants after repeated crossings of the Sweetwater River, and with the climb up rough and rocky ridges and hills and hollows behind them.

Another hundred miles or so and the wagons would roll into Fort Bridger. Some would not see the place, choosing instead a cutoff offering a more direct route to Fort Hall on the Snake River. But Captain Baker, Colonel Fancher, and some others had no intention of going to Fort Hall, either on a cutoff or from Fort Bridger. Rather, their intention was to follow the Mormon road from Fort Bridger to Salt Lake City to resupply—where they hoped prices would be better and goods more abundant than at either fort. So, as happened from time to time on the trail, wagons left one company to join another, thinking it advantageous to throw in their lot with another train, another route, another wagon master.

The shuffling got underway at the crossing of the Green River. Arkansas emigrants joined forces with wagon companies from the east that launched from Westport, Independence, Saint Joseph, and other points on the Missouri River. New companies formed and set out for Fort Hall, others organized for Fort Bridger from where they would strike the trail north for Fort Hall, and others laid plans for Salt Lake City from Fort Bridger. The Baker train lost no wagons, but gained a family from Missouri who left their Oregon-bound company in favor of California, hoping, like the Bakers, to add to their stores in Salt Lake City and trade for fresh oxen. As the new family set up camp, Polly watched a girl near her own age helping with the work.

Two days down the trail and two nights later, Howard drew rein. He tongued the worn-out cud out of this cheek, then scratched around in his pouch to assemble the last few leaves and strands of tobacco. As he fingered the small wad into his mouth he reminded himself to bum enough chaw to see him through to Fort Bridger.

Tired of standing, his mount snorted and tossed its head and pawed the ground. Howard jerked on the bit, then slapped the horse between the ears with the tails of the bridle reins. Squealing and shying from the threat, the horse lunged, and Howard hauled in the reins with a holler and planted both heels in the animal's flanks.

As he fought the horse, Billy Brown rode up. Howard, occupied with his mount, did not see him approach. The night was dark, lit only by the stars broadcast across the sky.

"You ought not treat a horse thataway."

Howard yanked the horse around until facing the voice. The two men were on night guard, circling the Baker herd in opposite directions.

"Damn you, Brown! You like to've scared the hell out of me."

"From the look of it, you got plenty of it to spare. You're treatin' that horse like you're the devil his own self. The Cap'n wouldn't like to see you do that to one of his horses."

Howard huffed. "Well, I reckon he's all tucked up in his bed and don't know the first thing about it—and he damn sure better not find out."

Howard could not see Brown's smile in the dark, but he could hear it in his voice. "Well, Howard, I don't suppose he would be surprised. He don't miss much."

"What the hell? Ain't much he can do about it just now. Somebody's got to tend to these stinkin' cows." Howard yawned, then mopped the escaping tobacco drool from his chin with a shirtsleeve.

"Yup," Brown said. "And just now that's you and me—and we had best get back to it."

Howard yawned again. "It ain't like we're missin' anything. Nothin' out here but you and me and them cows and some crickets." Another yawn. "And them damn coyotes."

"I heard 'em too. You don't suppose it could be Indians tryin' to fool us into thinkin' they're coyotes, do you?"

"Nah. I ain't never seen no Indians yet brave enough to be out after dark."

"Let's hope not," Brown said. He lifted the reins and clicked his tongue and his horse moved out.

Howard stepped down from the saddle to relieve himself, then decided to sit a spell. He jerked the reins and led the horse up an easy slope to a jumble of boulders barely visible in the dark, then hunkered down using one of the rocks as a backrest, squirming into the sun's warmth it still held. He was asleep before drawing four breaths.

Billy Brown wondered what had become of him, but the answer did not come until dawn. Abe Baker and Billy Red rode out from the wagons to bunch the cattle for the trail. Howard's horse whinnied at the new arrivals, and Baker saw the horse in the dim light on the low ridge. Howard awakened with the noise and scrambled to his feet. He slapped the horse on the jowl then swung into the saddle—not bothering to snug the cinch, as he had not bothered to loosen it before.

He joined the other riders as they pushed the herd together. "Where you been, Howard? I ain't seen you for a couple hours," Brown said.

"I had some business to tend to. It ain't like I missed anything."

Baker rode up at a lope. "You boys been sleepin' on the job? Looks to me like we're missin' thirty, maybe forty head."

"What?" Brown said. "I been ridin' 'round since I took up the watch. Only stopped but once." He nodded toward Howard. "Talked to Howard for a bit."

"What about you, Howard? You see anything?"

Howard spat out a stream of juice from the wad still in his cheek from before his nap. "Not a damn thing."

"You didn't see anything, Brown?"

"Nothing." Again, he looked at Howard. "Fact is, I never seen Howard after we talked."

"What about that, Howard?"

Howard had no reply beyond a shrug and a string of tobacco spit.

Abe glared at Howard, who returned the stare. When the silence grew uncomfortable, Abe shook his head and let loose a long breath. "Well, you boys stay here. I'll go find Pa and see what he wants to do. Somebody's going to have to go after them cows—I don't think they just wandered off."

While they waited, Billy Brown told Howard to help Billy Red keep the herd close, and he would ride a wide circle and see if he could find any trace of the missing cattle.

Howard spat. "Who the hell put you in charge?"

"What, you think you could do it? You're still so damn sleepy you couldn't find your ass with both hands. Just help Red, like I said. I'll be back soon enough."

Without waiting for a reply, Brown turned his horse and trotted away. He rode beyond the perimeter of the bed ground, well away from where he and Howard circled the herd, and started a wider round, watching the ground for any sign of the bunch-quitting cattle. It did not take long. He was no tracker, but Brown had no trouble finding the trail of the cattle, leading west. Also evident were the tracks of unshod horses.

Billy Brown made it back to the herd just as Abe Baker returned with his father.

"What the hell happened?"

Brown swallowed hard. "Well, Cap'n, it looks like somebody got in here last night and made off with a bunch of cattle."

"I guess you've got a reason to think so."

"Yessir." He pointed in the direction he had just come from. "Out yonder I found some tracks. Cows, and horses without no shoes."

Captain Baker's jaws clenched over and over, and deep lines creased his forehead. "I don't guess you've got any idea how it happened."

"No, sir, I'm afraid I don't."

"Howard—Abe tells me you were missing for a time. That so?"

Howard ducked his head and felt the flush rise from his throat. "Maybe for a bit. Not for long." He looked at the captain. "I was feelin' a mite poorly, is why."

Baker shook his head. "Well, you're feelin' poorly means this herd was only bein' looked after half as much as it ought to have been. Enough so's God knows how many Indians could make off with some of the cattle you were supposed to be watchin'."

Baker stood in his stirrups and turned to look at the country where Brown said the thieves had taken the cattle. He shook his head. "Well, there ain't nothin' to be done but go after 'em. Billy Red, you and Howard keep an eye on the herd. Let 'em spread out some and graze, but don't let any wander off. We can't afford to lose any more."

Howard said, "But Cap'n Baker—I been out here half the night already."

"Yes, boy, I know it. But from the look of things, you already got caught up on your sleep. So you stay here and do your job."

Howard said nothing, but answered with a long syrupy glob of tobacco spit.

"Abe, stay here and help these boys till I get back," the captain said. "I'll go tell 'em not to break camp. I'll round up some riders and we'll go after them cattle. Billy Brown, you come back to the wagons with me."

Brown cleared his throat. "If it's all the same to you, Cap'n Baker, I'd as soon ride after the missing cows."

Baker harrumphed. "Good Lord, boy—you been up since hours ago. You need to sleep. We'll be needin' men with sharp eyes, awake enough to pay attention. Can't afford to have nobody dozin' off on me and gettin' themselves or somebody else hurt."

"I'm fine Cap'n. I won't let you down—again."

"All right, then." Without another word, Captain Baker set off over the ridge toward the wagon camp.

Abe rode through the herd and did a count and determined the loss was not as bad as he had thought—there looked to be only twenty or twenty-five head missing. As the cattle spread to graze, he and Billy Red and Billy Brown took up positions on the perimeter of the herd, watching the cattle as well as keeping an eye to the west for sign of Indians. Howard sat horseback on the slope of the ridge, one knee cocked around the saddle horn, where he could keep an eye on the other riders and, should anybody ask, the cattle.

After a time, Captain Baker arrived at a trot, Colonel Fancher riding beside him, with half a dozen other men following. All had long guns in hand or hanging from the saddle, most with pistols holstered or shoved into waistbands. Trajan, unarmed, rode with them, leading a fresh horse for Billy Brown.

Abe and Billy Brown saw them coming and rode to the place Brown had found the trail of the stolen cattle.

"We'll follow the tracks for now," the captain said. "I asked Colonel Fancher here for his advice. He believes them Indians is Shoshoni. He's dealt with 'em before and figures they'll claim the cattle wandered off and will want a ransom for gatherin' 'em up. Colonel?"

Fancher cleared his throat. "It won't be the first time they've tried that trick. Happened to me when me and my brothers brung a herd through here years back. They're likely camped somewheres on Ham's Fork, west of here."

"Let's go find 'em," Baker said.

Abe questioned his father as they rode. The captain had no intention of paying for the return of his cattle. If it came to it, he was willing to fight. The trail was easy to follow, and it did not appear the thieves were in any hurry. But, a few miles along, the trail split, with the tracks of a few cattle and one of the horses peeling off to follow a dry wash. Baker stayed with the main trail, but reined up when the trail split again.

"Damn thievin' Indians," Baker said. "What had we ought to do, do you think, Colonel Fancher?"

Fancher tipped his hat back and wiped the sweat from his

forehead with a bandana, then retied the rag around his neck. He pointed out the trail showing the most tracks. "If it was me, I'd keep on after this bunch. Most likely, they're all goin' to the same place and just tryin' to confuse us."

Baker concurred and they rode on. They had not traveled a mile when two Indians—an old man and a boy of maybe twelve years—rode onto the trail out of a ravine. They did not look to be concerned at the appearance of the white men, but sat watching them approach. Baker stopped several yards short of reaching the pair and raised a hand to signal his riders to halt.

Fancher rode on ahead and stopped near the mounted Indians. He talked to them and drew no response, so resorted to hand signs. He and the old man exchanged signs for a few minutes, then Fancher reined his horse around and rode back to speak to Baker.

"Ask me, that old man understands English just fine, but he never let on. Don't know about the boy. Old man claims they're out huntin' meat—deer, antelope, whatever they can find. Said he doesn't know anything about no cattle."

Baker worked his jaw for a minute, staring at the waiting Indians. "What do you think, Alex?"

Fancher shrugged. "Hard to say. Could be he's tellin' the truth. Says he's the leader of a band that lives hereabouts and sees white men all the time and ain't never caused any of 'em any trouble."

Baker drew in a long, slow, deep breath and let it out the same way. "Come with me," he said to Fancher. "You too, Abe. Take down your rope." They rode up to the waiting Shoshonis and as they drew near, Baker unholstered a pistol and ratcheted back the hammer and brought it to bear on the old man. "Abe, put a loop around him."

Abe rode up beside the Shoshoni and slipped his rope over the old man's head and pulled it snug around his chest. The old man did not react, his eyes locked on the captain's.

"Alex, tell the young'un to beat it back to his people and tell 'em we've got the old man. If they don't bring back the cattle—every one of 'em—by nightfall, we'll kill him."

Fancher sat up straight in the saddle. "Don't you think that's a little harsh?"

"Tell him."

Fancher flashed hand signs at the old man, then turned to the boy. "I don't know if you can understand me or not. I think you can. You heard what Captain Baker here said. I think he means to do it if your people don't return the cows. You-all have got till sundown."

Baker reined his horse around and headed back down the trail. Abe pulled the loop tight around the old Indian and followed. Fancher fell in beside the Shoshoni, who did not seem to notice. Fancher turned in the saddle and watched the Shoshoni boy riding away, quirting his mount every stride.

Fort Bridger—Utah Territory.

Compared to Bent's Fort this is a shabby place. There are low rock walls in places but most of the walls are logs stood up like a picket fence and the buildings are log affairs as well; some of them old and run down. We have had some fresh food from the gardens but they come at a price. It is operated by Mormons. What little I have seen of them they seem ordinary enough. There is talk among them of coming troubles with the US Army but I know little of it and do not care to know more.

Since the crossing at the Green River I have made a friend—the first girl of my age in our train. She is from Missouri and her name is Sarah Wood and we have become fast friends. She walks with me most days as her father handles the teams and wagon for their family, which is Sarah and her mother and father and a boy aged 8. They are good people but poor compared to the Bakers. They hope to make good in California and so joined up with Capt Baker.

Again we faced difficulties with Indians. Howard fell asleep watching the herd of cows and some were stolen one night. Capt Baker captured an Indian meaning to kill him if the cows were not returned, which they were much to my satisfaction as I did not care to see the old man killed.

Sarah is much taken with Billy Brown and wears me out with questions about him but there is little to tell her. I say she should ask him her questions but she dare not out of shyness. I believe her father forbids her speaking to boys as well but she has not said as much and seems to know a good deal more about boys than I do.

We leave tomorrow for Salt Lake City and there is some ~~fear~~ worry about what we will find there with the rumors of the army coming as Capt Baker thinks it may make trading with the Mormons difficult.

Chapter Eleven

High in the Wasatch Mountains, some eight thousand feet above the level of the sea, there lies a small valley. A cirque, or bowl, one of many, carved and scoured by glacial ice. Here are two hundred acres of meadow and marsh, hemmed in by evergreen forest and confined by mountain peaks looming two thousand feet above. At the valley's lowest point, the glaciers left behind a tarn—a tiny lake—one of dozens that sparkle like diamonds in the clear mountain air of the high country. The lake has a name: Silver Lake.

To find Silver Lake from the Salt Lake Valley, follow Big Cottonwood Canyon, eroded by its namesake creek out of quartzite, shale, sandstone, and limestone for some nine uphill miles to reach the place where the glaciers had their way with the granodiorite that forms the top of the mountains. Go on for another five miles and, if you know where to look, you will find Silver Lake.

Summer is the time to go. Then, when the little valley is free of the five hundred inches of snow that fell there over the winter, the flowers grow. Columbine. Lupine. Yarrow. Fireweed. White Bog Orchid. Bluebell. Sego Lily. Indian Paintbrush. You may not see moose and deer, or bears and mountain lions there, but they will see you. Silver Lake and the snowmelt stream that feeds it are alive with cutthroat trout, beaver, and waterfowl.

On the twenty-third day of July in 1857, Brigham Young was on his way to Silver Lake. He was not alone. As his buggy negotiated the rough road up Big Cottonwood Canyon, he passed, by his own count, 460 carriages and wagons—all of which made way for the passage of their prophet and leader in all things, civil and religious.

In all, the conveyances that arrived that day at Silver Lake discharged more than two-and-a-half-thousand people, Mormons one and all. These Utah pioneers gathered at Silver Lake at Brigham Young's invitation to celebrate that evening and throughout the next day the tenth anniversary of the arrival of the Latter-day Saints in the Salt Lake Valley. Pioneer Day. The Twenty-Fourth of July.

Among the celebrants was Aaron Mendenhall, invited owing to his status as bishop of Springville. Jane, his first wife, accompanied him. He would have preferred the company of his second wife, Grace. But she, being in a delicate condition, was not up to travel. Mary, his third wife, was needed at home to see to the running of the household in his absence.

As the wagons out of the Salt Lake Valley communities plodded up Big Cottonwood Canyon, a spring wagon hurried toward the valley from the east. It had pulled out of Fort Laramie, more than five hundred hard miles back, just five days ago. Porter Rockwell handled the lines, a man known for his ability to push horses faster and longer without harm than anyone else on the frontier. His cargo was human, in the persons of Abraham Smoot, Judson Stoddard, and Eleanor McLean Pratt—she still fleeing Hector McLean and his quest to have her committed to an insane asylum.

Rockwell, traveling east on a mail run under government contract, met the others on the trail just east of Fort Laramie. Smoot and Stoddard, likewise carrying mail—or meaning to—had been in Missouri to collect letters bound for Utah when informed by the postmaster that the contract was void and that the government would no longer send mail to the Saints. Returning empty-handed, the would-be mail carriers encountered sizeable freight trains assembling in Kansas Territory and others already wending their way west. Smoot learned their purpose and destination: to supply the army bound for Utah Territory.

"Them government sonsabitches!" Rockwell said upon meeting his fellow couriers. "All them rumors is true, then?"

"For a fact," Smoot said. "Brother Brigham will not be pleased."

Rockwell snorted. "That ain't the half of it. He'll be mad as hell is what he'll be."

Stoddard heaved a long sigh. "I sure don't want to be the one to give him the news."

"Well, he's got to hear it from someone, Judson—you or me or Abe. Brig, he's used to hearin' bad news from me, so I'm game. Let's get these teams and wagons back to Fort Laramie. I'll find me a good saddle horse or two and make tracks for home."

Instead, the men opted to travel together. They acquired a light wagon and two teams of light horses Rockwell judged to be fit and rested for the journey to pull it, loaded a few supplies—along with the McLean-Pratt woman desperate to reach the protection of the Salt Lake Valley—and lit out across the plains and mountains.

Five days and three hours later, Rockwell whoaed-up the teams in Salt Lake City. "Where the hell is ever'body?" he asked the hostler at the Colorado Stables, one of his many business enterprises in the territory.

The stable hand handed his boss a flyer. The illiterate Rockwell looked it over, the engraving of a cannon the only thing on the word-filled page he could decipher, and handed it to Smoot. "What's it say, Abe?"

"It's an invitation from Brother Brigham. To a 'Pic-Nic Party at the Lake in Big Cottonwood Kanyon on Friday, 24th of July.' Tomorrow."

Rockwell looked around the quiet city streets. "Looks like durn near ever'body must've got one of the damn things."

"Brother Brigham will want our news without delay," Smoot said.

"And he'll damn sure get it. But it's too late to get there today. Go home. Get some sleep. Meet me here at half past four in the mornin' and we'll get up the canyon in time for the picnic."

Smoot and Stoddard showed up as planned to find Rockwell pacing about outside the stable, and saddled horses at the hitch rail.

The festivities at Silver Lake were in full swing. A tent city covered a good portion of the meadow. Children at their games darted in and out among the trees. Women organized communal kitchens to serve dinner to the crowd. Men gathered in conclaves and klatches, with talk of all things spiritual and temporal, of politics and policies, of news and rumor, of crops and livestock. Young and old alike paused from time to time to yawn and stretch, tired but happy from a long night of activity and a short span of sleep.

At midday, in keeping with Brigham Young's penchant for organization and precision, the dinner bell sounded. Saints gathered on the de facto parade ground. Helping hands lifted Dan Wells, counselor to Brigham Young in the church hierarchy and commander of the Nauvoo Legion, atop a boulder. He called the gathering to order, struck up the band, led the singing of a hymn, and offered an invocation.

He had yet to invite the people to eat when a rider, a lookout, galloped into the bowl. He skirted the crowd and made his way to where Wells perched atop his stone podium to convey his message.

"Brothers and Sisters," Wells said, raising his arms overhead for quiet. "Word has just arrived of the return of couriers from the prairies. Our capital city's mayor, Abe Smoot, along with Justin Stoddard and O. P. Rockwell, come bearing news from the States." He turned to the leader of the band. "Let us welcome them with a rousing tune. Then, Brothers and Sisters, enjoy the repast prepared for our pleasure."

As if on cue, the horsemen arrived at a trot, greeted with music, cheers, applause, and waving hats and scarves, their enthusiasm untempered by a lack of knowledge concerning what news, for good or ill, they carried. Brigham Young watched it all, and sent word to have the new arrivals join him, with Wells and other headmen of the Church, under the marquee adjacent to his tent.

"Missouri is as rife with Pukes and mobbers as ever," Smoot told the leaders once the welcomes and niceties were out of the way. "I went to pick up the mail in Independence, the postmaster showed me the door. 'The contract with the YX Company has been cancelled on account of the unsettled state of affairs in Utah Territory,' he said. 'The government will not be forwarding any more mail to Salt Lake City at present.' He offered no other explanation."

Young pursed his lips and worked his jaw as he chewed over the news. Loss of the contract meant the demise of his YX Company—YX being shorthand for Brigham Young Express—and its effort to improve mail service and shipping between the territory and the States. He waved off the news and the lost money with it, and asked Smoot about the army.

"By rough count, I saw seven hundred heavy freight wagons, either on the trail or readying to set out. As you might imagine, it is a slow procession and I do not believe they can reach here before snow falls.

"As for the soldiers, General Harney is in command and intends to have twenty-five hundred in the ranks. I do not believe the officers or soldiers want to come here. Many are deserting every day and will never reach here. Many are foreigners—Scotch, Welsh, English—and have been told many of the Saints are the same and they will not fight their own people. And the Americans swear that they will not fight Americans. Thus, they are in a fix and do not know how to get out of it. Officers have to stand with their revolvers and guard the soldiers to keep them from deserting."

"And yet they are coming, with Harney at their head."

"Yes, but they are not much more than started now. They are getting a late start and in a week or ten days the soldiers will have sore feet, and by the time they get to the Platte they will be so sore that lots of them will take themselves off."

Young harrumphed. Smoot reported on the federal officials the army would be escorting, including a new governor to replace the Mormon leader.

"One other thing, Brother Brigham—some soldiers and some Missouri Pukes asked how many men we could raise to go into the field." Smoot smiled. "I told them that I thought we could raise fifty or sixty thousand, more or less, but it was only a kind of rough guess. But I said it with a straight face, and I think they believed it."

Throughout the afternoon, the leaders of the Saints huddled in the shade of the marquee and talked over what to tell the people, and warn them what to expect—of themselves, and of the army marching toward them. The people, unaware of the depth or breadth of the discussions, kept up their celebrations with games, fishing, dancing, and singing. As the sun teased the peaks above the little valley's west side, a bugle sounded calling the Saints to assemble. They gathered before Brigham Young, the president, prophet, seer, revelator, and governor standing atop the boulder that served as a speakers' platform at Silver Lake.

"Brothers and Sisters, I have often said since arriving in these mountains and valleys that if the people of the United States will let us alone for ten years, we will ask no odds of them." Young got no further with his discourse, interrupted by cheering and applause. He allowed the people's cheers for a time before signaling for quiet.

"We are assembled here to celebrate those ten years. While we have not been left alone altogether, this people have prospered." More cheering. "Now, my brothers and sisters, the despots leading the so-called government of the United States are sending troops into our midst. Brothers Smoot and Stoddard have seen it with their own eyes." The pronouncement, while not surprising to most, still prompted a wave of shock through the assembly, that crested with murmurs and broke with boos, hisses, and catcalls.

When the ruckus abated, Young continued. "We are invaded by a hostile force, who are evidently assailing us to accomplish our overthrow and destruction. We should not quietly stand still and see those fetters forging around us, which are calculated to enslave us in subjection to an unlawful military despotism. The army will be followed by priests, politicians, speculators, whoremongers, and every mean, filthy character that could be raked up to kill off the Mormons."

Again, the audience interrupted the oratory with their ire. Again, Young stilled the crowd and continued.

"We have borne enough of their oppression and hellish abuse, and we will not bear any more of it. In the name of Israel's God, we ask no odds of them. If General Harney and his army cross South Pass, the buzzards shall pick his bones; we will no more submit to oppression either to individuals, towns, counties, states, or nation."

Rather than ire, enthusiasm and affirmation interrupted Young.

"Brothers and sisters, as I stand before you and before our God, I proclaim that this people constitute henceforth a free and independent state, to be no longer known as Utah, but by our own name of Deseret."

The crowd erupted in acclamation. But what happened next betrayed that the theatrics of Young's discourse were, to some degree, more planned than spontaneous. As the Stars and Stripes of the United States of America flew in the alpenglow, lighting the peaks and treetops around the valley of Silver Lake, one of Young's assistants joined him atop the boulder, shouldering a tall flagstaff. He unfurled the blue and white banner of the State of Deseret—assembled by Salt Lake City seamstresses in the weeks leading up to the celebration.

Other speakers took to the stone stump to further stir the crowd. Heber Kimball, Young's first counselor in the presidency, roused the biggest ovation when, after encouraging the Saints to, "Adhere to Brigham as your prophet, seer, revelator, priest, governor, and king," he harangued the distant government: "Send twenty-five hundred troops here to make a desolation of this people! God Almighty helping me, I will fight until there is not a drop of blood in my veins. Good God! I have wives enough to whip out the United States, for they will whip themselves."

The pioneers kicked up their heels through the evening and night. Dancing feet flattened meadow grass. Hurrahs, huzzahs, and three cheers for Deseret—countered with "three groans" for the hated state of Missouri—filled the mountain air. And a newly minted song filled the throats of the men of the Nauvoo legion:

Powder, bullet, sword and gun
Boys arouse we'll have some fun
As sure as fate the time has come
So fix your guns for shooting.

CHAPTER TWELVE

After months in the random chaos of the natural world, arriving in Salt Lake City in late July was like entering another world. The wide city streets, laid out in the cardinal directions of the compass, formed a grid of square blocks as routine and regular as the ticking of an eight-day clock. The city lay hard against the Wasatch Mountains, and as the wagons emerged from the canyon onto the benchlands—beaches left behind by the waves of ancient seas—Polly Alden saw before her down below more buildings in one place than ever before in her life. Glad to be off the dizzying mountain slopes and out of the oppressive craggy confines of the canyons, she eyed the spread of the valley, the mountain range defining its limits west and south, and the wide expanse to the northwest where the immense salt lake sparkled in the sun.

The wagon road angled down off the bench and turned due west, becoming Brigham Street, the main thoroughfare into the heart of the city from the east. The wagons rolled past homes set uniformly on city lots dividing the square blocks, each place with outbuildings in the rear, garden plots and fruit trees at the side, and fronted by dooryards. Irrigation ditches lined the streets, flowing with clear water fed by streams falling out of the mountains.

Horseback men sat at the intersections, keeping the train on the main road and out of the neighborhoods. When the cow herd came down, other mounted man intercepted the drive to lead it on a roundabout route skirting the city.

Abe Baker, riding at the head of the cattle, pulled up in front of the line of riders crosswise in the street. "What do you-all want?"

One man, older than the rest, his creped face fringed by a grayshot beard, stepped his horse ahead, a few paces out of the line. "If you will follow me, son, we will take you to the herd ground where you can pasture your cattle."

Abe's eyes flicked back and forth along the line of riders. They did not look to be armed, nor did they appear threatening. "If it's all the same to you-all, we'd as soon follow our wagons."

"I am sorry, son, but we cannot allow it."

"Why so?"

The old man watched the approaching herd as it snaked down off the bench for a moment, then turned his attention to Abe. "We are accustomed to emigrants coming through here. Every summer, wagons come through. They cause us trouble enough, but we allow it." The man shifted in his saddle, his weight in the stirrups rocking from side to side, the leather creaking as he sought a more comfortable seat.

"Cattle, now, that's something different. The animals leave behind a godawful mess. And they's as likely to go through a fence and tear up a garden or crop field as not. Fact is, sometimes the drovers will open the gates themselves and turn the critters into places they don't belong."

By now the body of the herd had arrived. Howard and Billy Red rode in front of the leaders to hold them, and the pause flowed back through the cattle like a wave. Howard rode up to stand beside Abe.

Abe said, "Well, sir, these cattle are trail weary and unlikely to cause any trouble. They've been handled all the way from Arkansas and are gentle as milk cows."

"All the same," the old man said, "you are to follow my lead around the city."

Abe stiffened. "And if we don't want to?"

The old man heaved a long sigh. "Son, it don't matter a whit to me whether you want to or not. You will do as we say, or your herd can go right on back up the canyon and all the way back to Arkansas so far as I am concerned."

Without a word, and so easily that no one noticed, Howard dropped the lash of his bullwhip to the ground. He raised his arm and snapped it ahead. The thong arced forward and the popper cracked like a gunshot close enough to the old man's face he could feel the whiff of air. Faster than either of the Arkansas boys could blink, sidearms appeared in the hands of the Mormon guards, drawn from under the fronts of their jackets and pulled from pockets. The metallic ticking of hammers snapping into place sounded above the lowing of the cow herd.

"Howard, you damn fool!" Abe said. "Wind up that whip and get the hell away!"

"You ain't goin' to let these Mormon sonsabitches tell us what to do are you?" Howard hissed.

"Just get back. You'll get us killed."

Glowering from one face to the other, Howard coiled his whip. Drumming hoofbeats announced the approach of Captain Baker, coming up the street at a run. He reined his horse around the line of men and slid to a stop between Abe and the old man.

"What the hell's goin' on here?"

Howard started rapid-fire talk, but the captain shushed him and asked Abe, who apprised him of the situation.

Baker turned to the old man. "Is it true, what he says?"

The old man nodded. "It's so. It ain't no different for your herd than it is for any other that comes through. If your boys will just follow us along, we'll get your cattle beyond the city to where they can bed down."

"Do as he says, Abe," Baker said, then turned to the old man. "There's another train right behind us. It'll be comin' out of the canyon soon. Led by a man name of Fancher. He's got a sizeable herd of cattle with him, too. We had best get these critters on the move, or Fancher's wagons'll be on top of us."

The old man nodded. "This way." He reined his horse around and started down a road leading south. Abe signaled Billy Red, who used his whip to get the lead cattle moving. Abe told Howard to get to work, and fell in behind the old man. As the cattle moved down the wide street, one of the Mormon riders would move out in turn to ride beside them, ignoring Baker's drovers.

The captain watched the trailing cattle for a time, then urged his horse into a trot to catch up to the wagon train, by now well into the city.

Polly had a time paying attention and staying abreast of her teams, her eyes wandering to the houses and commercial buildings they passed. The oxen paid no attention, plodding along as if the city streets were of no more interest than the fifteen hundred miles of trail their hooves had trodden to get here. But Polly marveled at the tidy houses and well-kept yards, the growing trees along the streets, the shops, and the multistory buildings with colorful signs advertising stores and offices.

She noticed behind a low wall an impressive building with a sculpted beehive topping its cupola, and the rows of gabled windows on the building next door, unaware she was passing the office of Brigham Young and the home of many of his wives and families. The wall continued along the block, encompassing the looming tithing office and its yards and pens. The next block was busy with stonecutters and excavators laying the foundations for what looked to be an immense structure.

People going about their business on the streets and sidewalks made way for the wagon train, stopping to watch the passersby. Polly saw few women alone; most were accompanied by a passel of children or with other women. She wondered if they were friends—or wives married to the same husband. Some of what she assumed to be families walked along like ducks in a row, an older man leading a parade of women—many with babes in arms—followed by a line of children of diminishing size. Similar family groups sat in buggies and carriages and watched the Arkansas emigrants pass. Most of the watchers were silent, but now and then someone would call out a question, wondering where the train originated, or where they were bound. Others made unkind remarks, encouraging a short stay or questioning their parentage and other insults.

The homes thinned out and the streets quieted as the train rolled westward. The wagons crossed a bridge over the Jordan River and turned to the south. After a few miles, the Mormon man serving as pilot signaled that the wagons had arrived at their campsite.

"This is it?" Baker said. "This is where you want us to lay over?"

The guide only nodded.

"Look around, man! This ain't nothin' but a dirt patch. And there ain't no firewood—that riverbank's been stripped clean of anything but willows."

The man shrugged. "This is the wagon camp. Your company is no different than the one that pulled out two days ago—or any other, for that matter. You can stay here or move on. Suit yourself."

"What about our cow herd?"

The man nodded southward. "Pasture's another mile or so beyond."

Baker looked that way. "It don't look none too green down

thataway. Is it as picked over as this place you call a camp? I see plenty of grass on south of there—east and west, too, and damn near everywhere else."

The Mormon sat for a time without answering. Then he shrugged and said that it had been dry the last few winters, and the grass Baker referred to was for the Saints' cattle and sheep, and that if the Arkansas cattle strayed onto communal pastures they would be seized, and there would be a steep price to get them back. He nodded farewell and rode back toward the city.

As the cow herd took its roundabout route past the city, Howard paid less attention to the cattle than the people they passed. Houses were spread out on the fringe of the city, and many of the streets were nothing more than two-track wagon ruts in the wide thoroughfares. He paid particular attention to the females going about their work. He watched women hanging out laundry to dry, at work in gardens, sitting on stoops and porches or under shade trees at some kind of needlework, and other tasks. The women came in all ages, from fresh-faced youngsters, to middle-aged and matronly, to the timeworn and elderly—and a good many of an age he thought ripe for plucking.

Most of the women paused at their work to watch the herd as it passed. Howard popped his whip from time to time to impress the spectators. He tipped his hat to those whose eye he caught, and offered greetings to some. Those he found most attractive were offered invitations, some bordering on obscene.

"Hey, Red!" he hollered at Billy Red, riding opposite him beside the ambling cattle. "You seein' all these women? A body ought to be able to find hisself someone to cuddle with at night."

Billy Red ignored Howard. But the Mormon escort riding a few rods ahead of Howard did not. He spun his horse around and waited, scowling at Howard as he rode up, reaching out to his horse's neck and snatching a rein. The man—a young man, perhaps a year or two older than Howard but taller in the saddle and carrying a good twenty extra pounds of muscle—jerked the Arkansas horse to a stop.

"From here on, you had best keep your mouth shut," the Mormon said. "You show any more disrespect to our womenfolk and I will pull you off that horse and thrash you but good."

Howard paled, but his temper soon overcame his fear. He leaned over in the saddle and spat a string of tobacco juice, barely missing the horse and the rider's stirruped foot. He wiped his mouth and smiled. "Hell, mister—I don't mean no harm. Just bein' friendly, is all. I don't know how you-all do things 'round here, but where I come from, folks is sociable."

"All the same, you watch your mouth. Not only that, while you are here you had best stay right away from the ladies."

"I don't see why I should. Hell, if you-all would content yourselves with one wife like ever'body else, there'd be plenty of women to go around. Ain't no reason I can see why some old man's got three or four pretty girls to keep him warm nights while I ain't got any. 'Sides, it'd only be for a few nights, then we'll be movin' on."

The Mormon's hand, still clutching the rein on Howard's mount, quivered enough to rattle the bit chain. His face and neck flushed red and his jaw clenched hard enough to crack teeth. His breath seethed and his eyes locked tight on Howard's. After a long minute, he let go of the rein and thrust a pointed finger at Howard's face, stopping just short of his nose. "Not another word," he said, barely above a whisper. He cleared his throat. "I hear any more out of you, you rude little bastard, I will forget my manners and beat you within an inch of your life."

Again, Howard blanched.

"Understood?"

Howard nodded. He did not spit out the tobacco juice that

filled his mouth. Instead, he swallowed hard and felt it burn its way down his throat.

The Mormon man turned his horse away and heeled it into a gentle lope until finding his place beside the herd, which plodded along unaware.

Chapter Thirteen

Alexander Fancher noted how much Salt Lake City had grown since his last trip through. As his wagons followed a Mormon pilot through the streets, his cattle, like the Baker herd, skirted the city. While accustomed to the arrival of hundreds and hundreds of emigrants every summer, the people in the city seldom saw two trains pass through on the same day. Much as Captain Baker had done, Colonel Fancher complained about the poor conditions at the campsite, and the sparse feed for livestock on the herd grounds. Like Captain Baker, Colonel Fancher received little sympathy and no alternative other than to press on down the road if circumstances were not to his liking.

So the emigrants set up camp in the dust and scoured the riverbanks for driftwood and overlooked deadfall to feed cooking fires. The cattle nosed the parched and sparse bunchgrass and denuded brush in the pasture, seeking a palatable mouthful. Despite the unfavorable state of affairs, most of the people in the trains looked forward to a few days' rest. And, they hoped to visit the city for the attractions a settled area offered—a diversion not available these past months on the road.

"What do you think, Polly—will there be any handsome boys in that city?"

"Sarah, your mind is too often on men."

"Well, it don't hurt none to look at what's on offer. A girl's got to look somewheres for her entertainments. I can't get two words in a row out of that darn Billy Brown."

Polly, unpacking a kitchen box with her back to her friend, smiled. "There's always Howard."

With a snort, Sarah said, "Howard! He's got plenty to say, all right. Trouble is, ain't none of it worth hearin'. Land sakes! That boy ain't got no better manners than Pa's off ox—and you've seen how contrary that critter is. No thank you! I'll sooner take my chances with the Mormon boys."

"You know that if you do, you might end up married to a man who already has a wife—or two or three."

"Oh, pshaw! That's just the old men. I'd get me one young enough he could still be taught proper ways. 'Sides, I ain't got no notion of hitchin' up with nobody just yet. Not till after I've had my fun. Maybe tomorrow we can go on into the town and see what's on offer."

"Maybe," Polly said. "If my work will allow me the time."

Polly went about her work, wondering how Sarah's attitudes about men could be so different from her own. About the only thing they agreed on, it seemed, was the unsuitability of Howard. Polly gave little thought to men and boys, outside of her day-to-day camp duties seeing to the well-being of the drovers. Any amusements men might offer were of no interest, and marriage was so far in the future it had no definable shape. The only advantage she could see was that marriage would mean taking care of one man rather than four or five, as would be her fate until reaching California. Of what might happen after that, she had no notion.

The rising sun revealed a beehive of activity in the camp. The wagon masters dispatched wagons and crews to the mountains to cut firewood enough to see them through their stay in the valley. Others were assigned to follow the leaders into the city to haul back supplies.

Those without appointed duties were free to come and go as they pleased. Except for Howard. Captain Baker, apprised of the boy's behavior toward the Mormon women, meted out punishment in the form of riding herd on the pastured cattle.

"Like hell I will!" the boy said, with his usual expectorated punctuation.

"You'll have hell to pay if you don't," Baker said. "Take the time to think on your manners—or lack of 'em. You've got no call to be rude to women—or anybody else—like you have done."

"Aw, Cap'n, I was just funnin'. Never meant nothin' by it. And it never hurt no one."

"So you say. From what I heard, you were damn lucky that Mormon boy never put the hurt on you. Sounds like he was fit to pound you into the ground."

Howard spat. "He might've tried. I don't think he could've done it."

Baker laughed. "All the same, boy, you stay here and keep an eye on the cattle. Make sure they don't wander onto that Mormon grass."

Howard looked at the cattle in the distance, most still on their bellies on the ground. "Don't look like them cows is any too interested in goin' any place." He extended an arm and a pointed finger in the direction of distant horsemen. "Besides, there's already Mormons out there horseback to see they don't eat any of their damn grass. Hell, you'd think the stuff was gold-plated."

"Mind your business and stay away from them," Baker said and headed for the wagons outfitted for town.

As he walked away, Howard sent a long stream of ropy tobacco juice in his direction.

Captain Baker and Colonel Fancher led the empty wagons into

the city. Each carried a list of supplies needed by members of their companies. The first stop, a large general merchandise store that fronted a warehouse, turned the buyers away all but empty-handed, the clerk claiming they had no bacon, no hams, no flour, no rolled oats, no cornmeal, no rice, no beans for sale. The only purchase the emigrants made was a crate of crumbling pilot bread. Two other outlets likewise turned them away with nothing but a single bag of rolled barley that would not feed the working horses for a day, a keg of vinegar, and a hundredweight of potatoes likely stored over the winter as they showed lengthy sprouts. A produce market would part with nothing more than a few boxes of wilted greens and a bushel of bruised apricots. Their visits to gunsmiths and armorers, looking to replenish their stores of lead and powder as well as to purchase additional firearms, were equally unproductive.

Undaunted, the wagon masters left town and struck the road for the mouth of the Big Canyon, called Parley's Canyon by some, named for the apostle who built a toll road through there and now lay dead and buried in Arkansas. They hoped the miller would sell them whole grains as well as milled flour. Again, Baker and Fancher were turned away. The talkative clerk at the mill, unlike the taciturn storekeepers in the city, let slip that Brigham Young had ordered his followers not to sell to "Gentiles"—as the Mormons called those not of their faith—as with the United States Army approaching and war pending, there was a need to store supplies for use by the Saints.

On the way back to camp, the wagons pulled up to watch a local militia unit put through its paces. The soldiers, despite a lack of uniforms, and carrying firearms of various kinds and quality, were well disciplined and well drilled.

"What do you think, Colonel Fancher?"

"Looks like they mean business, Captain Baker."

They watched the marchers for a few minutes before Baker

spoke again. "You think the government really means to send an army way out here?"

"You know what they told us at Fort Bridger. 'Course you can't take the word of the Mormons there, but I talked with some folks who come up the main trail, and they say they saw freight wagons hauling supplies, and that the army was already on the move."

Baker mulled that over for a time. "You think there's to be fighting?"

Fancher shrugged. "Wouldn't dare say." He nodded toward the militia. "Them boys seem to think so."

"Could be all for show."

"Could be—if we was anywhere else. Out here, there ain't nobody to put on a show for. And Brigham Young has 'em actin' like it's serious business. I ain't never been turned away when needin' supplies here before. You?"

Baker shook his head.

"When you can't trade gold for a filch of bacon, I guess you could say these Mormons are expectin' real trouble."

Before the supply wagons made it back to the camp, Polly and Sarah had spruced themselves up as much as conditions allowed and set off to walk the few miles to the city. Again, Polly was taken with the orderliness of the city, and overwhelmed with its scale.

The girls visited store after store, eyeing the variety of goods displayed for sale. There were mercantile outfits where you could dress from head to toe, harness a horse from bridle bit and brow band to crupper and breeching, then buy a wagon or buggy to hitch it to. You could buy food and fabric, farm implements and footwear, hats and hairpins. But, with Polly carrying only a few coins given her by Captain Baker for pocket money, and Sarah with nothing to spend, the girls limited their purchases to a sack of assorted hard candies each, and a hair ribbon admired by Sarah and paid for by Polly.

Sarah's hopes to meet boys went unfulfilled. The young men they encountered on the streets—all of whom they assumed to be local Mormon boys—either ducked their heads and pretended not to notice them in passing, or offered, at most, a tip of the hat and a word of greeting. They knew the boys were not blind, or lacked interest, as the girls could see them watching as they strolled the streets and sidewalks.

"I guess all the boys hereabouts is plumb shy," Sarah said.

"Either that, or they are only interested in Mormon girls."

Sarah chuckled. "Oh, they's interested in us, all right. You seen 'em lookin'. Ain't a boy alive what's got his growth who ain't interested in a pretty girl."

"Maybe we are not pretty enough for them."

Sarah stopped short, grabbed Polly by the arm, and spun her around to face her, grasping the other arm as she turned. "Why Polly Alden! Don't you never say such a thing! There's been more'n a few boys take a shine to me, and I been told by plenty of growed men that I'm right pretty." She gave Polly a shake. "And you—why, I can't hold a candle to you when it comes to pretty."

Sarah reached up and stroked Polly's cheek and tucked a stray wisp of hair back under her bonnet. "Just look at your cheeks—even with all the sun, they're smooth and soft as a baby's bottom. And they've got roses in 'em even 'thout you pinchin' 'em up." Polly blushed. "And your hair's all shiny—why, mine don't shine like that after a hundred brushes." She pushed Polly back a step and took her by the hands. "I don't never want to hear you say you ain't pretty 'cause I know darn well you are. And I'll tell you somethin' else—there ain't a man in our company—and them with Fancher's, too—who don't know it as well as I do."

On the way back to camp in the late afternoon, the girls

passed Howard, horseback and trotting toward town. The captain had released him, with a caution to behave himself. Riding beside him was a young man from the Fancher train called Skeets. He touched the brim of his hat and nodded as they rode by, while Howard removed his hat and swept it across his belly and bowed deeply off the side of his horse. "Ladies, we are off to town. But don't you-all run off, as we'll be back 'fore mornin'. If we ain't lucky in town, we may call on you-all." He turned in the saddle and shouted as he rode away, "See you in the mornin'—but not much before!"

Back at camp, Polly got her other drovers fed and went about the business of cleaning up and readying for the night. As she worked, a rider from Fancher's company came by, stopping at each wagon summoning the heads of all the families and the unattached men with wagons to assemble around a bonfire just taking flame between the two wagon camps.

"Gentlemen," Colonel Fancher said from his perch atop a packing box, "most of you-all know by now that Captain Baker and me had no luck buying supplies in the city. The Mormons are fearful of war, and they ain't inclined to trust anyone who ain't one of 'em. Captain, tell 'em what you was told."

Baker, who stood on a box beside Fancher, cleared his throat. "I stopped by a wagon yard to see about getting a spare king pin for one of my wagons. Fellow asked where we come from. I told him Arkansas. He got his hackles up and asked if we were the 'sonsabitches' that killed Parley Pratt. I told him I had no idea who Parley Pratt was. Can't say as he believed me. The thing is, it is clear that these people are hostile toward us—and, I dare say, anyone else who comes through here while the Mormons are fearing the approach of the army."

Fancher spoke up. "The captain and I have talked it over at length, and we believe the best course is for our companies to join up for safety's sake, at least till we get beyond Mormon country—which is good long way."

The announcement spurred some talk among the men, but no one raised an objection. Some men voiced a desire to go for provisions themselves, others to trade worn-out oxen for fresh cattle on their own. The wagon masters told them they were free to do as they pleased. The talk continued.

Baker raised his hands for silence. "Another thing, gentlemen. We intended to lay over here a few more days. But since the Mormons are reluctant—even downright unwilling—to sell us much in the way of supplies, we feel it best to be on our way. Perhaps, in the smaller settlements along the way, they will be less worrisome and fearful, and thereby more willing to trade with us. We will allow our animals another day of rest and make one more attempt to acquire supplies tomorrow—you-all can try to outfit yourselves as you wish. In any event, be ready to move on day after tomorrow."

A man in the crowd spoke up. "I thought we was to lay over here a week or more!"

"My teams need rest!" another said.

Other voices expressed similar sentiments.

"All true," Fancher said. "And we know it. But we ain't exactly welcome here, and might have a better chance of getting supplies in other towns."

That, too, spurred conversation among the company. Most were somewhat familiar, at least from reports, with the trail ahead, and knew other settlements were rare, even nonexistent. Fancher told the men they would not be taking the trail north to loop around the big salt lake and meet the main trail along the Humboldt River. He said he and Baker had been told more than once that, owing to a lengthy drought, there was little feed on the Humboldt road, and that the Shoshoni and Paiutes were raiding wagon trains on that trail. As a result, they would be taking the southern road to California, and that there were a number of Mormon communities along the way where they might find supplies. Any travelers who disagreed with any of the plans were welcome to leave the company and strike out on their own, or with others who were like minded, he said. But the colonel urged them to stay together, for safety's sake.

As the meeting at the camp wound down and the men formed in groups to talk things over, in the city Howard and his newfound friend Skeets, a Missouri boy from the Fancher train and also a drover, tied their horses to a rail and staggered into their fourth saloon. They intended to visit every grog shop in the part of the city called "Whiskey Street" before they were through.

The boys had plenty of money—at least Howard did—as he had harangued Captain Baker for an advance on his pay when the train was at Fort Bridger, claiming he needed tobacco money. Dissatisfied with the amount Baker offered, Howard opined they were at least halfway to California, and he felt he was owed half of his promised wage. Baker, rather than argue with the troublesome drover, crawled into one of his wagons and crawled back out with payment in gold coins.

Howard slid a gold eagle across the bar, still laughing at something Skeets had said when they entered the saloon. Skeets launched into song—if his wailing words could be called such—belting out the chorus of "Oh! Susanna." The barkeeper poured the rowdy newcomers drinks and left the bottle on the bar. He picked up the coin and examined it. "Where'd you get that, Sonny? We don't see too many of these around here."

"Aw, hell, that ain't nothin'. Man I work for, Cap'n Baker, he's got a wagonload of 'em. Unless I miss my guess, ol' man Fancher's got a right smart of gold hid away in his wagons, too."

Skeets nodded in agreement.

Howard turned away from the bar and hoisted his glass.

"Here's one for Arkansas!" he hollered, then drained the glass in one gulp. Skeets raised his glass, the movement causing him to sway from front to rear. Howard grabbed his free arm. "Steady, son."

Skeets pulled his arm loose and yelled, "Here's to Missoura!"

Before he had time to swallow, silence fell over the saloon like a blanket. Skeets, still swaying, looked at Howard. "What'd I say?"

"Who gives a shit?" Howard said. He slammed his glass on the bar and refilled it, splashing more onto the polished wood than into the glass. He turned back around to find three red-faced men facing off against Skeets.

"Whoa, boys! What's goin' on here?"

"Missouri, you say?" one of the men said through clenched teeth.

Skeets smiled, his lips as unsteady as the rest of him. "That's right—born and bred."

Another of the men spoke. "We don't like Missouri. You Pukes done gave us hell when we lived there."

Skeets smiled again. "That's all right, mister. We don't much like Mormons, neither." He turned to Howard. "Pour me 'nother one, Howard."

Howard brought the bottle around and poured the waving glass full, missing as much as he hit, and overflowing the rim.

"Fact is," Skeets said, his voice raised for the benefit of everyone in the room. "My pappy and grandpappy was with them that drove you damn Mormons out of Missoura." He swallowed half the liquor from his glass. "And, by damn, we'd do it again." More of the patrons had gathered in front of the two boys. "But from what I hear tell, we won't have to kick you-all's asses ag'in—the U.S. Army—bunch of bastards too, they are—is goin' to do it this time." He drained his glass. "Keep them damn soldiers out of Missoura, and get rid of you sonsabitches at the same time." He raised his glass again. "To Missoura!" he said, then noticed the glass was empty.

Skeets shrugged and turned back to the bar. He reached for the bottle, but found the bartender's hand already around it. The man drew the bottle back and leaned across the bar. "You've had enough, Sonny. Besides, I don't know if you've noticed it or not, but there's a whole bunch of folks about to give you a beating. Was I you, I'd shut my mouth and walk on out of here while you can still walk. And take your friend with you."

Howard, a little worse for wear than Skeets, grabbed his friend by the arm and took a step forward, only to find the men before them unmoving. He took off his hat and swept it past his belly and bowed. Upright again, he said, "If you-all gents will allow us the road, we'll be leavin'."

"You had better go," one of the men said. "And you had best not come back. You ain't welcome here, or anywhere else in the city—not in the whole of the territory, come to that."

Howard and Skeets walked as slowly and carefully through the crowd of men and out the door as their condition allowed, mounted their horses, and rode south.

Much has changed these past weeks in our travel and now there are to be more changes. The Capt and Col Fancher seem worrisome as they have been unable to get provisions in Salt Lake City and the Mormons are unfriendly.

I and Sarah paid a visit to the City and shops and stores were a welcome sight after these months in the wilderness. Never have I seen a City such as this with all its people and so many houses and big buildings. The people were not friendly, but neither were they ~~mean~~ unkind.

Sarah was disappointed that the young men we saw showed no interest in us. It may be more correct to say they kept it to themselves.

Sarah is keen to meet boys. I do not know how I feel. I do know that I have seen no one in the wagon trains that appeals to me in that way and for some reason I do not feel any loss because of it. As for the Mormon boys we saw, well I can only say I paid them no mind as our presence among them is to be brief and their dislike of us forbids familiarity.

Is there to be a gentleman friend for me? If so, will I know it? Sarah has set me to thinking of things I have not thought about before.

I wish Mother was here.

CHAPTER FOURTEEN

Tom kept the team at a trot. Other than rest stops for the mules, he would make this trip to the city without a layover. Otherwise, the wagonload of produce bound for market would spoil. Bags and baskets and boxes in the back held corn, beets, peas, cherries, snap beans, carrots, cucumbers, and potatoes grown in Springville. While tiring, the trip to Salt Lake City offered a welcome respite from the monotony of home life.

Hiram rode beside him, making his first trip to the city. The boy had begged and beseeched their father for permission, granted only when Hiram's mother, Grace, asked leave for the boy to go, claiming that having one less child to deal with in her delicate condition, even for a few days, would be welcome.

As always, Bishop Mendenhall had written out explicit instructions for Tom for the disposal of the produce, including a schedule of what vegetables came from which of his flock's gardens, with notes on quantity and quality. Also included were the bishop's estimates of what prices the produce should bring.

Dawn was just breaking as the boys passed Provo—unbeknownst to Hiram, as he slept, propped against Tom on the wagon seat. The sun rose and the day lengthened as the wagon rolled though Springtown and Pleasant Grove. Hiram peppered Tom with endless questions, pausing only to chew on sandwiches of thick bread and ham slices, packed for the boys by Tom's mother. American Fork came and went and Tom kept the mules on the trot through Lehi and the gap through Point of the Mountain.

As the wagon approached the Hot Springs Hotel and Brewery, a long southbound train of ox-drawn covered wagons filled the road ahead. Tom pulled off the track and stopped the team. The mules could use a blow, anyway. Hiram perked up at the sight of the wagons, again filling the air with questions Tom could not answer: who were these people, where did they come from, where are they going, how come them oxens are so big, how many wagons are there, who's that man on the horse, is all them cows back there theirs, how many cows are there, what's that noise, are they shootin' guns—and on and on. Tom could only smile and ruffle the boy's hair.

Captain Baker, riding at the head of the train, reined up beside the wagon. "Good day."

Tom nodded. "And you."

Hiram said nothing, doing his best to hide himself behind Tom.

Baker cast his eyes over the wagonload, covered with a canvas fly. "What are you-all boys hauling there?"

Tom did not hear the question, his eyes riveted to the girl handling the oxen on the second wagon in the train, just then rolling to a stop.

"Son?"

With a start, Tom turned to the mounted man. "Sir?"

"I asked what you-all are carrying in your wagon."

"Garden truck, mostly. Peas and beans and the like. Carrots and 'taters and such."

Baker shifted in the saddle. "Where are you-all bound? If you don't mind my asking."

"Salt Lake." Tom looked at the stalled wagons filling the road, and the herd of cattle milling back down the trail. "Look, mister, we got to be on our way 'fore this stuff ain't fresh no more. Folks back home is countin' on us to get it to market.

They need the money. Won't get much for it if it sits much longer."

"Market, you say? Could be I could take it off your hands. Mind if I have a look?"

Tom thought it over for a time, then set the brake and wrapped lines around the brake handle. He told Hiram to stay put, and stepped down off the wagon. He untied the ropes securing the canvas and rolled it back to uncover the load. Baker stayed on his horse, but rode up and stopped beside the wagon, looking over the load.

"Any reason you-all can't sell to me? Save you a trip, and I'll give you a fair price."

Again, the distraction of the girl with the goad kept Tom from hearing the question. Baker repeated it, and Tom mulled over the proposition. He shrugged. "I don't guess there's any reason why not—long as we get our price."

"And what might that be?"

Pulling Bishop Mendenhall's paperwork from the wagon's jockey box, Tom toted up the figures in his head, losing track and starting again twice. Then he checked the figures again. He gave Baker the amount the bishop expected the produce to bring.

This time, Baker took time to think. "Tell you what—we'll give you what you ask, plus another five dollars. Just so there's no question of us takin' advantage of you-all."

Tom smiled. "I reckon that to be more than fair, mister."

"You'll take payment in gold, I expect."

The boy's smile widened. "I expect so, sir." Gold was in short supply in Springville, and he had no doubt the bishop would be pleased to have it.

By that time, a crowd of the emigrants had gathered near the wagon. Baker set them to work unloading Tom's wagon, with instructions to stow it in his wagons for distribution to the company when the train made camp. All the while, Tom found it hard to look away from the girl at the second wagon. It did not escape his notice that she stole a glance at him from time to time. Baker returned with payment in gold coins, supplemented with a few coins of Spanish silver.

Baker offered his hand to seal the deal. "My name is John Baker, by the way. Most folks call me Captain Baker."

"Tom Langford." He pointed to Hiram, still sitting on the wagon seat, now looking more bored than wide-eyed. "That's Hiram. Hiram Mendenhall. He's my brother, kind of. My ma is married to his pa."

"Where you from, Tom?"

"Springville—it's on down this road. Left there before mornin', we did."

Baker asked if he knew of a place the train could lay over, as the day was getting late, and Tom directed them on past the Point of the Mountain to an oft-used camping place not far from a town called Lehi. He offered to lead the way if they would make room for him to turn the wagon around. Baker ordered the first three wagons to move on ahead and wait beside the road. Tom eased his wagon around and started back south. As he passed the second wagon he locked eyes with the girl with her goad, standing next to the ox teams watching him pass.

"Tom—how come we turned around? Where we goin'? I thought we was goin' to Salt Lake!"

"We don't have to go anymore, Hiram. These folks bought all the stuff we were goin' to the city to sell."

"But I want to go to Salt Lake! Ma said I could! So did Pa!"

"Sorry, Hi. Not this time."

The boy hunched his shoulders and folded his arms and bowed his head. He might have been sulking, or maybe praying for Tom to change his mind. In any case, he did not look up or speak to Tom for several long minutes as the wagon, empty save their camp equipment, rattled along the road.

"Say, Hi—how'd you like to drive?"

Hiram perked up. "Me? Drive the wagon? You bet!"

The boy's driving experience was limited, so Tom showed the boy how to hold the lines, cautioning him not to jerk or yank them. "You just hold on to 'em like that, and them mules will just walk on down the road. Shouldn't be no need to stop, but if somethin' happens, just draw back on them lines gentle-like and say 'whoa' a time or two, and the mules will stop."

"Don't you worry none, Tom. I'll do just fine."

Hiram sat tall on the seat, holding the lines as gently as if they had eggs for handles.

Tom sat beside him for a time. Then, "Think you can handle 'em all right?"

With a smile, Hiram turned to Tom and said he could.

"Well, you go on ahead, then. I'm goin' to step off here."

"How come?"

"Oh, you know—I just need to stretch my legs for a bit. But don't you worry—I'll be right behind you."

Hiram sat up a little taller, his eyes locked on the mules and the road ahead. Tom slid off the seat and, with a hand on the box board, swung past the wheel and lit on the ground. He stood and watched the wagon roll away, confident that the boy would have no trouble with the well-trained, docile team. The man walking beside the ox team drawing the first wagon in the train walked by. He nodded *hello* at Tom with a knowing smile. Tom walked behind the wagon and crossed the road as the second wagon drew near, so as to be on the same side of the road as the girl driving the oxen.

Tom took off his hat. "Miss . . ." He swallowed hard and shifted his weight from one foot to the other.

Polly Alden smiled. "Mister."

Tom swallowed again. "I thought maybe you could use a hand with them oxen." He put his hat back on and walked beside the girl.

"And who might you be?"

"I—I'm—my name is Tom Langford."

"Well, Mister Langford, I have handled these cattle every day since we left Arkansas longer ago than I care to remember. I suspect I can continue to do so without your assistance."

Tom's face flushed.

"But it is kind of you to offer."

They walked along in silence for a few minutes. Tom said, "Arkansas, you say? I ain't never been to Arkansas. What's it like there?"

"Oh, I suppose it is much like any other place. Not so dry as this, and trees are as thick as the sagebrush you people seem to grow so much of here."

"Oh, no, miss—we don't grow no sagebrush. It grows all on its own. It was already growin' here when we come."

Polly smiled. "Is that so, Mister Langford?"

"Yes it is, miss . . . I guess I don't know your name."

"I am not surprised, Mister Langford. I have not given it to you."

"Yes, miss."

"Would you like to know my name, Mister Langford?"

"Oh, yes, miss. It would be less awkward talkin' to you if I knew what to call you."

"Awkward, Mister Langford? You find it awkward to talk to me?"

"Oh, no, miss . . . I mean . . . Well, I just don't know what to call you, that's all."

"Polly Alden. My name is Polly Alden."

"Why, that's a right pretty name, Poll—Miss Alden, I mean."

"You may call me Polly if you wish, Mister Langford."

"Yes, Miss—Polly. I wisht you'd call me Tom."

"And so I will, Tom."

They talked as they walked. Polly informed Tom in answer to his questions that she was not traveling with her family. That she had lost her family and was in the employ of the wagon master, Captain Baker, to drive this wagon and see to the feeding of the drovers herding the captain's cattle. That, having no family and no prospects in Arkansas, she hoped for a fresh start in California.

"And what about you, Tom? Is that young man you abandoned to his fate on the wagon your brother?"

"No, he ain't my brother. I ain't got no family 'cept my mother. My pa and my little sisters and brother took sick and died on the way out here. Hiram, he's, well, my ma is married to his pa. So we ain't no kin, but we're family of a sort, I guess."

"What happened to Hiram's mother?"

"Grace. That's her name—Grace. There ain't nothin' wrong with her. She's got a passel of little kids 'sides Hiram. She'll be havin' another young'un some of these days."

Polly said nothing for a time, then, "So your father—stepfather, I should say—has two wives?"

"No, he ain't got two wives—he's got three. 'Sides my Ma and Grace, there's Jane. She's old, like the bishop."

"Bishop?"

"I guess you don't have no way to know how things is 'round here. When we got out here to Utah, Ma and me had no way to make a go of it, me bein' too young for regular work and all. So, someone—might've been Brigham Young his own self, for all I know—sent us down to Hobble Creek—they call it Springville now—to Bishop—Aaron—Mendenhall. He's the man in charge—the bishop. He's the head of the church in the town, and sees to most ever'thing else, besides.

"Anyway, the bishop, he took a shine to Ma right off and

asked her to be his wife."

Again, Polly took a while to measure her thoughts. "Your mother doesn't mind this? I mean, being married to a man who has two other wives?"

Tom shrugged. "I guess not. Lots of the old men hereabouts, especially the big men in the church, has got more'n one wife. It ain't too easy on Ma, though. Jane, she thinks she's somethin' special, bein' the first wife, and don't do too much. And Grace, well, she's kind of lazy, and it seems like she's with child most of the time, so she don't do much either. That leaves Ma with most of the cookin' and housework and tendin' the garden and such."

"That doesn't seem fair."

Again, Tom shrugged.

"And what about you, Tom Langford?"

"What about me?"

"What do you do?"

"Oh, I do whatever the bishop says needs doin'. Me and Hiram, we got barnyard chores to do. And we work out in the fields—plowin', plantin', choppin' weeds, puttin' up hay, takin' in crops come harvest time. Hiram, he ain't much help yet, but he's learnin'."

They walked along, talking more. Then Tom thought it time to get back to his wagon and relieve Hiram. "We'll be gettin' to a good place for you folks to overnight here pretty soon."

"What will you do then, Tom Langford?"

"I reckon we'll head on down the road. Get closer to home 'fore we crawl under the wagon for a sleep."

"It is getting late in the day, Tom. You won't get much farther before dark. Why not stay over with us tonight?"

"Oh, I wouldn't want to be no trouble for you, Polly. 'Sides, your Captain Baker might object to us bein' around."

"Captain Baker will not mind. And you would not be any

trouble. I am accustomed to feeding four or five young men, and having two more mouths to feed would not make any difference at all."

"Well . . ."

"Well, nothing. You are staying for supper—and breakfast—and that is the end of it."

Tom hurried ahead toward his wagon with a smile on his face.

Chapter Fifteen

The wagons were circled and cook fires kindled when Billy Red and Trajan rode in. The boys sat horseback for a moment, studying the unfamiliar faces at Polly's wagon. One, a young boy, sat on a camp box. The other, who looked to be a few years older than the drovers, stood holding a box with something green in it. The herders dismounted, tied their horses on the far side of the wagon, and loosened their saddle cinches. Trajan saw the water buckets next to the fire, their sides wet from sloshing.

"Miss Polly, you had no call to fill them water buckets. You know I don't mind doin' it. Wouldn't be no trouble a'tall for me to dip 'em in that there crick they call the Jordan River and haul 'em back."

"That's all right, Trajan. It was not me—young Hiram there was kind enough to do it for me."

Hiram hunkered down and ducked his head.

Billy Red walked over to him, bent over, and tipped up Hiram's hat brim. "And who might this feller named Hiram be?"

Tom, still standing and holding the box, saw the smile on the redhead's freckled face. "Hiram Mendenhall. He's my brother."

"And who are you? I'm Billy, by the way. Don't know why, but Polly, she dubbed me Billy Red. You-all can call me Billy or Red or whatever you care to, long as you don't call me late for supper. That one over there, that'd be Trajan."

Trajan stood back, but Billy Red extended a hand to Tom.

Tom shifted the box to balance it on one hip and shook his hand. "Tom Langford."

Billy said, "If he's your brother, how come you-all got different names?"

Tom set the box on the ground near the fire and wiped his hands against the seat of his pants. "We ain't brothers in the reg'lar way. My ma is married to his pa—so, we're just as good as."

Bending over the fire, Polly lifted the lid from a kettle hanging there, letting loose a cloud of steam. From the box, she picked out a handful of beets, rinsed them off, cut the greens off the roots all but a few inches and set them aside, then dropped the beetroots in the steaming kettle. She did the same until all the beets were in the pot, splashed in some vinegar, and replaced the lid.

"That looks mighty good, Miss Polly," Trajan said. "Ain't had no beets since I can't 'member when. You goin' to cook up them greens, too?"

"I sure am, Trajan. It is good to have some fresh vegetables for a change." She nodded toward Tom. "We are obliged to Tom, here—and Hiram—for having this food."

"No," Tom said. "I was just haulin' the stuff to market. Mister Baker, he bought it off me, so it's him you got to thank."

Polly wagged a finger at Tom. "Do not be so modest. Were it not for you, there would be no fresh food. No one in Salt Lake City would sell anything to us."

Tom's brow furrowed. "I can't imagine why that would be, Miss Alden—Polly. Why, there's all manner of stuff comin' on in the fields and gardens. There ought to be plenty for sale."

Billy Red spoke up. "All you-all Mormons is ascared of the soldiers what's comin'. Say they have to keep all the food for themselves—preserve what they can't eat. Same with flour and wheat and feed grain for the stock. Hard times is comin', they say."

The creases in Tom's forehead deepened. "I know all about the army and all. But I ain't heard nothin' about what you said."

Billy Red shrugged. "That's what Cap'n Baker says."

Polly, slicing bacon into a skillet, said, "There is no need to worry at present. We have plenty to eat. There is cob corn ready to roast in the coals. We have beans left over from yesterday. And there's biscuits." The last pieces of bacon she sliced did not go into the skillet, but into a deeper pot. When crisped, she broke it into pieces, dropped it back into its grease in the pot, poured in water, and when the steam dissipated, tossed in the beet greens and a dollop of vinegar.

"It sure does smell good, Miss Polly," Trajan said, scooting closer to the fire.

"Trajan, you act like you're half starved," Billy Red said.

"I am for a fact. I'm partial to beets, and ain't never got enough greens to fill me up. And corn! It ain't that I don't like what Miss Polly's cooked us up before—but this here supper is somethin' special."

While they waited for the meal to finish cooking, Tom and Billy Red talked. Tom learned all about Billy's work as a drover. Tom asked about handling such a large herd, and Billy took his bullwhip down from the saddle and demonstrated its use, the pops and snaps of the cracker punctuating their talk.

Billy said the work had changed these last few days since the Baker and Fancher trains combined. The cow herd had more than doubled in size, but with the addition of Colonel Fancher's herders, there were more than enough riders to keep the cattle plodding along. He told how the leisure allowed Howard—a drover he cared little for—to wander, and that he and Skeets, one of Fancher's drovers, had been sneaking off for the towns they passed since leaving the city.

"From what Howard says, they been raisin' hell and stirrin' folks up. He might be makin' more of it than what it is, but I wouldn't put it past him and Skeets to be causin' as much trouble as they claim."

"Well, I guess I ain't lookin' forward to meetin' this Howard."

"Oh, you'll meet him, all right. After me and Trajan has et, we'll be goin' back to the herd, and Howard and our other man—Billy Brown—will come in for supper. Maybe Abe, too—he's Cap'n Baker's boy and sometimes he eats with them 'stead of us." Billy cracked the whip. "Anyhow, was I you, I'd have nothin' to do with him—Howard, I mean. Billy Brown, he's all right, and so's Abe. But Howard, he's always tryin' to stir things up."

Billy looked around to make sure Polly was occupied. "Fair warnin', Tom—Howard thinks Polly is his girl. He knows better, but he's the kind that thinks any woman he takes a shine to is his by right, or ought to be. If he takes a notion that you're sweet on Polly—which he'd have to be blind and stupid not to see—could be he'll raise a ruckus."

Tom could not help blushing. "Oh, Polly, she ain't likely to pay me much mind, so I don't expect there'll be any trouble."

"Still, you had best keep a lookout—and don't turn your back on him."

Polly called out that supper was ready. Billy Red coiled his whip and hung it on his saddle. They got to the fire and took their places behind Trajan and Hiram, the boys already holding out their plates, waiting for Polly to fill them.

Trajan and Hiram sat down next to each other, leaned against the wagon's rear wheel with legs extended and plates on their laps. They found little time to talk as their mouths worked overtime on the food they shoveled in as fast as they could. But, by meal's end—a place reached only after refilling plates with second helpings—they felt like old friends. Hiram watched with envy on his face when Trajan mounted up to return to the herd. He reached behind the saddle and unlatched a saddlebag, pulled out a worn, but still serviceable, spare bullwhip. The coils landed on the ground at Hiram's feet.

"You go on ahead and try that out, Hi. Could be we'll make a drover out of you," Trajan said. He reined his horse around and urged it into a trot, following Billy Red toward the bedded-down cattle.

Tom carried his plate, sopped and scraped as clean as biscuit and fork could make it. "That was right tasty, Polly. You're a mighty fine cook."

Polly smiled as Tom slid his plate and fork into the washtub. The smile turned to laughter as Tom rolled up his sleeves and dunked his hands into the water.

"Tom Langford! What on earth are you doing?"

"Why, I just thought to help out—way of sayin' 'thank you' for the meal."

"I have never seen the like!"

"Oh, I help Ma out at home now and then. She's got more'n she can do, sometimes. Besides, dishwater never hurt no one."

Polly lifted a steaming kettle off its hook. "Mind your hands—I'll warm the water some. I find hot water cleans better."

"Yes'm."

Tom was scrubbing away on the plates and forks while Polly toweled them off and stowed them in their box when Howard, Billy Brown, and Abe Baker rode up. Billy and Abe stepped down and tied their horses to the outside of the wagon to unsaddle. But Howard rode between wagons into the circle and reined up a few yards shy of the cook fire. He sat, hands stacked on the saddle horn and a cocksure smile on his face.

"Well, well, well. What have we got here—a new chore girl?"

Tom looked up from the tub. Howard leaned over and spat

out a stream of tobacco juice. Polly tossed a tin plate into the box. It lit on the stack with a clang and rattle. She flung the dish towel over her shoulder and let it hang, propped both fists on her hips and stood facing Howard, legs apart and arms akimbo.

"Mind your manners, Howard—if you want to be fed, that is."

"Oh, I'll get fed, all right."

Abe Baker, washing up at the wagon, shook water from his hands. "Howard, get that horse out of camp where he don't belong. It makes a mess, you'll be cleanin' it up."

Howard turned to Abe and again spat a stream. He touched the brim of his hat with two fingers. "Yes, boss—no, wait a minute! You ain't no boss. You just think you are, on account of your old man runs this outfit."

"All the same, you get that horse out of here."

Billy Brown stepped up beside Abe. "Do as he says, Howard."

Howard spat again at the implied threat, jerked his horse around, and rode outside the circle. When he returned, Polly handed him a plate and started filling it with food, smacking the serving spoon against it each time. He managed to keep the plate from spilling under the assault, the churlish smile never leaving his face.

"Don't bother givin' me any of them greens. I ain't partial to what's rightly feed for hogs."

"No one else is complaining, Howard."

"They can eat what they please. Me, I'm satisfied with beans and bacon. A tater now and then don't go amiss."

"There are no potatoes tonight. You will have to make do with beets, like everyone else."

"I guess I ain't got no choice."

Polly smiled. "Sure you do, Howard. You can always go hungry." She clanged the serving spoon against the plate one last time as she served his beets.

Howard sat and ate in silence for a time. Then he turned to Tom, seated on a box on the opposite side of the fire. He sat next to Polly, with Hiram cross-legged on the ground on his other side. "Say, chore girl—who the hell are you? And who's that whelp with you?"

Abe said, "Howard, Polly already told you to behave yourself and I'm tellin' you again—mind your manners."

"Mind your business, Abe. I'm just askin' is all."

"I'm Tom Langford. This here's Hiram Mendenhall."

"What're you-all doin' here?"

Tom explained the sale of farm produce to Captain Baker, and Polly's invitation to stay for supper.

Howard, his plate empty, sailed it across the fire and it skidded to a stop just short of the washtub. He flipped his fork end over end and it splashed into the dishwater. "Well, Tom, since you're partial to women's work, get busy cleanin' up them dishes."

Tom stood. Polly reached up and grabbed his hand. "Just ignore him, Tom. Howard, leave it alone."

Abe said, "Do as she says. You had best get some shut-eye, Howard. You'll be goin' out on guard in a few hours."

Howard stood and stretched, forcing a yawn. "I guess I will get some sleep." He looked at Tom, Polly now standing beside him, still holding his hand. "I don't care much for the comp'ny 'round here anyway."

The other drovers turned in as well. While Polly finished cleaning up, Tom got Hiram settled in his blankets under the wagon. Then he and Polly sat up through most of the night talking, huddled next to the low glow of the fire.

I believe I am beginning to understand Sarah's ~~fascination~~ obsession with men. But with me it is for but one man. I met

Tom Langford just today and already I do not want ever to be apart from him. He is kind and thoughtful and ~~seems to be~~ is a hard worker if what he tells me is true, which I believe it is as I cannot imagine a lie passing his lips. After all our talk to(last)night there is little time left for sleep but I must try now for I must be about my morning chores soon. I hoped he might try to kiss me but he did not as ~~he~~ Tom—I cannot help saying his name—is a perfect gentleman.

Chapter Sixteen

The first stirrings at the wagons roused Tom from sleep well before dawn. He fought the urge to roll over and close his eyes and await the sun. Instead, he rolled out from under the wagon and sat up, scrubbing the sleep from his face with the palms of his hands. Hiram did not stir in his nest. Tom stood and stretched, enjoying the cool morning air, then set off into the brush to gather his hobbled mules. He returned, leading the mules with nothing more than a handful of mane, to find Colonel Fancher waiting for him at the wagon.

Fancher was habitually late getting to bed and always up early, seeming to others in the train to function on far less than his share of shut-eye. "Good mornin' to you, son."

"And to you, sir."

"I haven't had the pleasure of your acquaintance, young man, but I am Alexander Fancher."

"Yessir. I know who you are. I guess you know who I am." Tom slid the headstalls onto the mules and slipped the bits into their mouths, and went about laying on the harness.

"You are getting an early start, Tom."

"Yessir. Me and Hi ought to be gettin' on home. There's work to be done. But I'll be back."

"Oh? Why's that?"

The flush creeping up Tom's face did not show in the dark. "Well, Mister Fancher—Colonel—I've taken a liking to some among you and hope to, well, enjoy more of their company."

Fancher's smile, like Tom's embarrassment, went unnoticed in the dim. "I expect that would be that young lady who cooks for Captain Baker's drovers—Polly, I believe, is her name."

Tom, going about his business with the harness, did not reply, and Fancher did not speak again for a time. Then, "I'm hoping, Tom, that you can be of some help to us."

"Oh? How might that be?" Tom said as he hooked the cross lines on the team.

Fancher cleared his throat. "Y'know, son, I've been through this country before—twice, as a matter of fact. Last time about four years back. Me and my kin took cattle out to California and took up ranching out there. Both times, we was able to trade with your people to get what supplies we needed."

With the mules harnessed and ready to hitch, Tom reached under the wagon and took hold of the blanket under Hiram and dragged the bed, boy and all, out from underneath. "C'mon, Hi—wake up," he said, shaking the boy's shoulder. Hiram groaned and rolled over, pulling the cover over himself. Tom pulled it back. "Get up. We got to get goin'."

Fancher watched as Tom drove the mules to the wagon tongue, stepped one of the mules over the tongue with his voice, then lifted the end of the tongue and snapped the neck yoke to the collars, then hooked up the singletrees. He patted the mules on the rump, speaking softly to them. He told Hiram to roll his blankets and put them in the wagon, then stepped over to face Fancher.

"I ain't sure how I can help you, Mister Fancher."

"Truth be told, I'm not either. Like I said, I been able to deal with you Mormons before. But, with all this talk of war and such, we can't find much of anybody who'll sell us anything—and we're willin' to pay most any fair price, and pay with gold."

Tom said nothing, looking down and scratching a line in the dirt with the toe of his boot.

"Look, Tom, you must know people. Maybe you could ask around, see if anybody in these towns along here has got any flour or grain—that's mostly what we need—they'd be willing to sell to us."

Tom kept up scratching with his boot, then wiping away the mark and tracing it anew. "I ain't sure what I can do. Hiram's daddy is the bishop where we live, and if the apostles or President Young say not to sell, well, he—and most likely every other bishop—won't do it. And most folks do what their bishops say. There ain't none of 'em will pay any attention to me. Could be I'll catch hell when I get home for sellin' to Captain Baker like I did, even though Bishop Mendenhall never said not to."

Fancher let out a long breath. "I suppose you're right, Tom. Still, if you hear of anything, I'd be obliged to you if you would let me know about it. We'll be workin' our way down the valley slow-like, so you won't have any trouble findin' us."

The emerging dawn silhouetted the pinnacles of the Wasatch Mountains looming to the east. Fancher turned to leave, and as he walked away he crossed paths with Polly, hurrying toward Tom's wagon.

"Tom! You cannot leave already! Breakfast is not ready."

"I know it, Polly. And I meant to stay longer. But I got to thinkin' that Bishop Mendenhall won't be happy if me and Hi don't get back home soon as we can. There's work to do."

"But Tom!" Hiram said. "I'm hungry!"

"Shush, Hi. You won't starve to death 'fore we get home. If we get a move on, we could get there in time for dinner."

"Wait here," Polly said, then lifted her skirt a bit and hurried back through the parked wagons into the circle.

While he waited, Tom double-checked the buckles and snaps and ties on the harness. He had not finished the job when Polly returned.

"Here, take this," she said, pushing a cloth bag into Tom's hands.

"What is it?"

"Just some pone from day before yesterday. It is somewhat dry, but still edible. And there's some bits of leftover roasted beef I was going to stir into a soup with the vegetables you brought."

"Why, Polly, that's right kind of you—but we don't want to put you short—you got lots of hungry mouths to feed."

Polly smiled. "Don't you worry about that. Those boys would eat stewed shoe leather if I put it in front of them."

Tom looked at Polly, unsure what to say or do next. Polly threw her arms around his neck, crushing the bag between them. "Oh, Tom! I will miss you so!"

"You won't miss me long. I'll come see you when you get down the road a ways."

"I do hope so." Polly hurried away, back through the wagons.

They had not been on the road more than a few minutes when Hiram opened the bag and started gnawing on a corn dodger. He finished it and reached for another. Instead, he pulled out a folded paper.

"What's that you got, Hi?"

Hiram shrugged. "Don't know."

"Well, open it up and see what it is."

The boy carefully unfolded the paper once, then again, and a third time. Nestled inside was a snippet of Polly's hair, the mahogany curl tied with a green ribbon. There was something written on the paper, but Tom snatched it away and pocketed it before Hiram could decipher the words.

Bubbles rose in the water and dissipated into wisps of steam as Polly stood staring into the pot. She flinched when a stick of green wood in the fire popped, and remembered where she was and what she was doing. From the bag in her hand she tossed handfuls of cornmeal into the pot, pinched in some salt, then poured in some cold water and started stirring, waiting for the water to again come to a boil. She soon drifted away in the mindless routine of the task.

"Polly!"

The voice did not penetrate.

"Polly!" again, this time accompanied by a jostling of her shoulder.

She turned to see Sarah, blinked twice, then stared at her friend.

"Polly! Your bacon is burnin!"

Coming back with a start, Polly reached out and grabbed the handle of the skillet and let go, shaking the heat from her fingers. She wadded a handful of her apron front for insulation and pulled the frying pan away from the fire, splashing drippings as, barely slowing its descent, she let it fall to the ground.

"Land sakes, girl!" Sarah said. "I swan, you was someplace else when I come up here!" She took up the spoon and stirred the mush as Polly forked the over-crisp strips of bacon onto a plate.

"Just a bit tired, I guess."

Sarah chuckled. "And you can bet I know why. I saw you last night with that Mormon boy."

Polly flushed. "How is that mush coming along?"

"Just fine. And don't be changin' the subject on me, girl! Tell me all about it."

After a few moments of thought, Polly said, "I am afraid there is not much to tell. We talked."

"And talked and talked and talked, I reckon. I know you was up mighty late. What I want to know is, did he kiss you?"

Again, Polly blushed. "No! Never! Tom is a gentleman. He would not presume to do such a thing."

"Tom, is it? Do you like him?"

Polly hesitated. Then, "Yes, I do believe I do. He seems to be kind and considerate. He is different from other boys."

Sarah smiled. "I bet you wished he would've kissed you."

It was Polly's turn to smile. "Yes, Sarah—I confess the thought did occur."

"There's only but one thing to do at a time like that."

"Oh? What might that be?"

"Why, Polly, *you* got to kiss *him*!"

"Sarah! I . . ."

The boys came into camp from saddling up for the day's work. Sarah grasped both of Polly's hands and drew her close. "Remember, girl—if he don't kiss you next time, you pucker up and let him have it," she whispered.

Sarah giggled and hurried away. Polly, red faced, watched her go.

"What's for breakfast, Miss Polly?" Billy Red said, bringing her attention back to her work.

"Cornmeal mush. There will be milk for it when Trajan comes in from milking."

Howard fingered the cud out of his cheek. "Ask me, the only fit way to eat corn is to make it into whiskey and drink it."

"Aw, hell, Howard, if'n you had corn liquor you'd whine that it wasn't rye whiskey."

"That's where you're wrong, Red—I'm partial to either kind." He pulled a plate from the box and stepped up to the fire. He eyed the bacon, "Hell, Polly! This here bacon's burnt!"

Polly swallowed hard. "I apologize—I got busy with the mush and I guess it slipped my mind."

Billy Red took up a slice of the bacon and snapped off a bite with his front teeth. You could hear it crunching as he chewed. "Oh, it ain't bad. Not bad at all."

"Thank you, Billy Red. But it is overdone, I know. I am sorry."

Howard picked up a slice, studied it, and tossed it back onto the plate. It landed with a rattle. "So where's your fancy man this mornin'? Most likely that's why you burnt the meat—up all night with that Mormon boy, gettin' up to who knows what."

For the first time that day, Billy Brown spoke. "Shut your mouth, Howard."

"Oh? Yeah? And supposin' I don't?"

"Just shut up, that's all. You don't want to know what happens if you don't."

Polly cleared her throat. "It is all right, Billy Brown." She turned to Howard. "Not that it is any of your business, but Tom left early. Well before sunup."

"Tom, is it? I reckon you've seen the last of him. 'Specially if he got what he wanted off you."

Both Billys warned Howard to watch his mouth.

"Tom is not like that, Howard. Such behavior as you conjure up in your filthy mind would never occur to him. He was raised with better manners."

Howard laughed, but it was without humor. "You're just foolin' yerself, girl. If he's a man, it 'occurred' to him, all right. Peel off his hide, and he ain't no different than me—or any other man. Hell, bein' a Mormon, he's probably more that way than most. Takes two or three wives to keep them Mormon men happy. Even more, some of 'em. I hear ol' Brigham Young's got a hundred and twenty women in his bed."

Trajan came into camp carrying the milk bucket, with barely a slosh in the bottom. "Sorry, Miss Polly. That ol' cow never had much to give this mornin'. I guess the calf must've got at her somehow, else she's 'bout to go dry."

"It's all right, Trajan. There is enough for the mush. You boys go ahead and eat. I will be along to clean up later."

Polly walked to the wagon and lifted herself into the box. She folded her bedding and stowed it, thinking about what Howard had said. She wondered if it might be true.

Chapter Seventeen

Mary Mendenhall stirred up a batch of cream gravy seasoned with crumbled sausage and black pepper and slathered it over biscuits left over from breakfast. The boys had not made it home for dinner, and with supper hours away, she did not want them to go hungry.

"This is mighty good, Ma."

"Oh, Tom, it ain't much—but it will keep you till supper."

Hiram scraped the last smear of gravy from his plate with his finger, licked it off, asked to be excused, and dashed out the back door.

"Where's the bishop?" Tom said.

"You know, Son, you can call him Father. Pa, if you want."

Tom did not reply.

Mary watched her son eat for a moment. "Aaron has gone to Provo to meet with President Snow and the other bishoprics in the stake. He won't be home till late."

"What they meetin' about?"

"I couldn't say. Church business, I suppose."

Tom finished his meal. "I guess I'll go on out to the barnyard and see what needs to be done."

"Aaron penned a ewe in the barn. She seemed likely to bloat when he brought her in from the meadow yesterday. Give her a look-see and make sure she's all right."

Tom nodded, and went outside. He found Hiram playing with the bullwhip Trajan had given him. A red welt across his cheek revealed his unfamiliarity with its use.

"Looks like you've hurt yourself, Hi."

Hiram sniffled and wiped his watery eyes, and said it didn't hurt much.

"Lemme see that whip. I don't know much more about it than what you do, but Billy Red showed me a few things."

Tom carefully laid the whip out, raised his arm as Billy Red showed him, watched the thong falling behind him, and threw it forward. It took a few tries, but he managed to get a feeble snap out of the cracker. "That's how he said to do it, best as I can remember." He passed the whip handle to Hiram. "I guess it'll take some practice to get good at it. Be careful you don't smack yourself in the face no more—you could do yourself a damage."

He found the ewe in good health and decided to take her out to the pasture to reunite her with her lamb. The lambs were old enough to get most of their sustenance from grazing, but mother's milk was still an essential part of their diet. He put a rope around the ewe's neck, slipped a halter on one of the mules, swung a leg over, and set off riding bareback for the pasture with the ewe trotting along behind.

"Well, if it ain't Tom, Tom, the bishop's son!" Eli Price said as Tom arrived at the feed ground. "Stole a sheep and away he run."

Tom smiled. "Right. You can see I'm in a big hurry."

"Where you been?"

"Oh, the bishop, he had me take a wagonload of garden stuff up to Salt Lake to sell. I see they got you watchin' the stock today." Tom slid off the mule's back and led the ewe toward the other sheep, scattered across the pasture. Farther away, toward the lake that bordered the valley on the west before lapping up against the mountains, the town's cattle grazed. As he walked near, every sheep in the bunch raised its head to watch, ready to dash away if their feeble minds sensed danger. The ewe bleated and her lamb answered. Tom turned the ewe loose; mother and child trotted to each other and the lamb ducked its head and reached for her udder.

Tom walked back to where Eli sat and dropped down beside him.

"So, tell me 'bout this trip to the big city," Eli said.

"We never made it all the way. Come across a wagon train up by Point of the Mountain and they bought everything on the wagon 'cept me and Hi's bedding."

Eli's eyes widened. "You're likely to catch hell for that, Tom."

"Oh? Why's that?"

"Ain't you heard? Word's come down from Salt Lake that we ain't to have nothin' to do with none of these wagon outfits that come through."

Tom considered what his friend had said. "I knowed we was advised not to sell 'em no flour or wheat. But this was just carrots and beets and such."

"Things has changed. Your pa and mine and the others from the church has been meetin' with President Snow over to Provo yesterday night and today. Pa says the orders from on high is to leave 'em plumb alone. All of 'em."

Again, Tom thought it over. "I don't know, Eli. Them folks needs supplies. And we've always traded with emigrants before."

"Not anymore. Not with the army comin'. They say them wagon folks comin' through ain't to be trusted—could be spies for the army." Eli plucked a stem of grass and stuck it in his mouth. He chewed on it for a minute. "Speakin' of the army, we got militia tonight."

"Tonight? It ain't even Saturday!"

"Don't I know it. But they're havin' us march around more now—say we need sharpenin' up, need better discipline."

Tom flopped down backward and spread his arms wide and let out a groan. "I don't want to be no damn soldier." He rolled to his side and propped himself on one elbow and looked at Eli. "What do you think, Eli? You think there'll be fightin'?"

Eli shrugged. "Damned if I know. I just know that if we ain't there for drill there'll be hell to pay."

Tom rolled again onto his back and stared at the sky. "I'll tell you one thing—them folks that I sold to, they don't mean nobody no harm. They just want to get to California."

"I heard tell they're a rowdy bunch—been mistreatin' womenfolk and gettin' drunk and disorderly and such."

"There might be some of 'em that do—I wouldn't put it past this one kid I met—he's 'bout our age and full of the devil. Most of 'em in that company, though, they're just family folks."

"I heard tell they come from Missouri."

"Nah. Arkansas, mostly. Might be a few Pukes with 'em, but Arkansas's where most of 'em is from. Seemed good enough folks to me."

Eli chewed on his stem and Tom stared at the sky for a time.

"I met me a girl, Eli."

Eli sat up straight. "You what?"

"Met a girl. Her name is Polly. Polly Alden."

"Where'd you see her?"

"She's with that wagon train."

"With her family?"

"Nah. Just on her own. She's an orphan, she said. Hired on to cook for the boys herdin' the cattle."

"She purty?"

Tom rolled onto his elbow again and smiled at Eli. "Cute as a speckled pup. And I think she likes me. Gave me a lock of her hair all tied up with a ribbon."

Eli tossed his grass stem aside and plucked a fresh one. "I'd say 'good for you,' Tom—but I guess there ain't no point in it seein' as how you won't be seein' her again."

Rolling again onto his back, Tom said, "Oh, I reckon I will, Eli. I'll be seein' her again."

Captain Baker told the company not to hitch the wagons today. The grass was good enough along the river, and there was no hurry. Unlike the Humboldt road and the crossing of the Sierra, the southern route carried little likelihood of getting snowbound. Besides, slower progress meant temperatures would cool some, making crossing the harsh deserts to come less troublesome.

But it also meant a need for more supplies.

Baker saddled a horse and rode the few miles into the town called Lehi to see if he could arrange the purchase of flour and other goods. He hitched his horse under a sign saying Mulliner's Grist Mill, untied his saddlebags, slung them over his shoulder, and walked through the door. The makeshift office was small, holding only a desk, a file cabinet, a case on the wall with rows of cubbyholes holding papers, and a chalkboard listing costs for milling and prices for goods. An open door at the back of the room led to a warehouse storing rows and stacks of filled sacks. Beyond, from somewhere unseen, Baker could hear the sound of millwheels grinding. A thin haze of dust softened the dim light in the warehouse.

No one occupied the office. The captain stood for a while, waiting, until spying a bell with twine tied to the clapper fastened to the wall just through the doorway. He stepped through and shook the twine, dinging the bell several times. Soon, a man in a bib apron dusted with flour came up. He waved for Baker to go back into the office, followed him in, and closed the door. The man said nothing, eyeing the captain as if he expected trouble from him.

"What are you milling today?" Baker said with a smile and nod toward the back.

"Grist. Like the sign says."

"Wheat?"

The man nodded once.

Baker looked around the office, waiting for the man to speak. He did not. Baker gave a nod toward the chalkboard. "Those prices in effect?"

"Nope."

"What is today's price for flour, then?"

"Don't matter. Ain't no flour."

Baker listened to the faint hum of the mill, still audible through the walls and closed door. "Unless I'm mistook, it sounds like there's flour in the making. Your apron looks it, too."

"There is. Custom job. Not for sale."

After an uncomfortable silence Baker said, "You got any oats? Barley? Whole or rolled, it don't matter."

The man shook his head.

"What's in all them sacks stacked in there, and those barrels?" Baker said, nodding toward the door.

The man shrugged. "Some of it's sold. Some under contract. Some we hold in storage for customers."

"All of it?"

The man nodded.

Baker slung the saddlebags off his shoulder and dropped them on the desk with a loud thunk. Without hurry, he untied one of the flaps, reached inside, and pulled out a leather sack. Again taking his time, he untied the thong holding it closed, unwound it, stretched open the mouth of the bag, and tipped it up. Clinking and ringing as they spilled out, gold coins spread onto the desktop.

"I can pay with gold," Baker said.

The man stared at the coins, glistening in the light filtering through the window. He stared for a long while. He sighed. "Sorry, mister." He turned and walked through the doorway, closing the door behind him.

Baker cursed under his breath and with his hand, shoveled the gold back into its sack. He tied it off and stuffed it into the saddlebag and fastened it shut.

He rode down the town's main street, stopping at a general mercantile. A man and woman stood at the counter. The man answered Baker's every query about supplies in the negative. Baker waited around, handling the goods on display, until the man lost patience and went into the back.

The woman gestured him over and whispered. "Mister, I've some eggs I could part with. They ain't the freshest. Some might've gone bad, but I believe the most of them is still good. I imagine your folks would enjoy some eggs."

"They surely would, ma'am."

The woman looked over her shoulder toward the back, then turned back to Baker. "You have somebody here after sundown—in the alley out behind."

Baker nodded and left the store. Standing in the shade of the store's porch roof, he looked up and down the street. Three horses stood hipshot at the hitch rail in front of a saloon, two doors down on the opposite side. He recognized one of the mounts as belonging to him, and thought the other two looked familiar. Unwinding the bridle rein from the rail, he led his horse down the street and retied it in front of the saloon. He patted the neck of the horse he owned and checked the brands on the other two, seeing that they did, indeed, carry Fancher's connected *JF* mark, registered in the brand books of Arkansas and California.

Opening the saloon door quietly, Baker slipped inside. The light was dim, and as his eyes adjusted, he studied the occupants of the saloon. A bartender wielded a feather duster across the few bottles on the backbar. Two old men sat at a table rattling dominoes. Another stood watching. Four men sat at a table, their attentions on three young men standing at the bar. The loud, raucous talk from the men at the bar suggested they had been there for some time, sampling the bartender's wares. One of the drinkers was his drover, Howard. The other two were from Fancher's crew—one he did not know, the other the boy called Skeets.

Baker listened. The drovers joked about the women in the town, boasting of their intentions toward them. They suggested the Mormon men had more than enough women in their beds and ought to be willing to share the bounty. Their talk and laughter were directed at each other, but loud enough that the other patrons could hear.

Then Skeets turned to the men at the table. "Hey!—any of you-all got a spare woman I could borrow for a while? Hell, I'll even pay for the privilege."

The men said nothing.

"My pappy and grandpappy, they knowed themselves some Mormon women back in Missoura—till they run all the Mormons off!" Skeets laughed. The other two joined in, Howard slapping Skeets on the back and shoulder.

One of the men at the table cleared his throat. "So you boys are from Missouri, are you? My brother was killed there. Likely by some Puke like you."

Howard laughed. "Naw. I ain't from Missouri. Skeets here is. Me, I'm from Arkansas. So's he," he said, elbowing the man beside him.

"Arkansas, huh? That's where Parley Pratt was killed. Murdered. You know anything about it?"

"I ain't never heard of no Parley Pratt," Howard said. "But if he was one of you-all whoring Mormons, I wouldn't of minded seeing him killed—or maybe doin' it m'self."

"He was one of us, all right. Elder Pratt was one of the Twelve Apostles. One of the Lord's anointed. A great man. He did not deserve to die at the hands of ruffians like yourself."

Howard snorted. "Ruffian, am I? How'd you like to step outside and call me that? I ain't thrashed a Mormon since breakfast, and I am feelin' the need."

Baker stepped out of the shadows. "Howard!"

Howard spun around. "Cap'n Baker! What the hell you doin' here?"

"I'll ask you the same question."

Howard squirmed. "Oh, me and the boys here, we just wanted to unwind a little."

"That's right!" Skeets said. "Ain't nothin' wrong with havin' a little fun."

Baker ignored him and said to Howard, "Who is watching the herd while you 'unwind'?"

The boy swallowed hard. "I . . . I told Trajan to. He weren't set to ride today, but I told him to take my place. Said I had business to tend to."

"And Abe? He allowed it?"

"Your boy don't know nothin' about it. Leastways not till after we was already long gone."

Baker said nothing for a time. He looked at the old men playing dominoes, now ignoring their game to watch. The four men at the table also looked on and listened in. "Here's what's going to happen with you and your friends now, Howard. You-all are getting on your horses and getting back to the camp."

The boys started to object, but Baker's raised hand silenced them. "But first, you-all are going to apologize to these gentlemen. There is no cause for you to insult them like you done."

"Like hell I will!" Howard said.

Skeets said, "Me neither."

The other boy said nothing, standing with his head bowed.

"You will. And you-all will do it now. Right now."

Howard spat out a stream of tobacco juice, not bothering to

even aim at a spittoon. "Supposin' I don't?"

"That's up to you, Howard. But if you don't, I will fire you on the spot." He looked at the other two. "And I don't believe Colonel Fancher will mind if I give the two of you the sack." He let that sink in for a moment. "And then I will turn you-all over to these gentlemen. I suspect—and I think they will agree—that your talk is a whole lot bigger than what you-all can back up. And if they don't whip you enough to satisfy me, I will finish the job."

The boys said no more. They exchanged glances, studied the toes of their boots, scratched, hitched their britches, rubbed their faces, and thought. At once, they acted. Skeets drained off the last bit of beer in his mug, the other boy slid his mug away. Howard glared at Baker, turned his head and spat again, then started for the door. The other two followed.

Baker stepped in front of him. "Ain't you-all forgettin' something boys?"

"Aw, Cap'n," Howard whined.

"Do it."

The boys turned around and removed their hats and mumbled their *sorry*s. Baker stepped aside and let them pass. As the hoofbeats of their galloping horses faded, Baker said, "Gentlemen, let me apologize for the rude behavior of those boys. I assure you, they do not speak for our company. And when I get back to camp, they will be punished. We want no difficulties with you-all, only to pass through your territory in peace."

One of the men asked if it was true what the boys said.

"I cannot speak to what the one called Skeets said about his kin in Missouri and what they done in the past. Truth is, I don't know the boy. If he learned his manners from his father and grandfather, I wouldn't be surprised if it was true." He cleared his throat. "As for your man Pratt, I have heard about that.

Learned about it in Salt Lake City, and that was the first I heard. What I can tell you-all is that we were long gone from Arkansas 'fore it ever happened. And I was told it happened in Crawford County. Most of our folks is from Carroll County and Benton County. Some from Marion County." He paused again. "We wasn't there, and I doubt any of our kinfolk was. Now, I will bid you-all good day."

"Same to you, mister. We won't be sorry to see you go. And I don't just mean from this here room."

Chapter Eighteen

The flush in Bishop Mendenhall's face was so deep it seemed to redden his beard. "What in heaven's name were you thinking, Thomas? You were assigned to take the produce to market in the city! What prompted you to sell it to emigrants?"

Tom swallowed hard. The family was halfway through supper, a late sitting owing to the bishop's delay in getting home from church meetings in Provo. Tom's face was as pale as his stepfather's was florid. He put his fork down. "Didn't set out to do it—we just met 'em on the road. The man matched the prices you hoped to get at market, and then some. Seemed like a good bargain to me. Got me and Hi back home lots sooner besides." He swallowed again. "Checked on that there ewe you thought had the bloat and she was fine—took her out to the meadow, and her lamb mothered right up."

"Those sheep are the last of your worries right now. Surely you are aware that with the troubles to come, the brethren have forbidden us to traffic with this season's emigrants."

"I didn't know no such thing—I knowed we was to hold back grain and flour, but nobody said nothing to me about no garden crops."

The bishop took in and released a long breath. "Well, I suppose you have a point. But know this—yesterday and today I and the other bishoprics in the valley have been meeting with President Snow and the high council. Brother Brigham, the first presidency, the Twelve, and the presiding bishop are in agreement that we are to let the emigrants alone this season. We do not know their intentions. It may well be the army is using them as observers, and our preparations to meet the invaders are even now being reported. The same guidance from the brethren is being passed along to the Saints in every community. The wagon companies will be allowed to pass unmolested, but we are not to provision them at any price."

As his stepfather delivered the sermon, Tom stared at his plate, stirring the remnants of food around with his fork. He raised his eyes to the bishop, but not his head. "That don't seem right."

The bishop's fork clattered onto his plate. He sat upright. "What?"

"You're always preachin' about kindness and lookin' out for your neighbor, and quotin' scripture about helpin' those in need. Them folks in those wagon trains are in need. And if we don't help 'em they could be in real trouble down the road."

For a long moment, no one spoke. Even the children were quiet. The wives exchanged glances, and, under the table, Mary wrung the skirt of her apron.

When the bishop spoke, the family strained to hear his words. "Boy, do not presume to instruct me in the Gospel. Those in authority over us are called of God and their words are inspired. Our duty is obey. We are not to question. Understand?"

Tom scratched some more at this plate. "I hear what you're sayin'—but I can't say as I understand."

The quiet was gone from the bishop's voice. "What?" He slammed a fist to the table, rattling plates and knives and forks.

This time, it was Tom's voice that was quiet. "Well, it's like I said—you're always preachin' about helpin' those in need."

The bishop took several deep breaths as he collected his thoughts. "In ordinary circumstances, you would be right. However, when it is called for, the Lord allows us to depart from the usual commands. You are familiar with the story of Joseph in Egypt?"

Tom nodded.

"Then you are aware that it was revealed to him through the interpretation of Pharaoh's dreams that he was to lay up stores for seven years to provide for the people during seven years of famine that were to come. Understand?"

Again, Tom nodded. Then, "But . . . didn't Joseph give food to his brothers when they came with money to buy? Did it two times, if I remember right from Sunday school. Even had 'em come to live with him so's they'd have plenty to eat."

"But they were his family!" the bishop thundered.

Tom shrugged. "But there weren't nobody knowed that but Joseph. Far as anyone else was concerned, they was just folks—strangers—needin' food. Besides, ain't you always sayin' we're all God's children? Guess that makes them folks from Arkansas as good as blood kin."

Much to the relief of all at the table, the bishop did not burst into flames. His face, however, reddened to a shade that made it seem possible, and the family watched for evidence of wisping smoke. The working of his clenched jaws imperiled the soundness of his teeth. His grip on the edge of the table looked severe enough to leave indentations in the wood. He said nothing, only let go of the table with one hand and, the arm quaking, pointed at the back door. Tom looked to his mother, who gave him a faint nod.

"Excuse me, please," Tom said. He rose from his chair and hurried out the kitchen door into the yard. With the evening chores already done, he found nothing to do in the darkness but sit on the top rail of the fence and look toward the lake to the west and the dim indigo silhouetting the Lake Mountains rising above its far shore. He wondered when Captain Baker's wagon train and cow herds would make it this far. And he feared that when they did, the company—and Polly—would pass by and all he would see of them was their dust and perhaps campfires in the distance. He prayed it would not be so.

"Whatcha doin' Tom?"

Hiram's voice startled him. "Nothin', Hi. Just sittin'."

"Pa, he's right mad at you."

Tom nodded, the gesture unseen in the dark.

"I reckon we ought to've gone on in to Salt Lake."

Again, Tom nodded. "Likely so. But no matter what the old man says, I can't see not helpin' folks in need. It just don't seem right."

"Well, Mother Mary says for you to come on in now. Pa's gone into his room to do somethin' or other."

"Thanks, Hi. Tell her I'll be along in a bit."

Captain Baker and Colonel Fancher sat on camp boxes in the dim light of a campfire burned down to glowing coals, sipping coffee.

"Hot."

Baker swallowed the last of the liquid in his cup. "That it is. This time of year in this country, it don't cool off much even at night."

"True enough. But leastways it isn't sultry like it is back home. Here, the sweat on a man does dry off by and by."

Baker tapped the bottom of his coffee mug against his knee, the rhythm matching the beating of his heart. After a time, he picked up a stick and stirred the coals in the fire, sending a shower of sparks into the night sky. "You know, Colonel, we could be in a hell of a fix if these Mormons won't trade with us. Most folks that come with me counted on resupplying here."

"Same as us." Fancher sighed and dabbed at his forehead with a handkerchief. "Brigham Young and the other head men in the church has got 'em all so stirred up they're afraid of their own shadows."

"What do you reckon we ought to do?"

Fancher shrugged. "Not much we can do, other than keep goin'. We'll tell the cooks to put more water in the soup and thin out the pone batter some. Make the biscuits littler and the gravy thinner."

Baker cursed and tossed the stick he held onto the coals and watched as flames flickered and ate at its edges.

"There is one good thing," Fancher said. "By takin' this road south, we'll pass by a passel of Mormon towns. Had we gone to the Humboldt, there wouldn't have been a damn thing out there but scrub and Indians."

"Maybe when we get farther from Salt Lake, folks won't be so flighty. Could be the shine of gold will convince them to part with a sack of flour. That boy Polly is sweet on—the one who sold me them vegetables—maybe he can help us some."

"Maybe so. I talked to the boy myself. But one thing I've learned about these Mormons—they're more like sheep than cattle when it comes to followin' a lead. And Young and his toadies, they don't seem to have any trouble keepin' 'em lined out in the direction they want 'em to go."

Baker stood. "Well, Alex—I guess there ain't nothin' to do but see what comes. We got to keep askin'. Maybe someone will help, what with them claimin' to be Christians and all."

Fancher looked up at Baker's face, the glow of the coals accenting the deep creases that lined it. "One thing we got to do for sure."

"What's that?"

"Keep that damn Howard of yours and my Skeets away from any towns we come to."

There was no hint of humor in Baker's answering chuckle. "That's for damn sure. Had I a lick of sense, I'd have let them Mormons in that beer parlor take 'em down a peg."

"Oh, it wouldn't have done any good. With heads as hard as them boys have got, it don't matter how many dents you put in them. There still ain't no chance of anything getting through."

"I fear you're right. Still, we got to do somethin' about them."

Fancher stood, put both hands in the small of his back and pushed his elbows back with a low moan. "We'll keep an eye on them whenever we get near a town. Tie the contrary little bastards to the back of a wagon and drag them along if we have to. We can't have them stirring up trouble—we got enough of it as it is."

"I suppose we could send them down the road kickin' horse turds."

"We could do that. But I don't think them two would last a fortnight on their own. Besides, I promised Skeets's grandma, who's some kind of shirttail relative to my wife, that I'd see he got out to California safe. I wish to hell he'd stayed with them other Missouri folks who took the other road out from Fort Bridger."

"Why didn't he?"

"They wouldn't have him. His uncle run him off. Said if he couldn't stay on with me drivin' cows, he could go to hell. At the time, I needed him in the saddle. Had I known we'd be mixin' our herds and have more than enough herders, I'd have left him back there."

"Well, there ain't a thing holdin' me to Howard, other than the job I give him was to help see the herd through to California. I guess I feel some kind of obligation. I'll tell Abe to keep him on a tighter rein."

"If we both keep an eye on them two and they know we're watching, maybe they'll keep their noses clean."

Baker sighed. "I sure as hell hope so. Any more trouble and I'll turn Howard out." He smiled and shook his head. "I talk tough, but I keep hopin' the boy will smarten up. Hate to give up on anybody long as I can talk myself into thinkin' there's hope."

Polly could hear the wagon masters talking, but could not make out their words. She sat cross legged on her blankets in the wagon in the glow of a stub of candle. Her diary lay open in her lap. She laid the pencil in the fold and scoured both eyes with her fists, then yawned and stretched. Before closing the book and blowing out the candle, she read what she had written.

It seems an eternity since I have seen Tom but it has only been hours. I wonder if he has forgotten me already but Sarah says boys are not so soon to forget if they are good ones and I sincerely believe he is one of the best ones. Still I gave him a lock of my hair for remembrance so I would be on his mind and in his heart till we meet again, which I hope will be soon.

In the morning we move camp and the days travel will take me that much closer to Tom. I will ~~aski~~ be asking at each settlement for Springville. Alas I am told we will not reach that place for two or even three days. It is my sincere hope that Capt Baker makes haste and I will surely prod my teams along.

Even though I will not see my Tom on the morrow some lines I recall from a Shakespeare play we read in school come to my mind spoken by a girl young woman much like myself called Juliet—

Good night good night parting is such sweet sorrow that I shall say good night till it be morrow.

Chapter Nineteen

Utah Lake is the Mormon holy land's Sea of Galilee, connected by their River Jordan to a Dead Sea, the Great Salt Lake, to the north. The shallow water in Utah Lake stretches some twenty-five miles along the valley, its width half as much at most. The west shore laps at the base of the Lake Mountains. Gently rising to the east is a fertile valley laced by small streams flowing out of springs and snowmelt from the looming Wasatch Range. For time out of mind, before the arrival of Mormon settlers, bands of Utes populated the place, making a living off wildlife and plants on the land and bounteous harvests of fish from the waters.

The emigrants from Arkansas broke camp along the river and started southward toward the lake. The train bypassed the town of Lehi and struck the road toward American Fork, still in the shadows of the towering Mount Timpanogos. Alexander Fancher, riding at the head of the wagons, tipped his hat and offered greetings to the townsfolk standing in dooryards and along the road watching the travelers pass. No one returned his respects.

To the west and rear of the train, the cattle herd ambled through pasturelands nearer the lake, kept in line by the cracking whips of the mounted drovers. Howard, riding at the herd's left flank, eyed the settlement in the near distance, wondering what untasted pleasures he might be passing.

As the lead cattle waded through the reeds and shallow waters where the American Fork River started its spread into the lake, two boys from the town wandered by shouldering fishing poles. The dog with them barked and hopped and spun in circles and darted toward the passing cattle. The yapping upset the plodding animals, calves breaking away on the run, cows attempting to follow, steers and heifers surging forward, a bull hooking at the yipping mutt. The upset spread through the nervous herd, and the drovers worked to keep the animals from stampeding.

"Get that damn dog out of here!" Howard yelled as he galloped ahead toward the ruction.

One of the boys stood still as a statue, the other hollered at the dog, little more than a pup, and chased after it as it eluded his grasp and ignored his cries. The scruffy mutt dashed near the herd and stopped, bouncing on its front legs as its high-pitched yipping and yapping further upset the cattle. Howard slid his horse to a stop near the barking dog and struck with his bullwhip. With a yelp, the dog ducked away as the lash struck but Howard struck again, the stroke opening a gash across the dog's snout. The whip struck again as the dog whined and howled and pawed at the injury, then he struck again.

Howard stepped out of the saddle and, stretching a rein to keep his skittery horse in check, stood over the dog. The mutt bled from gashes on its forelegs as well as its face. Howard lit into it with a string of curses and blows from the whipstock. When the dog tried to crawl away, Howard dropped the bridle rein and grabbed the mutt by the scruff of the neck and continued beating on it.

The boy tried to push Howard away and the drover shoved him aside. Jumping astraddle of Howard's back, the boy yelled for him to stop and pounded his shoulders and head with a fist. Howard stood upright and pulled the boy off, spilling him to the ground. He raised the whip handle to hit the dog again—or perhaps the boy—but stopped when the lash of another whip popped near enough his face that he felt the burst of air.

Raising his eyes, Howard saw Trajan sitting horseback, ready to strike again. "Next one won't miss, Howard," he said in a voice barely heard above the bawling of cattle and the boy's crying.

The dog lay on its side, panting, eyes glazed over and tongue lolling, blood muddying the soil around its shattered skull. Dropping to his knees, the boy fell on the dog, wrapping it in his arms and burying his teary face in its fur.

Howard kicked at the dog, then stomped off to where his horse stood, dragging the reins and cropping at the grass. Trajan coiled his whip and turned his mount toward the herd. The cattle had calmed somewhat, the only memory of the fracas their hurried approach to the river crossing.

The train stopped for nooning a while later and when Howard rode to the wagons for dinner, Captain Baker intercepted him. Baker leaned out of the saddle and snatched one of Howard's reins and jerked it from his hand. Pulling the horse near, his face inches from the drover's, Baker hissed, "Howard, I swear you're as stupid as a mossy rock. What the hell did you think you were doin' beatin' that dog like that?"

Howard sat upright, tipping back from the captain. "Why—why—Cap'n, that there cur was after the cows. They'd be scattered from hell to breakfast and we'd be all day gatherin' 'em up had I not shut him up."

Baker tossed away Howard's rein and wagged his pointer finger in the boy's face. "You pull the saddle off this horse. When we pull out after dinner, you're to stay with the wagons."

"Like hell I will!"

"You'll do it, or I'll give you a whippin' worse than what you gave that dog."

Howard thought for a moment, smiled, then leaned over and spit a string of tobacco juice into the narrow gap between his horse and Baker's. "You could try, old man."

The captain's backhanded blow knocked the grin off the herder's face and toppled him out of the saddle. The horse shied away as Howard landed. The drover scrambled to his feet, fists clenched and face florid. Baker returned the boy's glare for a long moment. Then he heeled his horse into motion, rode over to Howard's horse and picked up the reins, and led the mount back. Tossing the reins to the boy, he told him again to get the horse to camp and unsaddle it and get some dinner. He said he would talk to him later, then turned and rode to the wagons.

Mary Mendenhall stood from her stoop labor in the garden, massaging the small of her back. She watched the grain patch as the breeze rippled the wheat ears on their stalks in waves and swells. In the next field, Hiram walked beside a mule team pulling a wagon with a hayrack as Tom forked the cured meadow grass onto the growing stack on the wagon.

As Tom grew older and stronger, and Aaron Mendenhall grew old and caught up in his duties as bishop, more and more of the work and upkeep on the place fell to the boy. Tom's dealings with the emigrants had so upset the old man that he heaped on even more chores as punishment. Tom took it in stride, but Mary knew her son's eyes were on the road, always watching for evidence of the wagon train and his newfound sweetheart.

Even before the Arkansas emigrants came in sight, news of their travels came to Springville. Home from church meetings for dinner, the bishop told of the altercation in Lehi, the dog beating in American Fork, and the failed efforts of the wagon masters to obtain supplies in Provo despite approaching nearly every merchant and several citizens.

"The emigrants are likely to come by here tomorrow," Mendenhall said. He turned his attention to Tom. "Boy, you are to have nothing to do with those people. We are to let them pass—unmolested, but unaided. This is to include that young girl of questionable character I am told you have kept company with. Understood?"

Tom sat upright, eyes widened. "How d'you know about Polly?"

"Polly, is it? You should know, if you don't already, that very little happens here that I do not know about. You are to leave the emigrants be—all of them. Understood?"

Tom nodded, but said nothing. He returned to haying after dinner, but was missed when the local militia met for drill that evening. Finding the wagon camp just north of the town of Provo and the river of the same name, Tom reined up his horse, winded from his hurried ride, and studied the wagons until finding Polly's. He dismounted and walked to the wagon and tied his horse to the rear wheel. Listening as he loosened the cinch on the saddle, he heard low talk from clusters of people scattered around the circle, resting from the day and letting supper digest. The cooking smells lingering in the air reminded him of his missed supper.

Stepping around the end of the wagon, Tom stood and looked for Polly among the emigrants but did not see her. He recognized some of the drovers she cared for—Howard sprawled out with his head pillowed on his saddle and his hat covering his face. Abe, Trajan, and Billy Brown played some kind of card game. Billy Red was not among them; Tom assumed he was guarding the herd.

From beyond the camp Tom heard laughter. He walked around the circled wagons, rather than passing through, and toward the willows lining the lakeshore. As he neared the water, he heard splashing along with the laughter. Several children waded and frolicked in ankle-deep water, the youngest in nothing but drawers, the older ones with pants rolled to the knees or dresses bound around thighs. Still, most were damp from head to toe from splashing water at each other.

Polly and another girl about the same age stood in the water apart from the playing children, deep in conversation, clutching the hems of their dresses to keep them dry. Tom edged along the shore to near where they stood and called Polly's name. She turned toward him. Wide-eyed, with a sharp intake of breath, she clapped her hands over her mouth. The skirt of her dress unfurled and the hem fell into the water. Paying it no mind, she splashed her way through the water, further wetting the dress. She threw her arms around Tom's neck and drew him close. Unsure what to do, Tom tried embracing her, pulled his hands away, dropped them to his sides, and, finally, placed them at her waist and gently pushed her away.

The girl's wide smile far surpassed Tom's embarrassed grin. "Polly!" he whispered. "Everybody's lookin'."

Polly saw that every child in the water stood stock still, watching. Some faces were surprised, others wondering, some smiling. The girl cleared her throat and stepped backward. She looked down for a moment, then lifted her eyes to Tom's. "I do not care. I am happy to see you and unashamed to show it."

"Well, all right, then." Tom wrapped an arm around Polly's shoulder and the other around her waist, turned and dipped her sideways, leaned over and kissed her.

He stood her back up. Now the girl was red-faced—whether from embarrassment or the effect of the kiss, Tom did not know. Or care. Polly patted her hair and smoothed the bodice of her dress.

"Land sakes alive! Don't you-all have any shame?" someone said.

Tom looked past Polly and she spun around toward the voice behind her. There stood Sarah, a teasing smile on her face.

"I 'spect this here fella must be Tom."

"Yes, Sarah, this is Tom."

"Well, I am glad to hear that. I would surely be taken aback to see you carryin' on so with somebody else after the way you've been jabberin' 'bout Tom Langford of late." She feigned alarm and looked at Tom. "I'm guessin' your Christian name is Langford—could be there's more than one Tom. I hope I ain't mistook."

Tom stammered, unsure how to respond. The flush on his face intensified. "I, uh, I—yes, miss, I, well, I'm Tom Langford, all right."

"Lord be praised!" She stepped forward and extended a hand. "I am surely pleased to meet you, Mister Langford—can I call you Tom? I got to say, you ain't nearly the catch Polly here has laid you out to be—leastways not to my way of thinkin'." She released Tom's hand after a vigorous pumping and stepped back, appraising him up and down. "Still, I reckon you'll do."

"Sarah! Leave Tom be! He did not ride all this way to have you poke fun at him."

Sarah smiled. "Oh, I know it, Polly. I's just a-teasin'. You don't mind, do you, Tom," she said, turning her mischievous grin on him.

Again, he stammered, eventually telling the girl that he did not mind her funning him.

"Tom," Polly said. "Why are you here? Are you all right?"

"Yeah. I'm fine. Little hungry, is all. Never had no supper."

"What I mean is, is everything all right at home? Are you in trouble?"

Tom told the girls of his stepfather's anger at him for selling the produce to Captain Baker, and that he had been forbidden to have anything more to do with the emigrants—these, or any others that would pass through. He passed along the anger in the towns over reports of mistreatment at the hands of the travelers.

"Well, it ain't like you-all have been neighborly," Sarah said.

"I know it. But folks is stirred up over the army comin' and whatnot. You got to remember that we come out here to get away from people. Your kind never was too neighborly with us, back in the States. Now you're a-comin' out here, and them that was ill-treated before is suspicious of what you're up to. They think you might be spyin' on us for the army."

"No such thing! Why, we don't know no more about no army than what we was told at Fort Bridger—just that soldiers is comin', that's all."

"Never mind, Sarah," Polly said. "Come along, Tom. I believe I can find you something to eat."

The trio walked back to the wagons to the sound of laughter and splashing, the children having lost interest in them and gone back to their playing. Polly led Tom through the center of the circle, drawing attention as they went. Sarah left them to join her family. The couple reached the ashes of Polly's cooking fire and she pulled a plate from a box and lifted the lid from a cast-iron oven and picked out some biscuits. From a skillet she forked up several slabs of bacon, the grease from their cooking already congealed on them.

"It isn't much, I am afraid," Polly said, handing the plate to Tom. "Just leftovers."

"It'll be right fine. I thank you."

The drovers looked on in silence, save Howard, since risen from his nap. He spat. "What the hell you doin' here, Mormon boy?"

Tom gestured with the plate. "Just about to have a bite to eat."

"You got a lot of gumption, comin' 'round here eatin' our grub when you-all damn Mormons won't sell us no flour to replace what's in them biscuits you're 'bout to shove down your neck."

"Mind your manners, Howard," Polly said. She poured a cup of bitter coffee, took Tom by the arm, and led him to the wagon. They sat on the tongue while Tom ate the bacon and biscuits.

"Seems like I ain't too welcome here," Tom said after he washed the last bite down with a swallow of tepid coffee.

"Oh, pay no attention to Howard. I have never known a person so contrary."

They sat on the wagon tongue in the fading light, talking. Tom remembered his horse and left to unsaddle it, lead it to water, then stake it out to graze. While he was gone, Captain Baker came by.

"Polly, Abe tells me that Tom came to see you."

"Yes, sir. He is here."

"Are you sure that's a good idea? His being here might cause further troubles with the Mormons."

"I don't see how, Captain. He has done nothing wrong."

"That might not matter. You know that the people in these towns resent us. They want nothing to do with us, and having one of their own coming around—well, it don't look good, that's all."

"You did not mind Tom coming around when he had a wagonload of vegetables to sell you."

Baker drew in a long breath and let it out slowly. "You're right. And I'd be tickled pink if he was to show up here with a wagon full of flour—and three more just like it. Fact is, it don't look like that's likely to happen. So it'd probably be for the best if you-all forgot all about each other. Most likely he's better off with his own kind—and God forbid you should end up among 'em."

"As long as I had Tom, I would not care."

"Maybe so. But you might not have Tom—them Mormons might force you to marry up with an old man who already has more wives than he needs."

"Tom would never let that happen."

Baker laughed. "Girl, I've always thought of you as bein' right smart. But, truth is, you don't know nothin' about these Mormons. If one of their head men says something, all the rest of 'em go along with it. Ain't Tom nor no one else has anything to say about it." He let that sink in for a time. "Your ma and pa would spin in their graves if I was to let that happen to you. Like I said, it'd be best if you was to send him home and tell him not to come back."

Dusk was gone and night had fallen. Polly could not see the man's reaction when she said, "I am sorry, Captain Baker. But I do not intend to do any such thing."

Chapter Twenty

Tom and Polly lay on their backs on a blanket, hands clasped and fingers interlaced, staring skyward. Countless stars littered the dark canopy, the stream of the Milky Way charting the trail the emigrants would follow southward. The quiet of the sleeping camp was interrupted now and then by the pawing of a picketed horse or mule, the huffing of an ox, or the cry of a child. They heard the changing of the guard as drovers returned from the herd and awakened replacements to take up their duty.

The young couple had talked through the hours, learning of one another's past, thoughts, feelings, hopes, dreams. They talked easily, voices hushed and laughter soft. They talked of lost parents, of abandoned homes, of times on the trail.

Polly yawned a yawn that became a sigh. "Captain Baker says no good can come from our keeping company."

Tom snorted. "There ain't much he'd agree with Bishop Mendenhall about, but they likely see eye to eye on that."

"I cannot see why it makes a difference to them. It surprises me they would care at all about the two of us."

"Me neither. It ain't like anything's goin' to change on account of us."

They watched the sky in silence for a time. Polly tightened her grip on Tom's hand. "I believe Captain Baker would be less concerned if relations with your people were better. He has been unable to find anyone in any of the towns we have passed to sell to us."

"That's so. Folks has been told not to. They're so worried about what's goin' to happen when the soldiers get here they don't hardly know what to do. Other years, tradin' with the wagon trains was the thing to do—people would line up for the chance to trade crops and such for household goods and whatnot that folks didn't want to haul no more on their wagons. That's how the bishop got the plow we use, matter of fact."

"Do you think you could find someone who would sell the captain flour? He will pay well—in gold."

"Me? Heck, I ain't nothin' in the sight of anybody—just a kid. First thing they'd do is tell Bishop Mendenhall what I was up to."

"But if you could . . . Well, it might change Captain Baker's mind about us."

They said nothing more until Tom asked Polly what she thought would become of them.

"What do you mean, Tom?"

"Oh, you know—I'll be goin' home to work, you'll be yokin' up your teams and movin' on down the road. Come tomorrow, you'll likely pass by my town. Then what?"

Polly thought. And thought. "I have no answer. All I know is that I cannot imagine being apart from you."

"What's that mean? The way I see it, you either quit the wagon train and stay on here, or I leave home and go with you. I can't see either way as bein' easy."

They said no more, and Polly's breathing slowed and she slept. Time passed and Tom watched the stars fade. He sat up and saw the sky rimming the Wasatch Range had lightened to indigo. He leaned down and kissed Polly on the forehead and she stirred.

"I'd best be goin'."

Polly sat up and wrapped Tom in her arms. "Whatever shall we do, Tom? I cannot bear the thought of being without you."

"I don't know. I'll think of something."

And then he was gone.

Tom rode hard to get home. The sun had yet to rise when he arrived. He did not enter the house. He tended to his mount and brought in the cows to milk, then fed the penned stock. After putting the milk in the cellar to cool, he stepped through the kitchen door.

Mother Jane, sitting at the table with a steaming cup of tea, sniffed when he came in. Mary, stirring up a batch of pancake batter at the cupboard, turned, the mixing bowl cradled in her arm. She did not stop stirring as she considered her son.

"You are up early, Thomas."

The boy ducked his head and studied his shoes.

"Or is it up late?"

Tom lifted his eyes and watched his mother, but said nothing.

Jane spoke. "The bishop says you shirked your militia duties yesterday."

"Yes, ma'am."

Mary asked where he had been.

"I been ridin'."

Mary smiled. "Is that all? And what business kept you riding all night?"

Tom shifted his weight from one foot to the other, and again, searching his mind for an explanation.

"I can guess where the boy's been," Jane said. "He's been out all night with that hussy from the wagon train."

"Polly ain't no hussy!" Tom said, glaring at his stepmother.

Jane sniffed. "Only a hussy lures a boy away from his responsibilities. I expect she has taken you to her bed, as well."

"No such thing! Polly ain't like that!"

"So you say."

"Darn right I say so!"

Jane sighed. "You are young, yet. With experience, you will learn that Gentiles are not to be trusted. For whatever reason, that girl has designs on you. Most likely she—or the heathen boss men she works for—will use you to finagle supplies for their journey."

Tom said nothing.

Jane swallowed the last of her tea and rattled the cup into its saucer, then stood. "Bishop Mendenhall will hear of this," she said, and left the room.

Mary watched Tom's expression turn from anger to worry as she stirred the batter. She turned and set the bowl on the counter, poured in a splash of milk, and started stirring again. "You had best get washed up, Son. Breakfast will be ready soon."

Tom did not move. "Mom, what am I goin' to do?"

Leaving off her stirring, Mary walked to her son. She grasped his shoulders and looked into his eyes. "I don't know, Son. You must listen to your heart. But that is not all. You must consider carefully what might happen, no matter what course you choose. And it would not be amiss to ask your Father in Heaven."

The boy shuffled his feet. "You know I ain't much for prayin'. It never did no good when Pa took sick when we was on the trail out here."

Mary released her grip, and smiled upon seeing faint handprints left on Tom's shirt from flour residue on her hands. She brushed at the prints. "Oh, Tom, we cannot always understand the Lord's ways. As He told Isaiah, 'My thoughts are not your thoughts, neither are your ways my ways.' Even so, we must not lose our faith or our trust in God. It won't hurt to pray—and it may well help sort out what's in your heart and mind. Now, go wash up."

We have yet to yoke up the teams today. It seems some of

the men believe they can do better at obtaining supplies than Capt Baker and Col Fancher and are going into the town to try their luck. With no chores facing me I take these moments to set down a few thoughts.

Sarah has been by this morning pressing me about Tom but I do not know what to tell her. As my sweetheart said ~~last night~~ this morning if we are to be together one or the other of us must abandon the life we know. As he says neither possibility ~~seems poss~~ will be easy. While there is nothing in the way of kinship binding me to my fellow travelers and my prospects in California are unknown I know even less about what life may hold for me if I leave my employment with Capt Baker.

As for Tom I do not know. I believe he would leave his stepfather willingly but of course his ties to his mother are strong and he shudders at the thought of leaving her. It is far from certain that he could throw in his lot with our company as we have mouths enough to feed and there is little another pair of hands could do to ease our travel. I suggested he could aid the Capt in negotiating with his fellow Mormons to provision us but he doubts his abilities to help in that way.

What oh what to do?

Isaac Goldstein's General Mercantile was the only "Gentile" business—a business not owned by a Mormon—in the town of Provo. Isaac Goldstein, a Jew, and his wife and daughter and son were the only "Gentiles" in the town. The Goldsteins were one of a handful of Jewish families in the Utah Territory, part of a small group that originated in Germany and came west in search of adventure and financial opportunity. His relationship with the people of Provo was amicable, although it had chilled somewhat of late as the Mormons turned inward, becoming suspicious of anyone not actively involved in their faith.

"What do you mean y'all ain't got any flour?" the man from Arkansas asked Goldstein. The merchant stood behind the counter, his wife beside him. "What's that in them sacks yonder?"

"I did not say I had no flour—I said I had no flour to sell."

"Y'all got any cornmeal?"

"Our supply is diminished. I have none I can part with at present."

"Rice?"

Goldstein shook his head. His wife stood, hands clasped at her waist, her face pale.

"Beans?"

Another head shake.

"Coffee?"

And again.

The Arkansas man turned to his companion, who had stood back and watched the exchange. "Can't see how a man can stay in business runnin' a store when he won't sell no goods to a payin' customer. Hell, they ain't even Mormons from the look of it." He turned back to the couple. "That so?"

"What is it you ask, sir?"

"Y'all Mormons?"

"We are not."

The man from Arkansas, hands on the counter, leaned toward the storekeeper. "So why won't y'all take our money? Y'all ain't bound to dance to the Mormons' tune are you?"

Goldstein considered his answer. "It is so that we are not of their religion. But we are members of this community and must maintain good relations. Your trade is only in passing—our neighbors, we must live with after you are gone. A sale now is not worth the risk of losing the business of the people of the town."

Pushing away from the counter, the man pointed at a jar of hard candy. "How 'bout a sack of that there candy? My young'uns would mightily enjoy that for a treat."

Goldstein shook his head.

His wife laid a hand on his arm. "Isaac—for the children?" She reached under the counter and came up with a small paper bag. She set aside the jar lid, retrieved the scoop within, and poured a measure of the candies into the bag, twisted it closed, and handed it to the man. "No charge," she said with a little smile.

"Rachel—"

"Now, Isaac—surely our neighbors will not take offense at a few pieces of candy. And in accepting no money, we have not violated their advice against trading with the emigrants."

The man from Arkansas nodded his thanks, tucked the sack of candy inside his vest, and left with his friend.

Others from the train, after visiting every merchant, the gristmill, livestock yard, and knocking on the doors of more than a few residences, were no more successful—less so, in fact, as they had not gotten so much as a sack of candy. The wagons gathered at the town's main intersection and the men shared complaints, fed frustrations, and threatened to take what they needed by force. Some spoke against it, but their voices carried little weight.

As the anger neared its climax, a man from the town, elderly with a long, gray beard, approached the emigrants, a dozen or so men following. He stopped a few yards shy of the wagons.

"Can I be of some assistance to you gentlemen?"

The most vocal of the Arkansas emigrants snorted. "Not likely. Ain't no one in this here town showed any inclination to be of help."

The old man nodded. "I see. It is an unfortunate situation. But in the present circumstances, I am afraid we are unable to render any aid to your company."

"Just who the hell are you, anyway?"

The old man grasped the lapels of his jacket. "I am James Snow. I am the stake president—the religious leader—in this valley."

"Religious leader, you say? Why the hell don't you remind these Mormons of yours what it means to be Christian—if you-all are Christians, that is."

With a nod, the old man assured him that Mormons were, indeed, followers of Christ.

"Then why don't you-all follow His teaching to do unto others as you would have them do unto you?"

Snow smiled. "Brother, if you knew of our history among those claiming to be followers of our Savior back in the States, you would know that we have had more than our share 'done unto' us at their hands. And now there are soldiers from your so-called Christian nation coming upon us to 'do unto' us again."

"Well, it wasn't us what done it, and we ain't got nothin' to do with no army. And I don't see how your sellin' us supplies would keep them soldiers from comin' on."

Again, Snow smiled as if the man were a child in need of teaching. "The intentions of the federal government toward this people are unknown. It could be we will be forced to flee, yet again, and a find a new home where we can live in peace. Or perhaps we will escape into the mountains and wait out the army. Maybe they will lay siege to us in our cities and towns. In any event, our leaders feel it wise to stockpile provisions. And so we will."

Snow paused and looked from one man on the wagons to another, allowing his words to settle. Then, "I can assure you, gentlemen, that you will find the same reception in every town in this valley, so it will do you no good to attempt to look there for supplies."

One angry man stood up from his seat on his wagon and pointed at Snow. "If y'all won't sell us what we need, we might just decide to take it!"

As if by some unseen or unspoken signal, the knot of men behind the stake president untied itself and the men spread out along an invisible line behind their leader. A pistol appeared in the hand of each, drawn from concealment in jacket pockets and from waistbands.

"Gentlemen," Snow said, "we mean you no harm. But we will not stand by and allow you to molest us. Please, be on your way and travel with our blessing."

The man standing on the wagon snorted. "Blessing? Blessing, hell! That don't mean a damn thing if you-all don't bless us with a load of flour!"

Snow said, "I am sorry, gentlemen." He turned and passed through the line of his followers and walked away down the street. The men followed.

Chapter Twenty-One

Bishop Mendenhall did not appear at breakfast. The family ate in silence, the attempts at conversation or questions from the children shushed or ignored by the wives. After the meal, as Tom pushed back from the table intending to go back to his haying, Jane stopped him.

"You are not to leave, Thomas. Bishop Mendenhall will see you in his study."

Tom blanched. "What's he want?"

Jane smirked. "I believe you know. If not, he will soon relieve you of your ignorance."

Through the narrow gap between the ajar door and the jamb, Tom could see the bishop's back as he hunched over his rolltop desk, entering figures in a ledger. He tapped on the door and pushed it open. "You wanted to see me, sir?"

The bishop said nothing for a time, continuing toting his figures, even dipping the nib of his pen into the inkpot to keep up the work. Tom stood in the doorway, waiting. After an uncomfortable interval, the bishop stood the pen in its holder, then turned on his swivel chair away from the desk to face Tom.

"Sit down, boy."

Tom stepped into the room and eased onto the edge of the rail-back chair against the wall opposite the desk. Mendenhall rocked back in his chair, laced his fingers over his belly, and stared at his stepson.

"Is there anything you need to tell me?"

Tom swallowed hard. "I don't know what you mean."

"I speak not only as your father, but as your bishop. Is there anything you should confess concerning your relations with the girl from the wagon train?"

Unable to speak, Tom shook his head, then bowed it to stare at the floor between his feet.

"Pray tell, then, what were you up to all night?"

Tom looked up at the bishop. "Nothin'."

After a moment the bishop asked why doing "nothing" took all night.

"I don't know, sir. We was just talkin'."

"And what do her parents think of her being out all hours with a boy—a boy who is, for all intents and purposes, a stranger?"

Tom cleared his throat. "Polly ain't got no parents. They died back in Arkansas."

The bishop stared out the window considering Tom's answer. "Who, then, looks after her? Surely a girl of her years is not on her own."

"No, sir. Captain Baker—one of the wagon masters—was friends of her folks. He's lookin' after her. Gave her a job drivin' one of his wagons and cookin' for the men tendin' his stock. He's got a right big herd of cows he's takin' to California."

Mendenhall turned his attention from the window to the boy. "I hope they do not delay in getting there. The sooner they are clear of the valley with their wagons and their cattle and their sinful ways, the better."

"Far as I been able to see, they're good folks. Ain't no more sin among 'em than what there is here."

"That is not according to the reports I have received. I have heard tell of threats of violence, improper advances toward women, and of the abuse of a dog and assault on a young boy."

Tom sniffed. "Yeah, that's so. But that's just one or two of 'em—mostly one of the herders name of Howard. He ain't much good. And he causes just as much trouble for the people in the wagons as what he does in the towns. I've had words with him, myself. He don't take too kindly to my keepin' company with Polly."

The bishop nodded. "I am also told that their people have pestered the Saints for supplies at every turn, never content with refusals to trade with or sell to them."

Tom shrugged. "Don't know how you'd expect them to do otherwise. They got a long road ahead, and they counted on gettin' supplies here—just like most all of the wagons that come through do."

"But in the present circumst—"

"—That ain't got nothin' to do with them."

"Mind your manners, boy. Do not interrupt me. And don't speak of things you know nothing about."

"Sure I do. I know about those folks."

"How do you know?"

"I've talked to 'em. Like I said, they're good folks. They don't know a thing about the army, and don't care. And they don't know nothin' about Parley Pratt gettin' killed back in Arkansas. They was long gone from there 'fore it ever happened."

"But they are not all from Arkansas. Some are from Missouri, I am told."

Again, Tom shrugged. "Some of 'em is. Polly's friend Sarah, her family's from Missouri. But that don't mean nothin'. Not everybody in Missouri is 'Pukes.' Some of 'em's good people."

The bishop shook his head. "Were you not so young, you would not be so trusting. The Saints who lived through the hard times in Missouri know better than to take anyone from that state at his word. Too many of our people have been stabbed in the back by people from that pestiferous excuse of a place to trust them. It is good counsel, plain and simple, to keep an eye on Gentiles—especially those from Missouri. They have caused the Saints trouble enough!"

They sat in silence, Mendenhall studying Tom, Tom studying the hat he held in his hands, rotating it slowly by the brim.

"Putting all that aside, the question at hand is what you intend to do now."

Tom asked what he meant.

"That girl. What are your intentions?"

"We don't know, sir. It's somethin' we ain't figured out yet."

The bishop sat upright in his chair and leaned toward Tom. "I can save you the trouble, boy. Here is what you are to do: nothing."

Tom's forehead furrowed over pinched eyebrows as he looked at the bishop. "Sir?"

"You are to forget about that girl, the wagon train, and everyone in it. You are forbidden to visit them, you are forbidden to see anyone from there who may call on you here. Once they have passed, it will be as if they were never here. Understand?"

Tom could not find any words.

"Do you understand? You are to have nothing—nothing—to do with the emigrants or the girl."

Tom swallowed hard and stammered until able to speak. "What—suppose—if—what if Polly wants to stay here?"

"She will not be welcome."

A flush crept up from Tom's collar. "Could be we'll want to marry."

The bishop laughed. "For one thing, you are too young to take a wife. You have nothing to offer that girl, or any other. Besides, she is not of our faith. You know the eternal consequences of marrying outside the Church."

"Maybe I don't care about that—maybe I don't give a damn

about the Church."

"I am sorry to hear you say that," the bishop said, shaking his head. "I trust you do not mean it. I hope it is but a result of your head being turned by that girl."

"She ain't 'that girl'! Her name is Polly. Polly Alden. And if she'll have me, I will marry her!"

The bishop said nothing for a time, squeaking his swivel chair as he rocked slowly back and forth. Then, "Listen to me, Thomas, and listen carefully. As I have already said, I forbid you to have any further association with that emigrant train. You are not to see or speak to anyone there. And that includes—especially—this Polly Alden. Understand?"

Tom did not reply, only stared at his stepfather.

"Furthermore, should you disobey, you will no longer have a place here—either in this household, or in this community. Understand?"

Again, Tom did not reply. Without taking his eyes off the bishop, he rose from his chair and sidled toward the door. Then, still without a word, he turned and walked through the door. He went to the bedroom he shared with Hiram, gathered up a rucksack from the wardrobe and put in a change of clothes from the skin out—which was most of all he had, save his Sunday best.

Hiram walked in as he stuffed in a pair of socks. "Tom, what are you doin'?"

"I've got to go, Hi. Your pa won't let me stay here no more."

"What do you mean? You live here!"

"Not no more."

"Tom!"

The boy stepped across the room and threw his arms around Tom's waist. Tom grasped his shoulders and pushed him away, holding him at arm's length.

"I'm awful sorry, Hi. But listen—you remember Polly, that

girl from the wagon train?"

"Sure. I 'member. She's nice."

"I'm goin' with her. Pa don't leave me any choice. There ain't nothin' else I can do."

Slinging the rucksack over his shoulder, Tom left the room, Hiram following close behind. He found his mother alone in the kitchen. Tears filled her eyes. They said nothing, only shared a long embrace. When Tom left the kitchen, his eyes were as full as his mother's.

Setting out to meet the main road through the valley, he cut through the pasture where the town's working stock and milk cows were out to graze. Tom's friend Eli Price was tending the animals and saw him coming.

"Hail, the weary traveler!" he called out when Tom drew near. "Where you off to, Tom?"

"Don't know," Tom said with a shrug. He dropped his rucksack and sat down on it.

Eli's questions peppered Tom like bird shot and Tom answered him as best he could. He told Eli all he knew about Polly, and how he could not be without her. About his visit to the wagon camp and their talk that lasted through the night. About Bishop Mendenhall's anger, and that he was forbidden any contact with the emigrants or with Polly. About his determination to be with the girl no matter what. And, finally, about his bewilderment about what to do.

"I wisht you wasn't goin' Tom. You're the best friend I got—'bout the only one, come to that."

"I know it, Eli. It's the same with me. But I don't know what else to do. I'll try to throw in with that wagon train. If they won't have me, I don't know where I'll go. If ever I get settled somewhere, I'll send you a letter sayin' where I am."

"Good luck, I guess," Eli said. He turned away as his friend stood up and left him. Then he watched Tom walk away until the heat waves rising from the land caused him to shimmer and finally disappear.

Hours later, Tom met the oncoming wagon train. He stood well off the road until Polly's wagon drew near. Their eyes met, but they said nothing. Tom tossed his rucksack onto the wagon seat and fell in step with Polly and the plodding oxen. After a while, he said, "Where are you folks goin'?"

"California," Polly said, without averting her eyes from the road ahead.

"Mind if I come along?"

"Do you have business in California?"

"Not that I know of. I was thinkin' maybe I'd find myself a woman and set up housekeepin'."

"Is there a particular woman you have in mind?"

"Can't say for sure. There was this one girl I met. She was an Arkansawyer, I believe. I kind of took a shine to her."

"Do you think she would have you?"

"I surely do hope so. I'll have to ask her next time I see her."

They walked on in silence.

Given the late start, the company covered only eight or nine miles before circling up for the night near Hobble Creek, between where the lazy stream left the town of Springville and where it poured into the bay on Utah Lake. Tom unyoked the ox teams while Polly unpacked the camp equipment from the wagon. He prodded the teams to water in the stream, then to a patch of brush and grass away from the wagons with the other Baker ox teams. As soon as Tom left off prodding them along, the cattle knelt on their front legs and lowered their hindquarters to the ground and propped themselves on their bellies to rest.

On his way back to the wagons, Howard rode up. He reined up his horse a few yards from Tom. With a naughty smile on his face, he leaned over in the saddle and let loose a long stream of tobacco spit, then wiped his mouth and chin on a shirtsleeve.

"Well, hell. If it ain't the chore girl. You been missin' cleanin' up after me?"

Tom said nothing, just stood watching the horseman.

"What the hell *are* you doin' here, anyways? I thought I told you to stay the hell away."

"I don't believe I'm obliged do your bidding, Howard."

"You might not think so, Mormon boy. But I say different."

Howard lifted his bullwhip from where it hung on the saddle horn, dropped the coils, whipped it back and lashed out at Tom. Tom raised an arm to ward off the whip, and the popper and fall spun and snapped around his forearm, ripping through fabric and flesh. Grabbing the thong with both hands, Tom jerked and almost pulled Howard from the saddle. But Howard pulled back, refusing to let go of the whip handle.

Hand over hand, Tom kept pressure on the leather as he walked toward the horse. The animal snorted and shuffled, unsure of what was happening. When Tom reached the horse, he let go of the whip, jumped up and grabbed a double handful of Howard's shirtfront as near the collar as he could reach. Twisting his hands into a firm grip, he fell backward, pulling Howard out of the saddle. The instant he touched ground, Tom used the momentum of the fall to roll back onto his shoulders, hefting Howard overhead to land beyond him. Howard scrambled and rolled to his belly but before could get his bearings, Tom was upon him, sitting astraddle his back. Howard humped up and tried to buck him off, but Tom grabbed a handful of hair and pushed Howard's face into the dirt. He grabbed an arm and bent it behind the drover's back and wrenched upward.

Howard grunted and groaned, turned his face sideways and spat out dirt and pebbles and ground litter. He cussed and swore, and Tom learned a few words he had not heard before.

"Let me up from here, you sonofabitch, and I will kick your ass."

Tom wrenched the arm harder. "You sure that's what you want, Howard? To get up?"

"Damn right."

Tom used Howard's back for a platform to push himself upright. He rubbed his abraded arm while waiting for Howard to find his feet. Howard did not stand. From a squat, he launched himself at Tom, reaching for his legs in an attempt to take him down. But Tom twisted out of the way and kicked Howard in the ribs as he went by. The blow knocked the wind out of Howard and he lay gasping for air. But, before long, he pushed himself to his knees and struggled to his feet. He staggered toward Tom with a cocked fist, swung, but missed his shot when, again, Tom stepped to the side. Tom's fist did not miss, forcing even more air out of Howard when it landed in his midsection.

Howard stood, hands on knees, fighting for breath, strings of drool dangling earthward. He got a breath, then another, and stood. He grinned at Tom and pulled an oversized knife from its scabbard on his belt. He lunged at Tom again, but the move was awkward and, again, Tom sidestepped and, again, landed another blow. This one rattled Howard's teeth and twisted his head sideways. He staggered, but kept his feet. He turned again toward Tom, still grinning, the blade of his knife snaking back and forth, looking for a place to strike.

Unnoticed by the fighters, a crowd had gathered. Captain Baker, horseback, pushed through the onlookers. He pulled a pistol from a saddle holster and fired into the air. He followed the report of the pistol with a shout.

"What the hell is going on here?"

CHAPTER TWENTY-TWO

Howard sat sulking in the saddle, slowly riding horseback around the herd. After the fight, Captain Baker had sent him out on guard, despite the drover's pleadings that it was his off-duty night; a rare chance to enjoy uninterrupted sleep. Instead, he watched stars appear in the darkening sky, and faint lights flicker on in the distant towns. His stomach reminded him that it had missed supper as part of his punishment, and that breakfast would be a long time coming.

Nearer the wagon camp, Captain Baker used a rock for a low stool, and Tom sat on the ground. At the wagon master's bidding, the Mormon boy had stood idle while the emigrants unpacked the wagons, prepared and ate supper, and readied the camp for sleep. Polly was still going about her clean-up chores, as the captain had pulled her aside earlier for a long talk. Tom could only guess at the upshot of the discussion.

"I've got a pretty good idea what you're doin' here," Baker said, "but I'd like to hear it from you."

Tom let out a long breath. "Well, sir, it's more tangled than what you're likely thinkin'. Fact is, I ain't got nowhere else to go."

Baker thought on that for a time. "I take it you've got trouble at home."

"I ain't had nothin' but trouble at home since I sold you that load of vegetables and such."

"Surely that's not all of it. That was days ago. I can't imagine your stepfather, your bishop, or whatever you call him, is still on about that."

Tom chuckled without mirth. "You don't know Bishop Mendenhall." He paused. "But, that's what set him off in the first place. And I guess it ain't helped that I keep comin' back here, missin' my militia duty and stayin' out all night—I made sure to get my chores done, and do what work needed doin', but still . . ."

"He sounds like a hard man."

Tom nodded. "He is. And all this business with the army and all is weighin' heavy on him."

"And yet here you are. Seems like you'd not want to upset him anymore."

"He made it so I didn't have no choice. He said I wasn't to have no more to do with Polly. And if I was to come out to see her again, I wouldn't be welcome at home no more."

Baker sat for a while without talking, snapping bits off a sprig of sagebrush he held in his hands. "You must think a lot of the girl."

"Yessir. I do."

"What do you-all intend to do? You and Polly are both mighty young."

"I know we're young, and so does Polly. Truth is, we don't need you nor Bishop Mendenhall to tell us that." Tom took in and let out a long breath. "As for what we're goin' to do—well, I don't rightly know. I ain't had time to figure it out."

"And what do you intend to do while you figure it out?"

"I don't know that either, sir. I was kind of hopin' I could tag along with you folks until me and Polly can decide what to do." Tom shrugged, unseen by Baker in the darkness. "Truth is, I ain't got any other ideas. All I know is that I don't want to be without Polly."

"And what about Polly? What does she think?"

Another shrug. "Don't know. Ain't had a chance to talk much with her since gettin' back here this time. You've talked to her. What did she say?"

Baker snapped off more of the sagebrush stem before answering, the aroma of the pungent plant hanging in the air. "She don't have any more idea than what you have. From what she says, I expect she's as determined to stick with you as you are with her. But, like I said, you-all are young, and I have seen more than a few young couples drift apart after a while. People change. And at your age, they change a lot, and they don't waste no time doing it."

"It won't be that way with us. I know it."

Baker stood and scrubbed the palms of his hands together, then held them to his face and inhaled the scent of sage. "Maybe it will, maybe it won't. But for now, you-all—at least you—have got other things to worry about."

Tom stood and brushed off the seat of his pants. "What do you mean?"

"You say you want to come along with us."

"I'm hopin' to, sir."

"Well, son, that ain't as simple as it might seem to you."

"Why's that?"

Baker explained that the train was fully manned. There were people enough to handle the working stock, enough to organize the camps, enough cooks, enough to repair wagons, and more than enough drovers for the cow herd.

"But that ain't the worst of it, Tom. There are those who would resent your being here."

"You mean Howard? I ain't worried about Howard. He'll stop ridin' me soon enough—if he don't he'll take a lot of beatings."

Baker laid a hand on Tom's shoulder. "Howard's the least of your worries. And not only because it looks like you can handle yourself just fine where he's concerned. But there are plenty of others who won't want any part of you."

"Why's that? What have I ever done to 'em?"

"It ain't you so much. It's that you're a Mormon. First off, your people haven't been any too friendly to us. Now, before you say anything, we've all heard about the army on the march to here, we've all been told how you Mormons feel like you were mistreated back in the States. But that don't overcome the fact that we planned on resupplying here, and we ain't been able to get it done. So a lot of families in this company will be on short rations all the way to California, and it could be some of 'em won't make it.

"I reckon some of these people is every bit as scared of what's to come as you Mormons are. The thing is, we can't do anything about what's threatening you-all, but you-all can sure as hell do something to help us. But you-all won't do it, and that don't set too well.

"Not only that, there'll likely be some who'll think Brigham Young or one of his men is using you to keep an eye on us—maybe put us into some bad situation."

Tom swallowed hard. "There ain't no such thing. And I wouldn't never do anything like that."

"They don't know that. All they know is the Mormons don't want anything to do with us, and all of a sudden here comes you, wanting to join up with us."

Tom thought for a time, then sagged all the way to the ground, sitting again in the dirt. Baker sat down on his rock. Tom said that if given a chance, he would prove himself. He would do any work asked of him, help in any way he could. And people would soon enough see that he meant no harm. Baker allowed that it might not be enough.

They sat for a time until Baker, believing the conversation had run its course, stood and turned to walk to the camp.

"Wait a minute, Captain Baker!" Tom said, hoisting himself to his feet in one motion.

Baker turned, but said nothing.

"Suppose I was to find a way to get you some flour? And maybe some sacked grain? Likely not as much as everybody needs, but some."

"How would you do that?"

"You'd have to pay—a generous price."

"Of course we'll pay. Whatever it takes. But you haven't answered my question. How?"

"This is Friday night, right?"

"Yes."

"You get me some teams and a wagon and a couple of good men to help load it, and you bring along some of that gold they say you're a-carryin', and tomorrow night about this time we'll go for a ride."

Baker stood thinking for a long minute. "Get some sleep. But find some place out of the way—you had best stay clear of Polly tonight. She can feed you come morning. You're welcome—well, I won't say welcome, but you'll be allowed to travel with us tomorrow. Just stay out of the way and don't bother anybody and there shouldn't be any trouble."

"Thank you, Captain Baker. I'm obliged to you. I won't bother no one, I promise."

As Tom went to fetch his rucksack from where it still sat on the wagon seat, he saw Polly sitting on the back of the wagon, legs dangling, with a book in her lap. A candle stubbed atop the sideboard of the wagon cast a halo of light. He said nothing as he passed, only nodding at the girl.

Polly smiled at him, but she, too, stayed silent. After Tom passed, she heard him walk out into the brush—looking for a place to bed down, she presumed. She raised her diary into the light and reread what she had written.

Tom has come back, I hope to stay. Capt Baker is not pleased but as I told him Tom has nowhere else to go and the reason for it started with his selling to the Capt. He took me aside after supper and talked as I suppose a father might speak to a daughter with all manner of questions about my feelings for Tom and his treatment of me and our plans for the future if we had any. Plans that is. Of that we have none but we are ~~strong~~ fervent in the hope that we will have a future together. Leastways I am looking forward to it. I cannot bear to think of being without Tom.

Capt Baker says that Tom being here will not set well with many in the company because of their bad feelings about the Mormons and the way they have treated us. But blaming Tom for such is as silly as the Mormons blaming us for whatever difficulties they have faced in other places in the past or are fearing now.

We shall see what tomorrow brings. If Tom is sent away from here as he has been sent away from his home I do not know what to do. I will ~~have~~ be forced to consider staying here with the Mormons should Tom be able to find forgiveness at home or perhaps we will be vagabonds searching for a home or at least a situation that will allow us to make a life together.

Oh how I miss Mother. Her advice at this time would be most welcome. There is no one I can talk to about these things except Sarah and to be frank she is not the most thoughtful or serious minded person. Her views lean more to the romantic than the practical.

Satisfied with what she had set down in the journal, Polly again took up her pencil.

Tom passed by a moment ago. We did not exchange

words only glances but in his eyes I can see the same love I feel in my heart. And now to sleep perchance to dream as that man Hamlet said in the play but unlike that sad man I do not equate sleep with death and I hope to see Tom in my dreams, which will make them happy ones.

We shall see what tomorrow brings. I pray it will be happiness.

The wagons rolled through Springville the next day. Tom walked beside Polly as she goaded the teams along. He tried not to look at the people—his neighbors—who watched them pass, not wanting to see the pity or even disgust he felt sure would be in their eyes. Eli walked with him for a ways but Tom had no answers for the questions his friend asked, and Eli soon stepped aside and, with thumbs hooked in his braces, watched the wagon train amble by.

As they passed the street down which the bishop lived, Tom looked and saw his mother standing outside the front door, holding onto a porch post. He started to raise a hand in greeting, but used the hand instead to wipe tears from his eyes. They passed the town's tithing office and bishop's storehouse and the clerk and Bishop Mendenhall and a few others stood on the walkway below the short flight of steps that led to the front door. Hiram was there, and when he saw Tom he shouted his name and ran out into the street but stopped and slouched back to the sidewalk at his father's order. For his part, the bishop stood still as a statue, his calling out to Hiram his only sign of awareness of what was around him. But Tom suspected, knew, in fact, that his stepfather was mindful of the goings-on and his choice to ignore his stepson was a deliberate one.

With Springville behind them, the emigrants pushed on to the town of Spanish Fork and the river of the same name. The cow herd was bedded down west of the town and the wagons circled up not far away on the banks of the stream as it meandered between the high mountains and the bluffs atop which the town sat.

Once settled, Colonel Fancher, with Captain Baker and a couple of the most strident men from the company, rode into the town in search of supplies and provisions. Once again, they were turned away empty handed.

But, tonight, John Baker thought as he unsaddled his horse back at camp, that may well change—if, that is, Tom Langford knew whereof he spoke.

Chapter Twenty-Three

The wagon sidled up the bluff to the benchland, following a seldom-used back road accessing pastures and hay meadows. Although the night was deep and dark, Tom dared not take the main road back to Springville. The wagon cover lay folded in the bed, the bows removed and left at camp, as starlight on the cover might reveal the passage of the wagon through the night. Leather thongs threaded through bit chains on the mule bridles and trace chains on the harness minimized the jingle, and cloth and leather bindings on other metal parts on the harness and wagon further reduced the rattle as the mule team moved the wagon along. A trio of loaded rifles, a shotgun, and a brace of charged pistols lay in the wagon box.

Billy Brown sat beside Tom on the wagon seat. A man from Fancher's company who Tom did not know rode in the wagon, and Captain Baker followed on horseback. The road skirted the foothills of the Wasatch Mountains, rising and falling through diminishing draws and ridges as it passed Union Bench, a small town at the mouth of Maple Canyon. Upon reaching Springville, Tom turned off onto the first street, with its few occupied lots, and stayed at the edge of the settlement until taking a street lined with closed businesses to the center of town and the building housing the tithing office and bishop's storehouse.

Pens behind the building held sheep, hogs, cattle, chickens, and one old mule that stretched his neck over the top rail of the corral and watched with interest. Inside the building were stored foodstuffs and other goods. All were contributions in kind from Springville Saints—their tithes to the church and donations to aid their needy neighbors. Surplus offerings unneeded locally, as well as tithes, were periodically transported to the main tithing office in Salt Lake City. It had been some time since such a shipment, so the warehouse held a goodly stock of stores.

Tom turned the wagon into the alley behind the building and backed up to the loading dock. Like most doors in the town, the sliding door opening into the storehouse was not locked, and Tom slid it back, wincing as it squealed along its rail. Once inside, Captain Baker lit a lantern and held it high to reveal the goods, loosely organized and stacked or binned along the walls of the room. The men located the flour, two barrels and several bulk sacks, as well as a number of smaller bags parceled out for home distribution.

Fancher's man wanted to take it all, but Tom refused, not wanting to cause a severe shortage in the town. Baker supported Tom in his caution. The men rolled out one of the barrels, and hefted about half the heavy sacks out to the loading platform where Billy Brown shifted the flour onto the wagon and arranged it in the bed.

Tom led Captain Baker through a doorway into the offices—a room inside the building's front door with a desk where a clerk kept accounts, and a small office where Bishop Mendenhall met with people contributing to or withdrawing from the storehouse. Baker had a reasonable idea of the going price for flour at the various mills and stores the emigrants had visited in the towns. He counted out gold coins equal to the value of the flour taken, and added half again as many coins to the stacks on the desk. They hoped the generous payment would counteract, to some degree, the theft.

After another round of debate with the Fancher man over the flour left behind, Tom slid the big door closed and drove the team away from the dock and back onto the street to retrace their route to the wagon camp.

Baker rode beside the wagon and asked Tom what would happen in the morning when the theft would be discovered.

"Ain't nobody'll know a thing about it tomorrow," Tom said. "That's why I wanted to come tonight. See, tomorrow's the Sabbath and folks will all be in church meetings most of the day. Won't nobody be in that office till Monday morning."

Baker chuckled. "I suppose they'll be right surprised to find that gold."

Tom agreed. "It'll take a while for that clerk to figure out why it's there. He'll soon enough notice there's flour missing, but it'll take some time to do a count to know how much is gone. Then he'll drag the bishop down there and explain what's goin' on. They'll know they got money enough to cover the loss and then some. But if I know Bishop Mendenhall—and I reckon I do—he'll be mad as hell anyhow, and will be wantin' to get to the bottom of it. I don't guess it'll take him too long to figure out where this here flour has got to."

"Then what?"

"Well, if we move along on down the road tomorrow—today, it is now, I guess—and get a good start the next morning, we'll be far enough away from here that the bishop might not think it's worth comin' after us."

"You think so?"

Tom sighed. "No, truth be told, Cap'n, I don't think so. But it could be the law, or the higher-ups in the church the bishop has to answer to, will figure the gold is payment enough and won't come for the flour. But you can bet that won't be the end of it."

"How's that?"

"Oh, they'll pass the word on down the line to be on the lookout for us—not that they ain't done that already—and to be extra careful to keep an eye on us. Any hope you have of tradin' with towns on down the road is long gone, unless I miss my guess."

Baker chuckled. "Well, it ain't like they were going to trade with us anyway, from the way it's been going. This way, we've at least got some flour. It won't be enough to see us through, but it'll help."

The Fancher man in the back of the wagon, perched atop a stack of flour sacks, snorted. "Hell, Cap'n—we could've had a whole lot more of the stuff had you-all not been so particular about upsettin' the Mormons."

"You're right—we could have taken it all," Baker said. "But, this way, they won't be as aggravated as they would have been. By not leavin' them with any more of a shortage than what we did, maybe they'll let us alone."

"Far as I'm concerned, the bastards are welcome to come for it. I'd be happy to shoot the first Mormon sonofabitch that tries to take it back."

Baker sighed. He dropped back behind the wagon and rode on in silence for a while. Then he moved up beside the wagon again. "You-all keep movin' along. I'll ride on ahead to the camp and roust folks out to be ready for an early start." With that, the wagon master heeled his horse into a trot, then an easy lope, down the road toward the circled wagons.

By the time the flour arrived, Baker had the emigrants ready to roll. The cooks had prepared a scant but quick breakfast while the men shifted loads, making room to secrete the flour in various wagons. Distribution for use would come later. The mules were unharnessed and turned out with the loose stock, the wagon bows and cover replaced, and teams of oxen yoked for the road. By the time the sun rose over the peaks of the Wasatch Mountains, the emigrants were moving south from the Spanish Fork River toward Peteetneet Creek, then on to Summit Creek where they circled the wagons after a long day on the road. Come morning, they would cross the low pass out of Utah Valley and into the Juab Valley.

Well into that valley, the emigrants stopped to overnight at a string of tree-lined ponds connected to Currant Creek. The women took advantage of the ample water to wash clothing, and the stock fed well on the lush grass bordering the creek and ponds. The campsite would have been a good place for a layover for a day's rest, but Baker believed it best to move on in the morning to put more distance between the wagon train and whatever trouble might be brewing on the back trail concerning flour that was bought but not sold.

The trouble arrived late the next afternoon as the train wended its way past the town of Salt Creek. A white-top buggy rattled by, drawn by a team of light horses. Tom, walking on the opposite side of the wagon, saw Bishop Mendenhall in the passenger seat. He recognized the driver as Porter Rockwell.

The buggy passed the lead wagon and Rockwell turned his team crosswise in the road and stopped. Captain Baker, riding point, saw the activity and came riding back at a lope.

"What's goin' on here, gentlemen?" he said. "Why are you-all blocking the road?"

The driver set the brake and wrapped the lines around the handle, then stepped down from the buggy. Baker watched the burly man approach, noting his lengthy, gray-streaked beard and long hair tied in the back and rolled into a bun at his collar. The man reached inside his jacket and Baker dropped his hand onto the grip of a pistol holstered to the forks of his saddle.

The man stopped and his hand froze, concealed behind the jacket front. "Were I you, mister, I'd leave hold of that pistol."

Baker said, "And just who might you be that I had ought to take orders from you?"

Raising his left palm to halt the conversation, he pulled his other hand from beneath the jacket and held it up to show a badge. "My name is O. P. Rockwell. Orrin Porter Rockwell. Most folks calls me Port. I am a deputy United States marshal."

"Well, Mister Rockwell—Port—Marshal, would you mind telling me why you are delaying our progress?"

By now, several men of the company had gathered, clustering between the buggy and the wagons, watching, with more men on the way. Some carried firearms.

Rockwell turned and studied the men, smiled, and turned back to Baker. "I take it you're the head of this outfit."

Baker nodded. "I share leadership with Colonel Fancher."

Fancher walked out of the crowd and past Rockwell and his buggy to stand next to Baker's horse and told the deputy he was Colonel Alexander Fancher.

Rockwell looked at Baker and said, "And who might you be?"

"John Baker. Most call me Captain Baker."

Rockwell smiled. "You're mighty fond of military order around here, I see."

There was no reply. Then Baker repeated his question as to why they were being held up.

Rockwell turned and nodded in the direction of his passenger, still seated in the buggy. "That there gentleman is Aaron Mendenhall. He's bishop in a town up on Hobble Creek called Springville. You gentlemen might recollect that town."

Fancher spoke. "Yessir. I seem to recall passing through the place a few days back. Folks there didn't exactly make us feel welcome."

Rockwell nodded. "I see. Well, it seems like, from what Bishop Mendenhall tells me, that there's some things missing from Springville since you was there."

"I have no idea what you're talking about," Fancher said.

Again, Rockwell nodded. "I see. So you're tellin' me you ain't seen a mostly growed boy name of Thomas Langford?"

This time Baker spoke. "Nobody is saying any such thing. Why are you asking? What are you on about?"

"Well, Thomas—Tom—he's the son of the bishop here. Stepson, if you want to be particular. The boy belongs to Mary, the bishop's wife."

"So?"

"The boy's mother misses him. Wants him to come home."

Baker squirmed in the saddle. "Supposin' the boy don't want to go home?"

Rockwell stared hard at Baker for a moment that stretched into uncomfortable. "He's a big boy, I reckon. Old enough, maybe, to make up his own mind. What say you bring out the boy and I talk to him?"

Baker thought it over, then stood in his stirrups and found Tom near the back of the assembled men. He nodded, and Tom came forward. "Tom, you likely heard that these gentlemen want to talk to you."

Tom said nothing, his gaze shifting back and forth from Rockwell to the bishop.

"Son," Rockwell said, "what are you doing with these people?"

Tom shrugged. "Hard to say. I guess I aim to go on to California with them." He glanced at Captain Baker. "If they'll have me, that is."

Rockwell asked about his mother.

"I feel right bad, leavin' Ma." He looked at the bishop. "Bishop Mendenhall there, he didn't leave me no choice."

Mendenhall scoffed. "Oh, come on!" he said to everyone, and no one in particular. "The boy has taken up with a girl from this company! Thinks he's in love! Ain't neither of them with enough age on them to know a thing about love."

Tom reddened. "Oh? And what about you, Bishop? You don't know the meaning of the word your own self! Ma ain't nothin' to you but a housekeeper and cook. And Grace—well, all you got Grace around for is so she can have babies you don't care about till they're old enough to work. And Jane—I don't know about Mother Jane. Bein' as she's your first wife, there might be somethin' there. But if there is, it sure don't show."

"Mind your tongue, boy! You will not speak to me like that!" He turned to Baker. "Far as I'm concerned, you can have the ignorant little whelp!"

Rockwell raised a hand. "Calm down, Bishop. Ain't no need to stir up a fuss." He asked the wagon masters if the boy was welcome to stay with them.

Fancher said, "It don't matter to me much one way or t'other. He's another mouth to feed, which we don't need—thanks to you-all Mormons not bein' willing to trade with us."

"And you?"

Baker cleared his throat. "The girl this man here spoke of, name of Polly Alden, she's in my care, she bein' an orphan. I admit I'm a mite concerned that the two of 'em is plenty young to be takin' up with each other in a serious way. But there are men and women among us—and likely among you-all, as well—that did the same." He shrugged. "I guess we'll leave that up to them. If we don't let Tom stay with us, then I reckon him and Polly will go off and try to make a life together wherever they can. He says he ain't welcome in what passes for his family no more, and that looks to be the case from what the bishop here says. At least with us, they'll have a better chance than they would goin' off on their own."

Rockwell said, "Then you don't mind the boy stayin' on with you."

Baker shook his head. "It ain't the best situation, but it's maybe the best there's goin' to be. Far as I'm concerned, we'll take him with us."

A voice in the crowd called out, "Bullshit!" Howard pushed

his way to the front. He spat and said, “I don’t want that little Mormon sonofabitch anywheres around me!”

Skeets yelled, “He’s right! The way we been treated by these Mormons, we sure as hell don’t want one of ’em right in amongst us!”

“Now, boys, I know you-all—Howard, leastways—have had your troubles with Tom,” Baker said. “But, seems to me, they’re more of your own makin’ than his.”

“Bullshit!” Howard hollered again, and punctuated the word with another gob of spit.

Another man stepped forward. “Maybe these boys are right. I don’t trust any of these Mormons. Could be they’ve sent this boy to spy on us—maybe cause trouble for us with the people in the towns on down the way.”

Other voices murmured in agreement.

Bishop Mendenhall said, “You people are talking nonsense. This boy hasn’t the wherewithal to do any such thing. And why would we care to cause you Gentiles trouble? We just want you out of here, the sooner the better. We’ve trouble enough facing us without worrying about a bunch of hateful Arkansawyers and Missouri Pukes. Be gone with you, I say! And take the boy with you!”

No one spoke for a time. Polly came out from the crowd and linked her arm through Tom’s. Captain Baker asked Rockwell to clear the road so they could be on their way.

“Not yet. There’s another thing. Has to do with a bunch of flour missing from the tithing office in Springville.”

Baker tipped his hat back with a forefinger. “Oh? When did this happen?”

Rockwell looked to Bishop Mendenhall for an answer, who said it must have been Saturday night, or perhaps Sunday night.

“Sunday? We were a good ways down the road by then, I suppose. Not as far away on Saturday night, but well past your town. If I recall, I believe we were camped on a stream called the Spanish Fork River—not that it's got enough water in it to merit bein' called a river."

"So you're a-sayin' you don't know nothin' about no stolen flour?" Rockwell said.

Baker smiled. "I can assure you, Deputy Marshal, that there is not an ounce of flour in this train that was not bought and paid for."

"That is madness!"

Rockwell turned to the bishop. "What's that you say, Aaron?"

"This is nonsense. That flour was as good as stolen! Sure, the thieves left behind money—but they had no business taking that flour!"

"You're a-tellin' me that whoever took that flour left money for it?"

"Yes, Port. Gold coins. Word is, these emigrants are carrying a lot of gold. It had to be them."

"Tell me Aaron, was it a fair price they left?"

Mendenhall stammered and stuttered and admitted the gold more than covered the value of the flour. "But that is not the point! Brother Rockwell, I demand that you search these wagons! I am certain you will find the missing flour! I want it returned!"

Rockwell stared at the bishop, worried about the deep flush on the man's face, and the sweat beading on his forehead and runnelling down his face. He looked at the line of wagons stretched out along the road and the cluster of people unhappy with being delayed.

"I dunno, Aaron. That's a right smart of wagons. And one sack of flour looks pretty much like another, far as I know. There ain't no way to know for sure where whatever flour is in these wagons come from. So I can't see that it would do any good to delay these people any longer."

From his seat in the buggy, the bishop pointed a trembling finger at Polly. "You! You Jezebel! You shameless hussy! This is all your fault!"

Tom turned, drawing Polly with him, and walked back down the line to her wagon.

Chapter Twenty-Four

The wagons rolled on past the town of Salt Creek a short way and circled up for the night. Abe Baker and his drovers moved the cow herd onto a stand of grass on the face of a low ridge. The animals drifted apart to graze, then most lowered themselves to lie on their bellies and chew cud.

Soon, a rider from the town galloped up and slid his horse to a stop where Abe and Billy Brown and one of Fancher's herders sat horseback, talking. The townsman, red in the face and wheezing from the hard ride, looked from one drover to the other.

"Who is in charge here?"

"I reckon that's me," Abe said. "What do you want?"

"What I want is for you to move these animals! This is our winter feed ground. If your stock crops the grass, then what will our cows and sheep eat come the winter?"

"Can't say it matters much to me." Baker swept an arm across the long, broad, valley. "Looks to me like there's plenty of room for you-all's critters to graze."

The man worked the reins to keep his horse under control, his agitation upsetting the winded animal. "But this is better pasture! This is our best grass for winter! This belongs to the people of Salt Creek! You must move off. Now! If you do not move them, we will do so! You will see!"

Fancher's man said, "You think this grass belongs to you-all?"

"Yes! I have said!"

"This is Uncle Sam's grass. We are his boys. We have a better claim on it than a bunch of rebel Mormons."

Without another word, the townsman jerked his horse around and, with the ends of his bridle reins, whipped it on the rump and flanks as his heels pounded its ribs, the driving hooves stirring up a rooster tail of dust on the way back to town.

"That feller was right upset," Abe said as he watched the man go.

"To hell with him," Fancher's man said. "Damn Dutchman!"

Abe thought for a long moment. "All you-all boys keep an eye on the herd. I reckon I had best get on to camp and tell the captain about this. As aggravated as that feller was, there could be more trouble."

Fancher's man chuckled. "That would be fine with me. I'd as soon shoot any one of them Mormon bastards as look at them."

"Well, try not to kill anybody—or get yourself killed—till I get back. Then we'll see." Abe told Billy Brown to keep a lid on things then rode for camp at a trot.

Abe huddled with his father and Colonel Fancher. Neither of the wagon masters thought anything would come of the altercation. But Abe thought otherwise, repeating the depth of the man's anger and threat that the men of the town would move the herd. "If they do, I reckon they'll stampede them. It could take days to round them up if they do."

Captain Baker considered the idea. "Maybe you're right, Son. I'll send the rest of the herders out soon as they've had a bite to eat." He turned to Fancher. "Alex, it might be best if you do the same. If they see all the boys out there watchin' the stock, them Mormons might be less inclined to cause trouble." Then, to Abe, "Go on back to the herd. If you sense trouble coming, fire a shot. We'll come a-runnin'."

The wagon masters set out in search of their drovers, and

Abe rode back to the herd. He stationed himself near the crest of the low ridge, where he had the best view of the town in the near distance. As the sun cast long shadows, he strained to see what was stirring up a faint haze of dust at the edge of Salt Creek. Before long he could see it was a group of men, afoot, marching in ranks. He swore under his breath and looked toward camp. Howard, Billy Red, Trajan, Skeets, and another of Fancher's herders were coming his way, laughing and prodding one another and getting up to other kinds of tomfoolery.

"Hey!" Abe shouted. "You-all get the hell over here! And fast."

The shout surprised the riders, and in an instant they spurred their horses into a lope, reining up in a semicircle around Abe.

"Boys, here's what I want you-all to do," Abe said, the words coming fast. "Trajan, you stay up here on the ridge with me. The rest of you-all ride around the herd and spread yourselves out along the bottom on the hill. Stay sharp."

Skeets, his brow furrowed, one eyebrow arched and eyes wide, said, "What the hell, Abe? What's goin' on?"

Abe pointed toward the town and the marching men, now near enough to count.

"Sonofabitch!" Howard said. "What's them damn Mormons up to?"

"There was one of 'em out here a while ago wantin' us to move the herd. Says this is where they graze their stock in the wintertime."

"There ain't but 'bout thirty of 'em, near as I can tell," Skeets said. "I say, let's light into 'em!"

Billy Red laughed. "Skeets, you're crazy. There's maybe thirty of them, and there ain't but eight of us. And me and Trajan ain't armed. I don't know about Billy Brown and that other man down below, but I'd be surprised if there was one gun between 'em."

Skeets started to protest, but Abe cut him off.

"Red's right, Skeets. Ain't no sense askin' for trouble. We'll wait."

"Wait? What the hell for?"

Abe didn't answer. Instead, he drew his pistol and fired into the air. The horses skittered and shied at the unexpected report, and the drovers had their hands full calming them down. Out on the flat, the Mormon marchers halted at the report. After a moment, they came on.

"Pa and the colonel will be sendin' help. Meantime, you-all get down there and spread out and wait. Don't do nothin' unless them Mormons make the first move. Don't be stirrin' up trouble—just protect the stock. You-all got that?"

Billy Red, Trajan, and Fancher's drover nodded. Howard smiled, spat, and offered a half nod. Skeets said, "All right. But if one of those sonsabitches comes anywhere near me, I'll plug the Mormon bastard."

The drovers rode off, some taking one way around the herd, others going the other direction. Trajan waited with Abe for a time, watching the approaching men, then moved off to his post on the crest of the low ridge.

The marching Mormons came on. Abe could see they were a ragtag troop with no semblance of uniforms and what looked through the distance to be a mishmash of long guns. The cadence for their march came at the hands of a small boy toting a drum that dangled from a shoulder strap, the bottom of the cylinder hanging below his knees. The leader signaled a halt a hundred or so yards from the base of the ridge and the onlooking drovers. At shouted orders, the militiamen reformed their ranks and went through a somewhat disjointed display of arms. Then drilling began, with the men—and boys, as Abe could now see—marching one way and then another, their unity less than precise.

While the militia from Salt Creek drilled, Captain Baker, Colonel Fancher, and a dozen or so men came along. Some were horseback, a few were mounted on mules, others trotted along afoot.

"What the hell?" Fancher said with a smile as he watched the show of force below.

Captain Baker said, "You think they mean trouble, Abe?"

"Dunno. They ain't done nothin' more'n what you-all are seein' right now."

Baker thought for a while, then said, "Well, Alex, let's you and me ride on down there and see what they have to say."

The two wagon masters rode slowly down the face of the ridge, wending their way through the loosely herded cattle. Some of the more skittish animals darted out of the way. Some hoisted themselves to their feet and walked a few steps before settling down again. Others stayed where they lay, jaws working over a cud, watching the horses and riders without much interest. By the time the two wagon masters reached the bottom of the ridge and crossed the flatland toward the militia, the drum was silent and the soldiers had formed into two long ranks facing the herd.

As he approached, Baker could see that some of the militiamen looked worried and some were frightened, but most looked unconcerned. A few faces looked belligerent. Baker and Fancher reined up facing the militia commander. Other than a thick fringe of white hair poking out from under his cloth cap, he looked to be a young man. But, as Baker studied the man's face, he could see his smooth cheeks were framed by networks of wrinkles at the corners of his eyes and mouth, and a lined forehead above dark eyebrows.

No one said anything for a long minute. Then Fancher spoke. "What are you-all doin' out here?"

The militia leader said, "I guess you might say this is a show of force, so to speak."

"Show of force? What the hell for?"

Turning to the ranks, the officer called out one of the men. It was the man who had confronted Abe and the drovers earlier, and the militia leader called him Hans. Hans explained that the place the emigrants had chosen to bed down their stock was set aside and protected by the town, held in reserve for winter grazing.

Fancher looked around the broad valley as he listened to the explanation and complaint. "Looks to me like there ain't no shortage of grass hereabouts. What makes this place special?"

Hans claimed the forage on the ridges had proven in the few years since the settlers arrived to be more nutritious for the cattle and sheep when cured in the winter than the grass on the flats. More than that, he said the Indians who frequented the area had long used the same country to winter their horses, and for the same reason.

Fancher smiled. "And what do the Indians do now, now that your critters is eatin' up their grass?"

The man looked embarrassed, unsure what to say. The militia leader said, "We do our best to get along with the Utes and Pahvants. But their use of the land is haphazard, and we, well, we have settled here and so our rights must take priority over the savages."

"I see," Fancher said with a faint smile. "How about our rights? This ain't deeded land and you-all are squatters, same as us."

Hans said, "It is not so! Our rights have priority, as we were here first!"

"Oh? And just how long have you-all been here?"

"It is six years now," Hans said. "Brother Brigham sent us to settle here in fifty-one."

Fancher's smile turned to a grin. "Well, gentlemen, I fear

you-all are wrong when it comes to you-all's rights having priority here."

Hans and the militia leader looked confused, as did those within listening distance in the militia ranks.

Fancher watched the confusion, then said, "I, myself, come through this country with a cow herd bound for California back in eighteen and fifty. My cattle fed on this very place a-way back then. And back then, there wasn't no sign of a town at all. So, I guess you-all are the latecomers."

"It is not the same!" Hans said. "You came and you went. But we—we came and we stayed!"

Hans had more to say, but Fancher halted the talk with a raised hand. "I know it ain't the same. I'm just funnin' you-all. But, I hear tell that you, Hans, all but threatened to stampede our cattle if we didn't move them. That so?"

Hans shuffled his feet and stammered before admitting that he had, perhaps, been too strident in his demands.

As the tension hung in the air, Fancher turned to Baker and held a quiet conversation. Then Baker said, "Just to be clear, gentlemen, you want us to move this herd to another place."

Both Hans and the militia leader and several of the soldiers nodded their agreement.

"Well, Colonel Fancher and I have talked it over and we will comply with your wishes."

The militia leader released a long breath, and it seemed to relax the strained air.

"But."

In an instant, the mood grew taut.

"But," Baker said. "You-all have to ask nice."

Hans snorted. "Like hell we will! We—"

"Hans!" the militia leader cut him off. He turned to the mounted men and cleared his throat. "Gentlemen, we, the citizens of Salt Creek, will be obliged to you and most grateful if you will please bed down your herd elsewhere, where their presence will not diminish the feed on our winter grazing grounds."

Baker smiled. "Why, thank you for asking, sir. Not wanting to cause any difficulties with the people of Salt Creek, we will comply."

The militia leader offered a snappy salute. "Thank you, sirs."

Baker and Fancher returned a casual salute with a finger to their hat brims. They turned and rode toward the herd. Baker used hand signals to tell the drovers to get the herd up and bunched and push them out onto the flats. Soon, the shouts of the drovers were punctuated by the snap and crack of popping bullwhips. Now and then Baker caught snatches of angry clamor from where Howard and Skeets went about their work, no doubt voicing their dissatisfaction with what they saw as kowtowing to the demands of the Mormons.

With the herd on the move, the leader drilled the militiamen into rank order, and, in time with the beating drum, marched the troops toward town. Hans, however, was not in the ranks. Rather, he hopped and skipped along with wild gyrations of hands and arms beside the commander, complaining loudly and vehemently about the officer's obsequiousness before the emigrants in bowing to their demands, and all but begging the damn Gentiles to move their damn cows.

I have not taken time to set down any words these past days. Much has happened. Tom is with me! He has left home and family to be with me but with the joy there comes difficulties. Some in the company do not accept Tom and believe his presence here is some trick on the part of the Mormons. How they could think such of Tom I cannot understand.

As for Tom he is at sixes and sevens. There is no work for

him really and he does not know what to do with himself. He yokes up the teams in the mornings and turns them out at the end of the days and helps with such camp chores as he can such as gathering wood and tending the fire and the like. He walks with me beside the teams and hopes to be of help but the truth is all the teams are so accustomed to their work that they follow the wagon ahead and need only the occasional prod to remind them to keep moving.

Today there was considerable excitement when Tom's ~~father~~ stepfather the Bishop caught up with our company and brought with him a lawman. They came to fetch Tom but the frightening looking man with the badge allowed that Tom was among us of his own free will and old enough to make up his own mind. There was talk of stolen flour also involving Tom but it was admitted that the flour was paid for and no cause for action. Upon leaving the Bishop called me a hussy and a jezebel and said unkind things not in keeping to my mind with his duties as a religious man.

This is a strange country the Mormons have chosen as their home. Their ZION Tom says they call it. It is dry and yellow and brown and gray and few things grow but brush and bunchgrass and small twisted trees on the sides of the mountains. Mountains surround us everywhere. A high wall is always on our left hand and other mountains rise in every direction hemming in the valleys the road follows. In time the road enters the mountains and climbs over them to reach yet another long valley that is much the same as the last except for being even more dry and barren. Why anyone would choose to live here is beyond me and yet the Mormons think it the promised land. I cannot wait to be away from this place and these mountains and again be at a place where one can rest in a shady grove and escape the heat of the sun. I pray we find such in California.

Still and all Tom is with me! Sarah is at me at every opportunity asking questions which are none of her business. I assure her that Tom acts the perfect gentleman but she will not let go of it and demands to know of every detail which I of course will not divulge. It is enough that he is here despite the trouble that comes with it. We are as the star crossed lovers of the poem or play I recall from my school days which now seem so long long ago.

CHAPTER TWENTY-FIVE

Alexander Fancher turned off the road and reined up in the shade of a cedar tree and studied the land ahead. Somewhere along the downslope lay a settlement called Buttermilk Fork or Cedar Springs, but there was nothing he could see to reveal its presence. No town had been there on his previous passage through here. Back then, there was a string of Mormon communities all along the road and there were more of them now, but the distances grew as the company moved south. It had been a four-day haul through valleys and over mountains and across the Sevier River since leaving Salt Creek, their longest journey away from a settlement since arriving in the heart of Mormon country. The heat, as well as the suspicion—even hostility—of the self-styled Saints made him question his decision to take the southern road rather than the more well-traveled Humboldt route. But there was nothing to do now but press on. Before him, the Pahvant Valley spread southward more than thirty miles, bordered by the Pahvant Range to the east and the Sevier Desert fading away into the west.

Standing in the stirrups and twisting to see the road behind, the colonel saw the wagon train now clear of the pass after a long, slow climb to the crest. Dust from the wagons and the cow herd in the rear hung low in the still desert air.

Fancher settled into the saddle and urged his horse on. He would ride on into Buttermilk Fork and look up the head Mormon in the town and arrange a place for the wagons to camp—as near to water as practicable—and to settle the cattle for the night. The people in the burg proved less than hospitable, directing the wagons on beyond the town to the skimpy waters of Pioneer Creek, most of which had been diverted by the Saints for irrigation.

The next morning, the wagons passed through Fillmore and the red sandstone multistory building meant to serve as the capitol of Brigham Young's sprawling kingdom of Deseret. Instead, the town served only briefly as capital city of Utah Territory. The emigrants' usual inquiries about supplies were met with vehement denial. The denials were met with anger, some in the train questioning the virtue of the town's women, others insulting their shabby log house abodes, some voicing blasphemous contempt for the Mormon religion.

Howard and Skeets, as was their wont, enjoyed deriding the townsfolk, hanging back long after the cow herd passed. Skeets unleashed a pistol shot at the vacant capitol, dimpling a sandstone block. He laughed, turning his horse in a tight circle in the street and waving the gun around, frightening the watchers—most of them women and children.

"Ain't there any men in this here town?" he hollered. "Bring 'em out, and I'll show y'all what a real man's made of! My kin drove all y'all Mormon sonsabitches outa Missoura, and by God I only wisht I was alive at the time to help 'em do it. I got half a mind, by damn, to ride back to Salt Lake City and take a pop at ol' Brigham Young his own self!"

Howard sent a shot skyward. He sat still on his horse in the middle of the street. "Listen up, you lousy Mormons! Y'all will rue the day you refused your Christian duty to aid the weary traveler! Uncle Sam has sent his army out here to kill every one of you treasonous bastards, and I'm more'n willin' to start the job right now!"

Another shot rang out—this one a boom from a big-bore

shotgun in the hands of a Mormon. The gunman, backed by a handful of other Mormon men, walked out of an alley into the street and stopped a few yards away from the drovers.

"In God's name, you boys curb your tongues!" the man said. "It is all I can do—and more than I want to do—to keep these men—members all of the legally constituted militia of Millard County—from shooting you heathens out of the saddle!"

Howard leaned over and spat and started to say something, but the man with the shotgun interrupted.

"I said hush up!"

The drovers heard the ratchet and hiss and click of cocking hammers and looked wide-eyed down the barrels of the guns aimed at them.

"Now, you boys get on out of town and don't come back. If there is any hint of further trouble from your company, I will call out the rest of the militia and lay waste to the lot of you. I expect those wagons would raise a right pretty plume of smoke when we put the fire to them. When we get done with you, there will not be a trace to betray your presence here."

Howard looked at Skeets. Skeets looked at Howard. They both looked at the militia leader, whose florid face contrasted with the pallor of their own.

"Now, get on with you!"

The drovers reined their horses around and set off down the street at a walk, soon urging their mounts into a trot, then a lope, then, at the edge of town, an all-out run toward the dust cloud left by the herd they were meant to be tending. They would say nothing to anyone about their adventures in the town—but word would get out.

It took all of the long day for the train to cross the remainder of the big valley. As the wagons rolled along, the emigrants passed dark buttes off to the west, remains of dead volcanoes whose frozen black lava flows and tuff and cinders erupted in scattered outcrops on the flats and ridges along the road. At the far end of the valley, not far from where the road started its climb up the mountains and over the pass leading to the next valley, they circled the wagons near a place called Corn Creek—this, a village occupied not by Mormons, but by a band of Indians with ties to the Utes to the north as well as the Paiutes to the south. The name of the band, which had lived there for centuries, had been given to the valley that was their home and the mountain range that walled it in—the Pahvants.

The Pahvant village, unlike any other Indian village the emigrants had encountered on their long journey, had what looked to be more than a hundred acres of land under the plow. Curious Indians watched the wagon train form a circle near the creek, and looked on as the drovers eased the herd onto the creek to water, then loose herded the cattle onto the broad swath of grass bordering the stream. The activities were no different than what the Pahvants had seen dozens and scores of times, as travelers going both directions on the road used the area for campsites. Seeing the curiosity of the Indians, Captain Baker told Abe to double the night guard around the herd.

Before the emigrants were settled, two northbound wagons came out of the canyon, accompanied by several horseback Indians and white men. The wagons halted no more than a stone's throw from the Arkansawyers and went about setting up camp, following the orders of a hefty man. As he shouted his orders, the big man removed his hat and mopped the top of his bald pate, then tossed the hat onto the seat of the wagon, pulled a thatch of hair from a pocket, and positioned the wig on his head and started toward the camp of the Arkansas emigrants.

Baker and Fancher walked over to make acquaintance and met the big man halfway. They learned the man was George Smith, one of the top men among the Mormons, on his way back to Salt Lake City. He said he had been sent by Brigham Young to the communities in the south to warn them of the approaching army and encourage them to prepare for the worst. Smith introduced them to Jake Hamblin, a missionary to the southern Indians and a man more familiar than most with conditions on the road.

The men moved into the shade cast by the low-hanging sun from a Mormon wagon. Smith sat on a folding camp stool, the others on the ground, as Hamblin answered their queries about the road ahead. He suggested the best camp sites and rest stops, including a place called Mountain Meadows—familiar to Fancher from his earlier sojourn through there. The Indians with the party, they learned, were the leaders of several Paiute bands. In the Mormon capital they would meet with Brigham Young to negotiate their cooperation in fending off the Americans in aid of the Mormons. Similar meetings had already occurred with the Ute and Shoshoni tribes to the north, Smith told them.

"Any danger from these Indians here?" Fancher said, pointing with his chin toward the Pahvant village.

"None whatsoever," Smith said. "Nor will you encounter any difficulties from the Paiutes down south—unless, that is, you mistreat or abuse them."

"These Pahvants pose no threat," Hamblin said. "They're a peaceable bunch. Kanosh, their head man, prefers a settled life. They've taken up farming and seem more or less content."

Smith swiped the wig off his head and used it to wipe the sweat from his forehead and face, then plopped it haphazardly back onto his head. "Tell me, gentlemen, should you encounter Indian difficulties, how many armed men have you in your company?"

Fancher and Baker exchanged glances, and Baker said they

figured they had forty, maybe fifty in a pinch, should it come to that.

Smith chuckled. "You would be safe here, and in the Paiute county, with half as many. These Pahvants would not even consider any outrage against such a well-armed company." Still, he advised maintaining a strong presence with the cow herd, as the animals sometimes tended to "wander away" in the night near Indian villages such as this one.

The wagon masters stood and dusted off the seats of their pants, thanked the men for the information, and set off for the circled wagons.

"They seem good enough folks," Hamblin said.

"Seems so," Smith said, "for heathen Gentiles. But I sense a cloud hanging over that party. I fear some evil will befall them."

Howard licked the remnants of food from his plate and swallowed the dregs of his coffee. He tossed the cup toward the washtub and it bounced off the rim and fell into the dirt. His aim with the plate was better. It sailed through the air and dipped into the tub, clattering into the mess of dishes already there. He whittled a cud of tobacco from a lint-covered plug and chewed it into a soggy gob, watching Tom come back from the stream toting a pail of water in each hand. Tom poured one of the buckets into the washtub, then warmed it up with a pot of water that had been steaming over the fire.

Tipping his head back, Howard spurted a thick stream of tobacco spit from his mouth, watching the syrupy string arc and splat to the ground. He wiped his mouth with a dirty shirtsleeve. "Say, chore girl," he said to Tom, "when you goin' to start earnin' your keep around here?"

Tom said nothing. He kept up his work at the fire, wiping out the pans and kettles Polly had used to cook the meal.

"Lover boy!" Howard said. "I'm talkin' to you."

Tom stood upright and glared at the drover, but still did not speak.

"Y'know you've been eatin' more'n your share of our grub ever since you got here. And you ain't done a damn thing to earn your keep 'cept women's work. I doubt you're even fit to do a man's job."

"Leave him alone, Howard," Polly said.

"Like hell I will. If you had a lick of sense, you'd be the one leavin' him alone. Ain't no future in takin' up with a mama's boy."

"Shut up," Billy Brown said, so quietly only Howard heard him.

"You mind your own damn business, Billy."

Billy Red perked up. "What? Me? I never said nothin'!"

"He's talkin' to me," Billy Brown said. "I told him to shut up. And he damn well better do it. Ain't no need to be ridin' Tom thataway."

Howard leaned over and spat a puddle between his feet. "What the hell do you care? Ever'body else has to earn their keep—why not him?"

"How many biscuits did you have with your supper, Howard?"

"I dunno. Six. Maybe eight," he said with a shrug.

"Well, you damn fool—you wouldn't've et half that many were it not for Tom. You know damn well most of the flour we got, we got on account of Tom."

"Who cares about that? Hell, I could've gone into any one of them Mormon towns and come back with a load of flour. I'd've shot the sonsabitches to get it if I had to."

Abe Baker stood. "Shut up, the both of you. All your bickering wears me out." He walked to the tub and dropped in his dishes. "Red, get on out to the herd and send Trajan back for supper. Brown, Howard—you two get some rest. You'll be goin' out later. We'll be keepin' a double guard most of the night."

"Damn Indians!" Howard said. "A man can't get a good night's sleep no more with all these damn savages around."

"Abe," Tom said. "I'd be pleased to help out."

Howard laughed. "You? Hell, chore girl, I'm guessin' you're ascared of the dark."

Tom bristled. "You can think what you want. I can ride as good as any of you, and I can handle cattle, too. Give me a gun and if it comes to shootin' I can do that, too."

Howard laughed again.

"That's all right, Tom," Abe said. "We won't need you tonight. With them Mormons camped yonder, Captain Baker wants you to stay close."

Tom's jaw dropped. "What? He don't trust me?"

"I don't know about that. I do know he wants to talk to you. You had best leave this to Polly and go find him."

Chapter Twenty-Six

As twilight faded, Tom crossed the camp to the wagon occupied by Captain Baker. He found the wagon master outside the circle with Colonel Fancher, supervising a handful of men unloading food supplies. Indian men sat on the seats of the two buckboards, watching the white men at their labors. The wagons were nearly empty, the workers dragging out bags of beans and sacks of potatoes and wheat to stack alongside what looked to be at least thirty bushels of shelled corn.

Captain Baker saw Tom looking on and walked to him. "What do you think, son? It ought to hold us for a while."

"Yessir. Looks like these Indians is more inclined to trade what they grow than the people in the towns. Must be a reason they're willing to ignore Brother Brigham and the other church leaders."

"Colonel Fancher organized it. The Pahvants were reluctant. They weren't too interested in gold, but let it be known the offer of firearms, powder, and bullets might persuade them. Alex had a good supply of such laid by for California. He traded some of his own, and found others in the company willing to part with some of what they carried."

Tom watched the men unload the last of the food. "Abe says you want to see me."

"Come with me." Baker led Tom away to a quiet place near the creek. "Those men in the other camp—do you know them?"

"Can't say I know them. But I know who some of 'em are.

The fat man, he's George Albert Smith. He's one of the Twelve Apostles in the church. Last couple of years him and Jeddy Grant—he's a counselor to President Young—has been stirrin' up people over their need to repent from sin and get rebaptized and tattle on their neighbors and to show more obedience to what the priesthood leaders say to do. I reckon he's been down here raisin' Cain about the army comin'."

Baker nodded. "What about the fellow with the chin whiskers?"

"Don't know him—leastways not to speak of. But I've seen him now and then when he come through town and would stop to visit with Bishop Mendenhall. His name's Jacob Hamblin, and he's been down south amongst the Indians there for the last few years, tryin' to keep 'em friendly to the settlers—leastways that's what I gathered from hearin' him talk."

"Do you think they would mislead us as to conditions down there?"

Tom thought for a minute. "Can't say. I wouldn't think so, most times. They're both good men so far as I know." Tom paused for more thought. "But what with all that's goin' on, maybe . . . Well, I don't believe they'd tell you any lies, but they maybe wouldn't tell you everything, if you know what I mean."

"I see." Baker laid a hand on Tom's shoulder. "Thank you, son. It is getting late and we'll be rolling out of here early. We had best get some sleep."

Polly's cook fire was barely visible, its coals burned down to a faint glow when Tom arrived. Light showed through the cover of her wagon, leading him to believe she was writing in her journal. Why she bothered with all that escaped him, and he could not help but wonder what might be said about him in the words she wrote. He rolled out his blanket and stretched out, staring at the stars, hoping his mind would soon settle.

"Where you been?"

Tom bolted upright at the question. "Howard? What're you doin' here? Ain't you supposed to be out watchin' the herd?"

"Yeah. I reckon I'll get out there soon enough. I was just restin' up for it when you come a-stumblin' in here and woke me up."

Tom heard Howard yawn, and could imagine him stretching and scratching at himself.

"I asked you where you been."

"I can't see that's any of your affair, Howard."

Howard snorted. "You prob'ly been over yonder reportin' on us to them Mormons."

"What? What on earth could I be reportin' on? And why would I?"

"Ever'body knows how you damn Mormons stick together. You might be foolin' ever'body else about why you're here, but you ain't foolin' me."

"Well, you can think what you like, Howard. You had best be gettin' to work. Me, I'm goin' to sleep now."

"Go on ahead, chore girl. Get your sleep. Just keep in mind I'll be keepin' an eye on you."

Tom rolled over onto his side, pillowed his head on his arms and closed his eyes. No sooner, it seemed, had he drifted into sleep when the rattle of pots and pans awakened him. He sat up, squinting his eyes tight, then scrubbed his face with the palms of his hands. Polly's smiling face greeted him when he opened his eyes. She squatted before him in the dim light of early dawn.

"On your feet this instant, Tom Langford, or I shall be forced to fetch water on my own."

Tom reached out and took Polly by the hands, pulling her toward him. She rocked forward until overbalanced and dropped onto her knees before him. He let loose of her hands and hugged her around the shoulders, drawing her close. She pulled her head back and turned seeking a kiss.

"Oh my, Polly. You don't want to be kissin' me—my mouth tastes like somethin' died in there."

Polly laughed. "Go fetch that water and before long I'll have coffee on. That will scorch that foul taste out of your mouth. Or maybe make it worse."

Tom got to his feet and gathered the water buckets. He dropped them at the edge of the creek, jumped across the narrow stream, and stepped into the willows on the opposite bank to relieve himself. Back on the other bank, he dipped the pails into the flow one at a time and after they filled he palmed up water, swishing it around to rinse his mouth and spitting it back into the creek, then laved up more to drink and scrub the sleep off his face.

On the way back to the wagons, he noticed the people camped with George Albert Smith and Jacob Hamblin starting to stir. An arm reached out the door of a wall tent and shoved the flaps aside. The apostle stepped out. He had britches and boots on, but only underwear up top, his bald head showing white in the growing light. Tom looked for any hint of recognition as he watched Smith watching him, but saw none—but that did not mean Smith did not know who he was.

"Here's your water, Miss Polly," Tom said as he lowered the buckets near the fire.

The pails had barely settled when she hefted one and filled a trail-worn coffeepot, then poured more of the water into a kettle and hung both vessels over the flames to boil. Bacon already sizzled in a big skillet. "Only bacon and oatmeal this morning. Captain Baker says we are to get an early start."

Tom yawned. "He said as much last night."

"Don't know why he is in such an all-fired hurry. This is a fine place for a day of rest if you ask me."

"Well, I don't know 'bout you, but he sure never asked me

for my opinion. I believe he wants to get away from the settlements quick as he can. He seems a mite worrisome."

"It's not like there is no reason for it. You Mormons have not exactly been friendly."

Tom smiled. "Why, Miss Polly! I thought I'd been right friendly." He wrapped an arm around her waist and drew her close until their hips bumped. "I'd be right pleased to be an even better friend if you're amenable."

Polly turned to face Tom and held him close. "Oh, Tom! What is to become of us?"

"I can't rightly say. I suppose we could say to hell with it all and get hitched up. Captain Baker might not like it, and my kin would pitch a fit if they was to know, but I don't care anymore. It don't seem right, us worryin' more about if other folks is happy instead of us bein' happy."

"But how could we, Tom? Get married, I mean."

"That's easy enough. Next town we come to, we could look up the bishop and he could marry us."

"But would he? With me not being a Mormon and all?"

Tom shrugged. "He don't need to know. Or we could tell him you was if he was to ask. We'd just say we hooked up with this company to make our way to California. There's some Mormon towns down there. We'll say we got kin there."

"I don't know as I could lie, Tom. Besides, it doesn't seem right starting out a marriage with a lie."

"Maybe they got a judge down in Parowan. It's the main town down there. It wouldn't have anything to do with church—even if the judge happens to be the bishop, too."

Polly said no more, only held Tom close. She turned loose when the lid rattled on the coffeepot as steam from boiling water lifted it. She dumped a handful of ground coffee into the big pot and set it aside to steep, then tossed a handful of salt into the other pot, almost ready to boil, and slid the skillet with the bacon off the fire. She poured rolled oats into the kettle when the water boiled and stirred the mix with a wooden spoon.

Abe, Billy Red, and Trajan walked into camp carrying their saddles. "Somethin' sure smells good, Miss Polly," Billy Red said.

Polly wiped her hands on the front of her apron. "Not much for breakfast this morning. I'm afraid Captain Baker and Colonel Fancher want to be on the road by sunrise."

"You got that right," Abe said around a yawn. "The boys are already gettin' the cows on their feet and bunchin' them up. Soon as we've et, we'll be saddlin' fresh horses and gettin' back out there. Then Howard and Billy Brown will be in to eat."

Trajan said, "Miss Polly, is there anything you need? I ain't been much help to you since that ol' milk cow dried up."

"No, Trajan. But thank you. Tom, here, he fetched water for me. And there was firewood enough left over from yesterday." She stirred the oatmeal and judged it ready. "Grab your plates, gentlemen. Breakfast is ready."

"Don't bother chewin' it boys," Abe said. "We ain't got the time."

Breakfast was hurried throughout the camp. By the time Billy Brown and Howard came in to eat, Polly was already cleaning up and Tom was loading camp equipment into the wagon. He brought in the ox teams and yoked them up and hitched them to the wagon, then topped off the load with the last of the kitchen boxes.

The road angled up in a long, slow climb through the desert mountains, up and down ridges and draws, around outcrops, rattling through sagebrush and clumps of cedar trees. The road twisted down a canyon, dropping onto a wrinkled upland for several miles, climbed again over yet another divide, across a meadow watered by the marshy waters of Indian Creek, then climbed another low divide to fall slowly into a big valley and the town of Beaver out in the flats, some forty miles and more in three long days of travel since leaving Corn Creek.

Jaded animals and weary travelers alike leaned into the pace the wagon masters demanded of them since leaving the Indian village. Although no one in the company had heard the Mormon apostle's divination of evil hanging over the emigrant train, perhaps Captain Baker or Colonel Fancher felt a similar foreboding. Whatever the reason for all the hurry, the stop at the town was a welcome one—but the town was not welcoming.

The emigrants who visited the burg called Beaver noted a difference in their treatment by the residents. The frosty reception since arriving in Mormon country fell several more degrees in the southland. The fire in George Smith's sermons had turned Mormon faces away from strangers, making the townspeople's fear and anxiety in the presence of the emigrants palpable. Refusals to sell to the travelers came before the question could be asked, with doors latched and window shades drawn at their approach. The only villager not behind closed doors was the local lawman, who sat in a rocking chair on the porch of his office, a shotgun propped against the wall at his side. He whittled on a stick, adding to a scatter of shavings around his feet on the porch.

Alexander Fancher sat horseback and studied the closed-down town, then rode to the lawman's office. "Afternoon," he said, with a tip of his hat.

The lawman only glanced at him, his concentration fixed on peeling wood off the stick in his hand.

"Mighty quiet around here."

The whittler did not respond. Fancher listened for a moment to the slow hiss of the slicing blade and the rhythmic creak from the rocker or a porch board beneath it.

Two women and three men from the wagon train stopped to stand beside the mounted Fancher. One of the men stepped forward and said, "Say, mister—we'd be obliged if you could say when these stores will be open for business."

The rocking chair stopped in the middle of its curve. The man studied what was left of his stick and, satisfied with his handwork, dropped it. He folded the jack knife and slipped it into the pocket of his vest, on which a tarnished star was pinned. "They won't be openin' up today—or tomorrow, if you folks are still here."

"Why's that?"

The lawman shrugged. "Merchants hereabouts won't be tradin' with you. Fact is, I'm here to see they don't."

Fancher asked if there was something wrong with their money.

"Don't know. Don't care. Only thing that matters is that we've been counseled by those in authority not to do business with strangers." He stared at the emigrants in turn, then cast his eyes about the street where others wandered. "You folks might just as well get on back to your wagons. You're welcome to what feed and water you need for your livestock out there, and what firewood you can scrounge up to do your cookin'. But the sooner you are back on the road, the better. There ain't no point in lingering hereabouts."

The emigrants, seeing no hope of obtaining fresh food, went back to camp. Later, one mother among them walked back into Beaver after sundown. She walked the streets in the gloaming, a patchwork quilt folded and draped over her arms, hoping to attract the attention of someone willing to trade for the family keepsake, hauled all the way from Arkansas.

Other than curious eyes peering past curtains pulled aside, she drew no interest. But as she passed a well-kept cabin on the way out of town, a woman stepped out from behind the house and signaled to her. She looked around and, seeing no one watching, turned at the corner of the fence into a driveway beside the house. The woman in the yard said nothing, only gestured for the quilt.

"This is fine handiwork," she said, after examining the stitching and binding on the quilt. "Yours?"

"No ma'am. That was stitched by my ma and my grandma, back in Carroll County, Arkansas."

"Yet you are willing to part with it?"

"Yes, ma'am. My children—they are poorly. What I've got to feed them fills their bellies, but they ain't had milk for weeks now, and we ain't been able to get no fresh garden truck. It ain't good enough, and one of my girls is frail."

The woman shook her head and sighed. "Wait here."

There was little light left in the sky when the cabin door opened again and the woman walked out. A man stood watching, leaned against the open doorway, silhouetted in the faint lamplight from within. The woman held out a basket. "Take this."

The basket held a small wheel of cheese and a crock of milk, butter, as well as carrots, turnips, radishes, and beets.

"Thank you. Oh, thank you!" the emigrant woman said, clutching the quilt. "It is more than generous." She held out the quilt.

"No. You keep that."

The emigrant woman stepped back. "No, ma'am. I can't take no charity."

"It is little enough. Much less than the value of the quilt. But I have no more to offer."

After a pause, the emigrant held out an arm and the Mormon woman slid the handle of the basket into the crook of her elbow.

"Thank you-all," the woman said, with a catch in her throat, glancing from the woman to the man in the doorway. "May God bless you-all."

The woman turned and went back inside. The man watched for a moment, then closed the door. The emigrant woman stepped over to the door and laid the quilt on a bench then walked out the driveway to the street. Night had fallen, but there was enough light for her to see a man coming along the street toward her, a long gun dangling from his hand. She recognized him as the local lawman, and she hurried away toward the wagon camp.

He did not pursue her. She looked back over her shoulder and saw the lawman turn into the yard of the house she had visited and pound on the door.

Chapter Twenty-Seven

Across the flats south of Beaver the wagon road unraveled, parallel tracks spread several rods wide over the sagebrush plain. Some ruts cut deep, filled with dust ground fine as flour, other traces barely visible as they wended their way. To the east rose the Tushar Mountains, the highest peak reaching above twelve thousand feet, some six thousand feet higher than the plain over which the train traveled. The road headed for the Black Mountains to the south, their slopes darkened with thick stands of cedar. The next town, Paragoonah, lay more than two days down the road.

Atop the divide in the mountains, a narrow upland valley led the way for several miles, then opened up into the Little Salt Lake, or Parowan, Valley. The towns there, Paragoonah and Parowan, tucked into the southern end of the valley, some five miles apart, against the red wall of the Hurricane Cliffs. East and a little north of Paragoonah, Little Creek cut through the cliffs, its canyon floor trodden by the hooves of countless mule strings packing trade goods along the Old Spanish Trail on its way from Santa Fe to California. From here on, the southern road the emigrants followed would shadow the tracks of the mule trains.

The Arkansawyers set up camp outside of Paragoonah in a deluge, thunderstorms pouring summer rain onto the valley and mountains. Runoff overflowed the creeks and filled the canyons, carrying with it floods of red mud onto the farms and fields.

But, as is typical of summer storms in desert country, the clouds passed, night fell, and morning dawned clear and hot.

Single-minded in cleaning up the mess, the Mormons in the towns were of two minds concerning the emigrants. Most, stirred by Apostle George Smith's recent oratory and the exhortations of local leaders, shunned the outsiders, refusing them food or aid. A few, contrary by nature to a degree all but unheard of among the Mormons, believed their leaders too zealous, too fearful, too antagonistic. One such was the local miller, who ground the Pahvant corn for the emigrants. Another townsman, in the midst of negotiating to trade his fresh oxen for trail-weary emigrant draft cattle, abandoned the bargaining when a zealous neighbor, upholding the will of his leaders, held a knife to the man's throat.

"Tom! Thomas Langford! Is that you?" The call startled Tom as he walked down a Parowan street hand in hand with Polly. He turned to the source of the voice, finding a man and woman working in a garden beside a house. He shaded his eyes and studied the man for a time before recognizing him from the company they crossed the plains with years before.

"Henry? Henry Farnsworth?"

"As I live and breathe! I'll be damned! I hardly recognize you, boy—you appear to have got your growth these years since I last laid eyes on you."

Farnsworth stabbed the blade of his spade into the soil and left it standing. He walked to the picket fence, reached across, and shook Tom's hand, the enthusiasm of the greeting rattling all the way to Tom's shoulder.

"How's your mother? I trust she is well."

"She's doin' fine. Bishop Aaron Mendenhall up in Springville took her to wife. He—I guess I should say his other wives—there's two of 'em—work her pretty hard. But she's took care of, far as it goes."

As they talked, Henry's wife had come out the front gate to stand by Polly, the two of them engaged in quiet conversation.

Henry said, "Well, I am glad to hear it. Now, what brings you away down here to our country? And who's this pretty young thing with you?"

Tom bowed his head and pondered how to reply. Then, "Henry—Mister Farnsworth—that there is Polly Alden. She ain't said so yet, but I intend to marry her as soon as she'll have me."

Henry smiled. "You have chosen well, young man. And?"

"And?"

"You never said what brings you to Parowan."

Tom swallowed hard. "Truth is, Mister Farnsworth, I had a fallin' out with Bishop Mendenhall. Me and Polly, we're travelin' with this emigrant train. Bound for California to try our luck there."

Henry smiled and asked his wife if she could make a pot of tea, then invited Tom and Polly inside. Tom avoided adding any detail to his story, instead peppering his host with questions about crops and cattle and other small talk about life in the far reaches of the territory.

"Oh, it's a good enough life, I suppose. We try to keep up the faith, but it's tested at times. It don't rain enough around here to wet the sole of a pissant's shoe, and then when it does rain, it's likely to be a duck drownin' storm like we just had, doin' as much harm as good."

Once wound up, Henry could not stop talking. He carried on about the fear permeating the town. "I swear, it's got most of my neighbors chasin' their own tails. Listenin' to old George A. Smith carry on lately stirred 'em up plenty, and there's been reports—rumors, I call 'em—of soldiers comin' right in here from over east, and soldiers comin' in from California, so as to steal a march on Salt Lake. And folks up and down the line carry on about emigrant trains—the one you're with, I reckon, bein' one of 'em—stirrin' up trouble and makin' threats and what all. Can't talk sense to some of these people—they're as stirred up as outhouse flies. Bill Dame, he's the head of all the militias down here, he's had us marchin' and drillin' to where my feet's wore off and I'm walkin' on my ankles. Not only that, he's been sendin' his toy soldiers up the canyons and out into the hills lookin' for places for the women and kids and old folks to hide out when the army comes. Down to Cedar City, they're even worse. Isaac Haight runs everything down there—he's the stake president and mayor and runs the Iron Works and is commander of the local militia—thinks he's king, he does—he's so het up he'd send his militia boys out to fight the American army tomorrow if only Dame would let him—and if only there was an American army within a thousand miles of here to fight." He paused to take a breath and shake his head. "Nuttier'n squirrel shit, the whole lot of 'em. You folks in that wagon train had best watch your backs, I'd say."

Back outside, the Farnsworths showed off their kitchen garden. Polly admired a row of onions. "Oh, I do wish for onions," she said. "Anything to spice up what I feed the boys. They are not shedding any pounds with what I feed them, but the fare is bland most of the time. I fear."

"Don't say another word," Henry said. "You're welcome to all the onions you want." He retrieved his shovel and proceeded to unearth onion bulbs. When Polly called it enough, he did not stop. He pulled up radishes, plucked cabbages and collard greens, picked squash and melons, stuffing all into a gunnysack as he went.

Just as the harvest wrapped up, a neighbor stormed across the street, shouting. "Farnsworth! What are you doing?"

"Settle down, Abijah."

"I'll not settle down! What is the meaning of this?"

Henry smiled. "Just doing my Christian duty, neighbor."

"But you have been counseled otherwise! We have been told in no uncertain terms not to provide for the outsiders!"

"Surely you don't mean that, Brother Abijah. Besides, this young man is no outsider. He's been a Mormon boy most all his life, if not the whole of it. I crossed the plains with his family when we come out from Kanesville. He is Thomas Langford, lately of Springville and the household of Bishop Mendenhall there."

Abijah snorted. "That matters not a whit! He is traveling with the Gentiles, and your aid to this boy aids those godless emigrants as well! You have been told to leave them alone by your priesthood leaders from the bishop all the way up to an apostle of the Lord!"

Henry watched his neighbor stew for a moment. The man's forehead wrinkled as deep as the furrows in the garden, and radishes paled in comparison to the flush on his face. He smiled and placed a hand on Abijah's shoulder. "But surely there is a higher authority, brother."

The man bristled. "Oh? And what might that be?"

" 'But whoso hath this world's good, and seeth his brother have need, and shutteth up his bowels of compassion from him, how dwelleth the love of God in him?' First John, chapter three, verse seventeen."

Abijah rumbled with a growl or bitten-off roar and pulled and pried and tore a picket from the fence. With a grunt and a snarl, he swung the picket, the swing ending when the wood splintered against the side of Henry's head. Henry fell to the ground. With a final snort, Abijah tossed the fence picket aside, turned on his heel, and stomped back across the street into his own yard and house, slamming the door behind him.

By that time, Henry was sitting up, somewhat goggle-eyed, blood dribbling down into his shirt collar. Tom knelt beside him, attempting with little success to stanch the flow. His wife had run into the house and soon returned with a bowl of water and a handful of rags. She handed it off to Polly, telling her to clean the wound, and returned to the house.

Polly mopped up the blood, drizzled water over the gash, and pressed a clean rag against the wound. Then came Henry's wife, tearing a strip from the edge of a bedsheet as she came. She left the soaked rag in place and wrapped the makeshift bandage around and around her husband's head, the earliest layers showing pink above the wound as fast as she could wind them.

Tom helped Henry into the house, lowering him onto a kitchen chair. "I'm awful sorry, ma'am. We didn't mean no harm to come to no one."

"It's all right, son. My Henry, he's good-hearted and wouldn't have it any other way. It is not the first time he has tangled with that wild-eyed Abijah. Were it not unseemly in the eyes of the Lord to do so, I'd call him a crazy sonofabitch. Of course, with me being a lady and a churchgoer, I'll be damned if I'll use such language for fear I would burn in hell."

"Now, dear—you know Abijah can't help himself," Henry said, his voice shaky and soft.

"Just the same, I won't have you nail that picket back onto the fence. I aim to keep it handy for the next time that man steps into our dooryard."

Henry took a deep breath. "Tom, you and Polly had best gather up that gunnysack full of vegetables and go. Once Abijah calms down some—which won't be much, as the man don't know no more about how to relax than does a honeybee—he'll head on over to the bishop's house to report me. If you and the evidence are gone, he'll have a hell of a time proving any of it." He managed a weak smile. "Me, I'll be too addled in my head to offer any recollection or opinion of the matter."

Back at camp, Polly divided the produce with the other Baker wagons, then shared what was left among the other emigrants. She fended off questions about how they obtained the food, some of the travelers finding it suspicious that the Mormons would share with Tom but not them—further proof, they contended, that Tom was in league with the Saints and somehow plotting against them. Polly cast such claims aside, but her concern lingered—not about Tom, but about the disquiet of others concerning him. Long into the night, she burned a candle to a stub putting pencil to paper.

Tom, oh Tom, why did I fall in love with you, Tom? You are as fine a man as ever there was, of this I am convinced and I ~~feel~~ know my love for you is true. Why cannot Capt Baker give leave for me to marry you? I know he could not prevent our union but still I do not want to act against his wishes. I do not believe he opposes our marriage but fears the upset it may cause in the company as many paint my Tom with the same brush as the Mormons they despise so. Tom has said he could find someone with authority to perform a wedding in these towns or the one that lies ahead but to do so we may have to ~~disguise~~ lie about our circumstances as it is unlikely the Mormons would allow one of their own to wed a gentile, as they call those not of their faith.

But we will not have to struggle with it much longer as Capt Baker tells me the Mormons will be behind us in a week or so save what few we may encounter traveling on this road to or from California. Those in the towns are more and more unkind to us and my fears grow that they or some of the men in our company will become violent. It will be a relief when it ends. How any of them can lay claim to being Christians yet be so hateful escapes me. I know there is good both in our company and among the Mormons but it sometimes seems the bad outweighs the good.

Tomorrow morning we move on from this place and two days hence will be in Cedar City where we shall once again attempt to obtain provisions for the many remaining miles to California. I sometimes wonder if we shall ever get there. I am weary to the bone of traveling and look forward to reaching the place where Capt Baker says we will rest ourselves and the stock. That place he calls Mountain Meadows.

Chapter Twenty-Eight

The whiskey was harsh and seared the throat, but still they imbibed. The liquor—sagebrush whiskey, it was called—came from a dilapidated distillery on the edge of Cedar City. This was the last community of any account the emigrants would pass until reaching the Mormon outpost of Las Vegas on the Mojave Desert, some two hundred miles down the road. Bad as it was, the whiskey did its job. And in light of the fact that there would be no alcohol in any quantity for weeks to come, the men quaffed in quantity.

Howard and Skeets were among the imbibers, their horses tied to the wheels of the wagons that brought the others to this place. The place was a gristmill, across the street from the whiskey mill, owned by a man named Philip Klingensmith, the Mormon bishop in Cedar City. Had the man been present, it is unlikely the mill would be at work grinding down wheat for the emigrants. The wheat itself was theirs by happenstance. A lapsed Mormon who farmed a few miles south of the town at a place called Fort Harmony knew of the approach and plight of the Arkansawyers and, with Klingensmith away, saw in it an opportunity to shift some stored wheat at a price more attractive than any he could hope to obtain elsewhere.

As a result of the man's avarice, the wagon train led by Baker and Fancher came into possession of fifty bushels of much-needed wheat, at the expense of a trove of gold coins from the rumored riches of the travelers. Soon, the grain would all be milled into flour courtesy of Klingensmith's millstones turned by the currents of Coal Creek.

"C'mon, Howard, let's get the hell out of here. Let's go see what there is on offer in this one-horse town."

"I'm with you, Skeets." Howard untied his horse and, after three tries, managed to find a stirrup with his foot. Once mounted, the boys headed for the main part of town, the horses steadier than the riders.

"This place ain't much like these other Mormon towns," Skeets said as they rode past ramshackle houses with farm implements squatting in the yards beside broken-down wagons and discarded parts, refuse piles outside back doors buzzing with flies, odoriferous outhouses, and pens and corrals tumbled down to the point that holding animals was only a matter of faith. Even the iron works that gave the town its origin were rusty and run-down and did not look up to the job.

"What do you mean?" Howard said through the haze fogging his brain.

"Well, seems like most of the towns out here has been poor, but leastways the folks was tidy. These here people don't seem to care much for show. Kind of like the white trash back home."

Howard yawned. "I guess so."

Barking dogs darted out of yards as they rode by, milk cows and horses staked out to graze the ditch banks raised their heads to watch them pass, and uninterested pigs rooted through trash heaps. Out front of one house, chickens scratched in the dirt as a woman wearing a patched and tattered homespun dress sat on a split saw log that served as the step up into her house.

Howard reined up, watching the chickens and studying the woman shooing away flies as she sat. "I sure would fancy me some fried chicken."

The woman looked his way, waving at the flies, but said nothing.

"How much for one of these chickens?"

"Ain't for sale," the woman said. "These here is settin' hens. They's for layin' eggs and hatchin' chicks as needed. They ain't for eatin' till they're old and wore out and find themselves in the stewpot."

"But I'm hungry now," Howard said.

"Don't care. You ain't eatin' none of my hens."

Howard pointed with his chin toward a young rooster with patches of bare skin showing and skimpy tail feathers. "How 'bout that rooster there?"

"Nah. Gotta have roosters if'n we want any baby chicks."

"C'mon, Howard. Let's go."

"You just sit still, Skeets. I'm dickerin' on a dinner for us." He turned to the woman. "Lady, I want me one of them chickens. And I mean to have one."

"Well, you ain't gettin' one. Kick that horse of yours in the belly and ride on."

"Like hell I will." Howard lifted his bullwhip from where it hung on his saddle and let the thong, fall, and cracker drop to the ground. He set his eyes on a fat speckled hen, then drew back and popped its head nearly off with a single stroke.

The woman rose to her feet with a yell, but in an instant Howard's whip lashed out again and decapitated a red hen. The woman hollered and cursed as Howard coiled and hung his whip, dismounted, and gathered the dead chickens, still flopping around in the dust, their bodies as yet unaware of their fate. With the four legs of the two hens in hand, he swung back into the saddle. The woman, shaking a fist and cursing, walked toward Howard and he dropped the reins and pulled his pistol, waving it in her face and answering her curses with some of his own, questioning the woman's parentage, her appearance, her virtue, and spouting all manner of insults.

"Lady, I offered to buy from you. I'd've been content with one chicken, but I've taken two. You missed your chance for pay. Now you just sit back down and shut up your squawkin' or I'll blow your damn head off. Hell, you sound as bad as one of them damn chickens screechin' like that. Hush up." He rode off, the hens dangling from his hand.

Skeets trotted up beside Howard. "Hell, Howard, how'd you do that, drunk as you are? How'd you handle that whip so?"

"Damned if I know," Howard said with a crooked grin. "I just hope Polly will fry these up for supper."

"That woman back there ain't goin' to be happy about what you done."

"Ah, to hell with her. Ain't nobody goin' to do anything about it."

The boys had yet to reach the wagon camp when the woman pounded on Isaac Haight's door to complain. It was not the first complaint he had heard since the arrival of the emigrants. Most were trivial, no worse than what occurred with the passage of any emigrant train. But conditions being what they were, he added the affray between Mormon laying hens and an emigrant bullwhip to the growing list of grievances—some real, others imagined—against the Arkansawyers. And to think they had been here less than half the day.

Summoning police chief John Higbee, Haight provided a description of the men and their mounts and sent him out to arrest the miscreants. Higbee found the boys, still in their cups, sitting by the wagons and attempting to pluck the chickens. A group of men stood by, listening to Howard's story and laughing at his escapades.

Higbee stepped up. "Boys, where did you get those chickens?"

Howard said he did not see that it was any of the man's business.

Pulling the lapel of his jacket aside, Higbee revealed the badge pinned to his vest. "This here badge makes it my business. I've had reports that those chickens are stolen. Theft is against the law in this city. I'm also told you insulted the owner of those chickens in a most vile and repulsive manner. Such is not allowed here, and you will be called to account. I am placing you under arrest."

Dropping the half-denuded hen to the ground, Howard rose to his feet, pulling his pistol as he rose. "No you ain't, mister. You won't be arrestin' me today."

Staring down the bore of the pistol aimed at him, Higbee swept the tail of his jacket back and placed a hand atop the pistol tucked in his waistband. The move was answered by the slide and snick of steel against steel as some of the emigrant men cocked hammers on firearms. Higbee swallowed hard, let his hand drop, and took a step backward.

"You go on now, get out of here," Howard said. "I offered to pay the woman for a chicken but she wasn't havin' it. Name a price and I'll pay you for the scrawny damn things if it'll make you happy. But I ain't goin' to jail. All you-all Mormons'd string me up for nothin' more'n chicken stealin', and I won't have it. Now, get on out of here!"

Higbee backed away, flushed and flustered. Back in town, he reported to Haight and they argued about assembling a posse and effecting the arrest. Higbee allowed it would only lead to violence, and he did not intend to die for the theft of two laying hens.

Haight stewed for a time. "Well, by damn, if the police can't do the job we'll call up the militia."

Higbee, an officer in the militia but subordinate to Haight, pointed out that such could not be done without authorization from Bill Dame in Parowan, commander over them both and all the militias in the region.

Haight summoned one of Higbee's policemen and sent the man with a hastily scrawled note up the road to Parowan for delivery to Bill Dame. "See he gets this, and don't come back here without a reply. And don't let him waffle and go all wishy-washy like he usually does. And hurry, for God's sake, or it will be too late."

The correspondence, seeking permission to activate the local militia, claimed the difficulties with the emigrants were more than the town's police force could cope with. Along with reporting the failed arrest, Haight passed on an account that one of the travelers threatened violence when refused service at a store. Another complainant said an emigrant called one of his oxen "Brigham" in a sign of disrespect for the Mormon president. A woman told Haight a drover claimed his father shot Joseph Smith back in Illinois, and that he had the pistol that did the deed. Haight passed along other such protests about the emigrants neither knowing nor caring if they were true, and knowing that similar if not identical complaints were lodged against every emigrant train that passed through his city.

In a postscript he added that there were rumors the Arkansawyers intended to lay over at Mountain Meadows and there await the arrival of troops from California, then return with the soldiers to wipe out the Saints in Cedar City and every settlement up the line.

The messenger spent hours into the night on the porch of Dame's house, listening to the debate and arguments of a group of men assembled to assess the threat and determine how to respond. By the time the courier carried the reply back to Haight, the emigrants were long gone, having pulled out late yesterday on their way to the Meadows.

Haight tore open the missive and read, his face flushing as he mouthed the words on the page. He cursed, wadded the paper, and flung it toward the cold stove in the corner.

"What did he say?"

"Not a damn thing, in the end," Haight said. "Same old nonsense about keeping the peace and letting them go their way, just like he always says. He says, 'words are but wind' or some such bullshit about their threats being meaningless."

The messenger, standing hat in hand, allowed that at least the emigrants were gone.

"Gone, are they? Gone where? And for how long? We ain't got no idea of their intentions! So we're just to sit here and let them go on their merry way with all them cattle and all that gold, and us not knowin' if we've seen the last of them. I swear, how anyone expects Dame to run the militia is beyond me. Man ain't got the guts to act, no matter what!" Haight muttered and murmured and finally slapped the desktop with both hands. "Damn! I'm probably going to have to go up there myself and try to talk sense into the man!"

Haight stewed for a moment, then slapped the desk again. "No, by God! I'll deal with this without Dame and without the militia! Get me John Lee!"

John Lee, longtime and faithful Mormon and close associate of Brigham Young, lived at Fort Harmony. Indian agent for the area, he dealt with the various Paiute bands around about, attempting to turn them into farmers—farming being an occupation and enterprise at which he himself was a success. But the Paiutes were less than fascinated with white man agriculture and preferred the ways of life their people had followed time out of mind.

At the end of the day, Lee rode in from Fort Harmony and found Haight in the town square. "I'm told you wanted to see me, Isaac."

The familiarity annoyed Haight. He would have preferred "President Haight" or "Major Haight" in respect of his offices, or even the informal Mormon address as "Brother Haight." But he and Lee had clashed over the years and had their differences, so he overlooked the indignity from his sometimes-rival.

"Yes, Brother Lee. There are troubles afoot. I would appreciate your coming with me, away to somewhere quiet where we can talk."

Haight was building a new brick house and led Lee inside the walls of the yet unroofed structure. The men found seats on sawhorses and crates but, as night fell and their talk continued, stretched out on the raw floors where they eventually slept. Lee had already heard of the difficulties with the emigrants, and as Haight amplified the details, the firebrand's anger intensified.

"I've met with men in the city and we are in agreement that the emigrants cannot go unpunished—not only for their deeds traveling through the territory, but for the threat they pose if they meet the army, or even get to California and guide soldiers back here."

"I believe you're right, Isaac. And knowing you, I expect you've already laid plans."

"Yes, Brother Lee, and that's where we need your help. We figure to stir up the Paiutes, give them arms and ammunition, and turn them loose on the wagon train."

"You think the Indians will do that? They'll rob and steal, but they ain't generally inclined to fight that way."

"Those emigrants are trailing a big herd of cattle—several hundred, maybe a thousand head. We'll tell the Paiutes the cattle are theirs if they'll fight for them."

Lee mulled it over. "It might work. But you know, don't you, that if the Indians get the upper hand, there'll be a lot of killing—and it won't stop with the fighting men. Could be they'll lay waste to the whole lot of them."

Lee could not see it in the dark, but Haight only shrugged at the suggestion.

"How do you see it happening?"

Haight passed along the talk from his earlier meeting. Most had agreed it best for the Paiutes to attack the train on the move, as a pitched battle against encamped and somewhat fortified emigrants would narrow the odds. "Out past the Meadows, down in the narrows where Magotsu Creek meets the Santa Clara, looks to be the best place for a fight. You know the place. The wagons will be spread out on the road and vulnerable to attack."

Lee agreed. "So what do you want me to do?"

Haight said they had already sent men ahead to gather the bands and parley with the Paiutes, but Lee's familiarity and leadership among them would likely be required to organize the details, perhaps even persuade the Indians the risk was worthwhile. Other riders would overtake the emigrant train and urge them not to linger at Mountain Meadows, as the people of Cedar City were stirred up and that it was all the local leaders could do to restrain them from seeking revenge for the emigrants' misdeeds.

"Brother Lee, our success will depend in large part on your ability to convince the Paiutes to act. If the lure of cattle is not enough, find some, any, other reason for them to want to take revenge on the emigrants—hell, make something up if you have to. Invent some atrocity that they cannot overlook.

"And remember this, John. Even if we let the Paiutes have the emigrant cattle, there's a lot of plunder in those wagons the Saints here could use. And, word is, they're carrying a wealth of gold."

When dawn broke, Lee was already up and about the town, assembling supplies for his foray into the mountains. By sunrise, he was on the road toward Mountain Meadows.

Chapter Twenty-Nine

Tom and Polly pulled the last of the camp equipment and kitchen boxes out of the bed of the wagon. Buckets in hand, Tom walked to the spring for water. With plenty of time left in the day to prepare supper, Polly took a seat on a smooth rock in the shade of a cedar tree, opened her diary, and put her pencil to work.

We have arrived at the place called Mountain Meadows and with how much mention it has gotten from Capt Baker and Col Fancher in the days leading up to it I confess I expected more. It is no more than a narrow valley among the low mountains and looks no different than hundreds of other such places we have passed. There is I suppose more grass and less of the ever present sage brush on the floor, and that will be good for feeding the oxen and the cow herd.

While I have grown by necessity somewhat used to the mountains and having them ever on the horizon no longer troubles me, I am still uneasy being in among them as we are now and have been since leaving the Cedar City valley. There is nothing to be done for it and despite my hopes to the contrary Capt Baker tells me California is a mountainy country as well.

My Tom assures me we are in no danger from the Mormons in Cedar City despite our troubles there. As has so often been the case Howard was the cause of much of it, but the Mormons there were more hostile than any others we have encountered. Capt Baker says we will stay in this place for a few days rest despite the warning from some Mormon horsemen to move on.

Tom continues to be ever attentive and kind but I sense disappointment that we did not seal our union in one of the towns. Capt Baker says once we reach Calif he will arrange a wedding but the wait ~~disturbs~~weighs on Tom and I confess impatience of my own to begin acting as husbands and wives do. Sarah says we should not wait to share our affections and sometimes when in Tom's embrace I feel the same, but Tom resists the temptation. How long he will hold to his belief that only man and wife should indulge their passions in that way I cannot say.

He is a gentle soul and misses his mother, but is putting that life behind him in favor of a life with me. Many in our company are yet distrustful of my Tom and resent his presence among us. He takes it in stride for the most part and avoids those people but he is ever more troubled at our own fire by Howard goading him and only the intervention of Abe and Billy Brown have prevented their fighting.

The afternoon is fading and I must see about supper. With the cow herd on pasture the drovers will have little to do in the daytime and so they will hang around camp and are always hungry, but I think the hunger at such times results more from boredom than lack of food, which they continue to devour by the bushel it seems.

The deadfall limbs cracked and snapped as Tom broke them apart, prying upward against a foot pinning the branch to the ground. Despite the continued use of the Meadows as a campsite for many years, dry firewood was still available if one scoured the ravine cut by Magotsu Creek down the center of the narrow valley. An ax leaned against a wagon wheel to break apart heftier pieces of wood and to split kindling.

"Get a move on it with that firewood, chore girl," Howard said, his insult punctuated as usual with a discharge of tobacco spit.

"Hush up, Howard, or you'll spend supper time out guarding the herd."

"To hell with you, Abe Baker. I already had my turn and I'll be damned if I'll take another."

"You'll ride when I say so."

"Yup. And it could be I'll just keep on ridin' right on out of here."

Abe laughed. "Where you goin' to go, Howard? Back to Cedar City? I'll bet them Mormons back there would be glad to see you."

"Just don't you worry about it. And you don't need to worry about the chore girl there, neither. He don't mind my ribbin' him. Do you, chore girl?"

Tom snapped off another length of firewood and stood upright. "Truth be told, Howard, I don't mind a thing you say. No more than I pay attention to the squawking of these magpies around here, or the yappin' of a coyote at night. It's all just noise and there ain't none of it means a thing."

Howard smiled and spat. "See what I mean, Abe? He don't mind."

Billy Brown said, "It's a good thing, Howard. 'Cause if that boy ever starts to pay attention to your blather he's likely to kick your ass."

Howard laughed. "Oh, that scares me. Puts the fear of God in me for certain. Why, even if I was as black as young Trajan there, the fear would turn me as pale as Billy Red's bare backside."

Every eye in the camp locked on Howard.

With a sloppy grin, he looked from one face to another. "What? What's the matter with you-all?"

Polly sighed. "Howard, why don't you try to be nice for a change? There is no need for you to insult everyone and be so mean spirited all the time."

"Mean? Hell's sake! You-all ain't seen mean from me yet! I'm just funnin' and you-all know it." He stood, spat again, wiped the dribble from his chin with a shirtsleeve, then dusted off the seat of his pants with his hands. "Ain't a one of you-all got any sense of humor a-tall. I'm goin' to find Skeets. That boy knows how to have a good laugh." He started away, stopped, turned back and said, "To hell with you-all," and was gone.

Howard wandered among the wagons, somewhat spread and scattered across the meadow. The emigrants, weary from the hurried exit from Cedar and long days to reach the place, had not formed into the tight circle usually employed for security, but parked and made camp in a haphazard fashion. He found Skeets stretched out flat on his back under a cedar tree, an exposed root serving as a pillow, with his hat over his face. Howard kicked his friend on the sole of one of his boots.

"Skeets! What're you doin' down there?"

Skeets lifted the hat and squinted at Howard. He hoisted himself to sit and chafed his cheeks with the palms of his hands. He yawned. "Well, Howard, I wasn't doin' a damn thing 'cept inspectin' the crown of my hat for leaks. I wouldn't want to get my head wet should it cloud up and rain." He yawned again.

Howard lowered himself to sit cross legged. "I'm half tempted to soak my head in the stream yonder. Feels like that herd of longhorn cattle we been tendin' is stampedin' around in there."

Skeets laughed. "Well, hell, Howard—what do you expect?

You swallowed enough of that rotgut whiskey in that town and what you brung with you since to float one of these wagons. You ought to've slacked off some, seein' as how you ain't never learned to hold your liquor."

"You're a fine one to talk. You can't tell me your head ain't poundin' like a blacksmith hammer on a anvil."

Skeets yawned and stretched. "I was just wonderin', Howard—whatever become of them chickens we was pluckin'? I don't recall ever eatin' any fried chicken."

Howard scooped up a handful of soil and shook his hand back and forth, winnowing out the sand and dirt, leaving his palm full of pebbles. One by one, he picked them out and tossed them at his friend.

"Quit that, damn you," Skeets said, dipping, ducking, and dodging the assault. "What about them chickens?"

"I can't rightly say," Howard said, spilling the last of the pebbles to the ground. "I guess after that lawman tried to take me in and ever'one was in such an all-fired hurry to get out of town we must've just left 'em layin' there half plucked. I sure didn't get none of 'em to eat. Likely some of them cur dogs in that town or maybe a rootin' hog got them."

Skeets laughed. "Like I said, Howard, you got to learn to hold your liquor. Then you won't be so forgetful." He yawned again, then stood. "C'mon. Let's go see what there is to see. Won't be long now till supper and I don't want to miss it. My belly wasn't in no mood to eat earlier and now I'm gaunted up so bad I can't hardly keep my pants up."

The boys came upon a crowd of men around an ox stretched out on the ground. There was no ox sling at Mountain Meadows, but that lack did not prevent the need to replace worn or lost shoes. The men knew the use of ropes and hitches and leverage and balance, and could lay an ox down and restrain it while a cloven hoof was re-shaped and fresh shoes tacked on.

Alexander Fancher supervised the shoeing of another ox, this one needing only work on one hind leg. The animal was tied close to a wagon, and two men held either end of a pole threaded under the hock, lifting the leg high enough for the man with knife and rasp and hammer to do his work.

Fancher saw the boys watching and called them over. "Boys, we're changing up guarding the herd tonight—and likely for as long as we're laid over here. We'll run but two shifts so as to have as many herders out with the cows as we can."

Skeets snorted. "Aw, hell, Colonel! I thought we was here to rest! And I don't mean just the stock!"

"From the look of you, you've been gettin' some rest already. Them twigs and trash and dust all up the back of your pants and shirt didn't get there in no windstorm. Besides, the new shifts won't bother you any—leastways not tonight. We lost a bull and maybe six or seven head of cows and a few calves back where we camped last night. They either hid out, or maybe the Indians got them. Skeets, I want you to gather up Charlie and the two of you-all to go back and find them."

"Aw, hell, Colonel. It ain't but a few head. And if there's Indians out there I sure as hell don't want to be tanglin' with 'em. I say leave them missin' cows be."

Fancher sighed and shook his head. "Skeets, you ain't got a say in the matter. Just do your job and don't be bawlin' like a calf that's lost its mother."

Skeets tromped away muttering, but said no more that Fancher could hear. He turned to Howard. "Captain Baker will be expectin' the same of his drovers come time to ride night guard, Howard. You had best go look him up, or maybe find Abe."

The thought of a long night in the saddle brought a frown to Howard's face. "I don't get it. What for are we all goin' to be ridin' guard?"

Fancher inspected the farrier's work and told the men to turn the tethered ox loose. The other animal was still down, a man with a hammer tapping nails into a shoe on a forefoot. The colonel dusted off his hands as if he had been handling the cattle, then answered Howard. "Likely there's wolves and maybe bears around. But mostly, this here is Indian country. Could be they drove off them missin' cows I sent Skeets to hunt for.

"If there are Indians about, you-all most likely won't even see 'em. But Paiutes and other Indian bands wander all over this country, all the way across the desert to California. They're wily, and can crawl right under your horse's belly while you're sittin' in the saddle without you even knowin' it. They'll steal a few cows here, sneak off with a couple there, drive off another bunch or two tomorrow night, and some more will go missin' the next night, and before you know it they've made off with the whole damn herd.

"So you-all had best be keepin' your eyes open and not dozin' off in the saddle. Any sound is likely to be Indians sendin' signals, and they'll make a noise to draw your attention to one place while they take cattle from somewheres else. All you-all drovers will have your work cut out for you, and damn well be ready to do your jobs. Now, go on and get your supper so you'll be ready to ride when the captain sends you to work."

Howard shuffled off toward Polly's wagon where he found supper in the works. He smelled bacon, and caught a whiff of baking biscuits when Polly lifted the lid from a cast iron oven. "Step up, boys," Polly said.

Abe, Billy Brown, Billy Red, and Trajan lined up, plates in hand, for Polly to fill them with fried bacon, boiled potatoes, beans, and biscuits. Tom stood by with pot in hand, ready to fill coffee cups. Howard fetched a plate and fork from a kitchen box and elbowed his way into the line ahead of Trajan. When he reached Polly, she withheld serving his outstretched plate.

"I believe it is Trajan's turn."

"The hell it is," Howard said. "Give me my supper!"

Polly leaned over to see past Howard. "Step up, Trajan."

Trajan bowed his head and spoke softly. "It's all right, Miss Polly. I ain't in no hurry. Go on ahead and serve Howard."

"I will not. Rude behavior and ill manners will not be rewarded in my kitchen. They never have been, nor will they be now."

Howard shifted to block Polly's view of Trajan. "Damn it, woman! You had bett—"

Before he finished the word, Tom had him by the shirtfront and shoved him aside. Howard, unsteady, swung the empty plate at Tom's head, but Tom dodged the blow. He kept his grip on Howard's shirt and shoved again, hard enough this time that Howard sat down on the ground.

"Damn you!" Howard said from where he sat. "Damn your Mormon hide!" Howard scrambled to his feet, dropping the plate and fork and clenching his fists.

He faced a rank of eight doubled fists, Abe and both Billys having set their suppers aside to stand beside Tom.

Abe said, "You've got two choices here, Howard. You can pick up that plate and get behind Trajan and get your supper, or you can get the hell out of here and go hungry. Now, what's it going to be?"

Howard bristled and raised his fists, his eyes boring into Tom.

"I guess there's another choice come to think of it, Howard—you can keep coming and we will beat you back as often as you like," Abe said.

Howard snorted, turned aside, and spat. Having already shed his customary cud in anticipation of supper, the weak speck of spittle did not have the desired effect. He sniffed and dropped his fists. "You sonsabitches." He picked up his plate and took his place behind Trajan, the heat seething off him as intense as that from the fire.

As the drovers ate, Abe explained the situation with night guard. "Brown, you and Howard and Trajan will take the first shift."

"Why me?" Howard said. "I had last shift this mornin' so I ain't been to bed since."

Abe laughed. "Howard, I was out there with you and I know you slept most of the night. Had to wake you up to come in for breakfast, for a fact. You likely don't remember on account of you being so drunk you couldn't have hit the ground with your hat if given three tries."

The insult prompted a laugh from everyone, further upsetting Howard.

"Well, that ain't neither here nor there. It ain't fair me bein' out there ridin' half the night while chore girl here is cuddled up in his blankets all night long."

"Don't you worry none about Tom," Abe said. "He'll be taking the second shift with me and Billy Red."

"Finally! It's about time he earned his keep." Howard turned to Polly. "Since your lover boy'll be replacin' me at the herd, how about I replace him in your bed?" Howard laughed and turned to see Tom's reaction, just in time to see the boy's boot coming at him. The instant widening of his eyes was the only reaction he had time for, as the toe of the boot landed just under the point of his chin, knocking him over backward. His plate spilled, but he still held the fork in his hand, its tines piercing a chunk of boiled potato. He did not move.

Abe chewed a mouthful of bacon, contemplating the scene. After a moment he swallowed. "Well, Tom, it looks like you'll be swapping shifts with Howard. I doubt he'll be awake in time to take the first shift."

The other boys tried not to laugh.

Tom helped Polly clean up while someone somewhere among the wagons plucked and strummed a slow tune on a banjo. As the sky darkened, he and Polly talked until Trajan rode up leading a saddled horse.

"Here you go, Tom. Abe says you're to ride this horse. He's a good'un. I've rid him on night guard m'self and he'll do you fine."

"Thanks, Trajan," Tom said, standing and taking the reins.

Polly stood and threw her arms around Tom's neck, kissing him hard on the mouth. She drew back and whispered to his surprised face. "Oh, Tom! My Tom! Do be careful—I could not stand being without you should something bad happen."

Tom swallowed hard, searching for his voice. "Don't worry, Polly. There ain't nothin' out here that's goin' to hurt us."

CHAPTER THIRTY

John Lee had Indian trouble. No one of the Paiute bands he had tracked down showed much interest, if any, in attacking the Arkansas emigrants. He mentioned the abuse wagon trains had heaped on them over the years—destroying their gardens, killing off wildlife they relied on for food, fouling streams and springs, abusing their women, taking revenge on them for depredations committed by others, and sometimes shooting their people for little more than sport. And he suggested the emigrants were in league with the American army, which was coming to destroy the Mormons and, along with them, their Indian friends. Fight now, Lee advised, or die tomorrow at the hands of the Americans.

Still, most hesitated. The temptation of ownership of the cattle herd and plunder from the wagons was insufficient to sway them. They claimed to lack firepower against the well-armed emigrants, and doubted Indian agent Lee's promise that their Mormon friends would provide guns and ammunitions. Despite his best efforts, Lee and his subordinates convinced only a few dozen Paiutes to gather near a Mormon village called Pinto near the Meadows to prepare an attack on the emigrants.

While Lee and his men attempted to stir up the Paiutes, Haight stirred the pot in Cedar City until it boiled over and spilled out onto the region. Word went out to out-of-the-way Mormon settlements—Fort Harmony, Enoch, Fort Santa Clara, Washington, Johnson Fort, Pinto—for assistance. With every telling, the evils perpetrated by the emigrants intensified, and the need to act against them escalated. Some members of the militia in those towns, as well as in Cedar City, gathered their arms and marched for Pinto to join Lee and the Paiutes assembling there to await further orders.

In a Sunday sermon, Haight memorialized persecution of the Saints in New York, in Ohio, in Missouri, in Illinois. "We went into the far wilderness where we could worship God according to the dictates of our own conscience without annoyance to our neighbors. We resolved that if they would leave us alone we would not trouble them." His preaching turned to thunder and lightning. "Have the Gentiles let us be? No! They have sent an army to again drive us from our homes or exterminate us! I have been driven from my home for the last time! God being my helper I will give the last ounce of my strength and if need be my last drop of blood in defense of Zion!" All the sins against the Saints and the danger of the American army were focused on the Arkansas emigrants, raising anger and ire and turning it toward action.

Following the public meeting, Haight gathered leading men from Cedar City and surrounding communities into council. A blacksmith from Johnson Fort was late to the meeting. Sensing the fury in the room, he asked what was up. He was told the question under consideration was how best to destroy the emigrants in order to preserve the lives of the Saints. The settlers, he was told, were not only under threat from the approaching army, but some said the Arkansawyers had threatened to remain in the area and help the soldiers "destroy every damn Mormon." That could not be allowed to happen. Instead, some said, the wagon train must be destroyed, and if the Paiutes could not be counted on to do it, the task should fall to the militia.

The blacksmith paled. "Do not our principles of right teach

us to return good for evil and do good to those who despitefully use us? To fall upon them and destroy them is the work of savage monsters, not civilized men! The evils you lay at the feet of the emigrants—even if true—do not merit killing. How can we justify shedding innocent blood?"

Haight rose to his feet. "Damn it! There will not be one drop of *innocent* blood shed if every one of the damned pack are killed, for they are the worst lot of outlaws and ruffians that I ever saw in my life!"

Some in the meeting wondered if the wagon train Haight accused was the same one they had witnessed passing through just days ago. But few expressed their doubts in deference to Haight's positions of leadership.

"What does Colonel Dame have to say about it?" came a question from the back of the room.

Haight's wandering answer only occasionally crossed the line of truth. No two men in the room understood it the same way, but most believed Dame must have given his blessing to punish the emigrants. Dame, in fact, had ordered otherwise. Despite all of Haight's arguments, and despite any sense of unified opposition, the council could not reach consensus.

The blacksmith rose to his feet. "Here is what we must do. Dispatch an express rider for Salt Lake City. Seek counsel from President Young. His word will be the final one on the matter." As he sat down, the blacksmith saw two men—some of Haight's supporters—slip out of the room. He wondered at their intentions and determined to take a back road home to Johnson Fort out of fear of being waylaid in the dark.

The men sitting in council saw the blacksmith's suggestion as a way to delay action, if not avoid it altogether. For some, it was a way out—a way to shift blame for whatever happened onto other shoulders. Haight had hemmed and hawed, but finally agreed to seek the advice of Brigham Young. But he would not act until the next day, and then not until further prodding to follow the direction of the council. It would take nearly a week of hard riding to get to the city and back. He watched the rider gallop out of town on the road to the north, knowing the matter would be settled before he ever returned—and, perhaps, before he even reached Salt Lake City.

Haight had dispatched other riders to Pinto the night before to report the outcome of the meeting—or lack of it—to John Lee and his ragtag assembly of militia members and Paiutes. Whether ordered by Haight to act or to hold fire, Lee did not say.

Taking with him a few scouts, he rode to a hilltop overlooking Mountain Meadows to surveil the emigrant camp. By the light of a moon nearly full and from the glow of campfires, he saw the wagons parked haphazardly, rather than joined in a tight defensive circle. He studied the layout of the camp as his mind worked. *Perhaps,* he thought, *there is a better way to do this.*

Far into the night, Tom and the other herders on the first shift shuffled back into camp, dragging their saddles. Without ceremony, they unspooled bedrolls or wrapped in blankets. Rather than dip into the water bucket, Tom walked out to the spring for a drink of fresh, cool water. Back at camp, the other drovers were already breathing regularly or snoring. He sat down on his blanket and was straining to pull off his boots when he heard the creak of the nearby wagon.

Polly slid off the back of the wagon and walked to where Tom sat. "Come with me. Bring your blanket."

The second boot came off and Tom tossed it aside. He gathered the blanket and followed the path the girl had taken past the wagon. She waited a few rods away, near a cedar tree on the lip of the ravine cut by the creek. She took the blanket from his hands, fluffed it upward and let it settle to ground.

Taking Tom by the hands, she pulled him close and kissed him, lowering herself to sit. He followed.

He caught his breath and whispered, "What're you doin' Polly?"

She answered with another kiss, squeezing Tom tight.

"Polly?"

"Hush, Tom." Another kiss.

Tom's breaths came fast and his heart pounded. "We ought not be doin' this."

"We are not doing anything wrong, Tom. Aren't you enjoying it?"

"Well, sure. But—"

Another deep kiss interrupted Tom, and he pulled away. "You've been talkin' to Sarah, ain't you."

Polly groaned and flopped down, lying on her back. "Don't you love me, Tom?"

He stretched out beside her and lay looking at the stars for a long moment. "Sure I do. You know I do." He felt Polly shudder beside him and propped himself on an elbow to look into her face. Tear-filled eyes glistened in the moonlight. "Polly! What's wrong?"

"Nothing." She sniffed. "It's just that we are stuck in this kind of limbo. We should be married but we are not. And I do not know when we ever will be."

Tom leaned over and brushed her cheek with his lips. She threaded fingers through the hair on the back of his head and guided him down to her mouth. They spoke no more. Lingering kisses and groping embraces eclipsed the passing of time.

Sometime later, beyond the reckon of either of them, Tom broke free and bolted upright.

"Did you hear that?"

"What, Tom? What is it?"

"Listen . . ."

It took no longer than the ride of a few miles back to Pinto for John Lee's plan to take shape. He gathered Moquetas and Big Bill, who led the Paiutes, and the officers who had convinced some of their militia members to march against the emigrants. Tossing fresh wood on the fire, he waited for it to flame up and, by its light, sketched out a map in the dirt.

The men discussed, debated, and deliberated over Lee's strategy. "Then we ain't waitin' for 'em to pull out?" one said. "I thought the plan was to hit 'em on Magotsu Creek down in the narrows there by the Santa Clara."

"That was the plan, all right," Lee said. "But we don't know how long they'll camp there in the Meadows. We sent riders to tell them to move along, but it doesn't look like they are going to. As it is, they're scattered around there by the spring, and their cow herd is off a ways in that bowl. From what we could see, they look to have a lot of riders keeping an eye on the cattle, so that separates their fightin' men somewhat. And if we catch them unawares, we can have the thing over and done with before they can mount any kind of a defense."

"I don't know, John," someone said. "I can see how we want that wagon train gone, but I don't see how killin' a bunch of 'em will help anything. Might make things worse. I say we put the fear of God into 'em and wait and see."

"Sure, we could do that," Lee said. "And we can get out our knittin' needles and crochet hooks and sit and gab like a bunch of women while we wait."

"I think Lee's right," a man said. "I say we get it over with."

"But we ain't had no orders from Haight nor Dame on it."

"That's right. If we was supposed to do this, the whole damn militia would be out here. Where the hell are they?"

"Who cares? We can't be worryin' about what anyone else is or ain't doin'. We come here to do a job and I say let's get to it!"

Moquetas had not commented, sitting quietly and studying Lee's map. He stood and raised a hand for silence. "This plan. I do not see anything but trouble in it for my people. Where are your people?" He squatted and poked the map here and there with a finger as he spoke. "Here and here. And over there, where there is no danger. Where you will not even engage with the Americans! And where are my people? Here!" He stabbed at the place on the map again and again with the finger. "Here, where the Americans could hit us by throwing stones! It is we who will be killed. We will not do it. This is your fight, yet we are the ones who will die."

Big Bill agreed. Lee wheedled and cajoled but could not convince the Paiutes until offering to send some of the Mormon militia members with them. He chose the men for the assignment, then told everyone to prepare.

Indians and Mormons alike darkened faces and applied war paint.

"You are imagining things, Tom. Come here."

"Maybe so." The kiss continued until Tom raised his head in response to Polly's gentle pressure on his chest. "What is it?"

"I was thinking. Back home, when folks live away from towns or where there is no preacher, or maybe only a circuit rider who comes around from time to time, and especially among the colored, well, when a couple intends to marry and there is not a way to have it solemnized or made official, they will declare themselves and jump a broomstick as a sign of their union."

Tom sat up. "Jump a broomstick?"

Polly giggled. "Yes."

"I ain't never heard of no such thing. Are you funnin' me?"

"No! I mean it! It's true. Folks have been doing it for years—long before anyone ever came to America. I have read about it in books besides hearing of it back home."

"So you're sayin' that's what we ought to do? Jump a broomstick?"

"Do you have a better idea?"

"I don't guess so. You sure it's legal?"

"I don't know, Tom. I know it is better than nothing. We can always make it official later—whenever we find a preacher or a judge."

Tom shrugged. "I reckon it's worth thinkin' about."

"Come here, then, while you are thinking." She reached behind his neck and pulled him down into another kiss. But Tom pulled away, sat up again, and cocked his head. "What is it, Tom?"

"Listen."

"I do not hear anything."

Tom looked around the camp and the meadow and the surrounding hills but saw nothing in the dim light of the emerging dawn. He shrugged and leaned into Polly's affectionate arms and stayed there for some time. The sky continued to lighten and Tom suggested they should get back to the wagon. People in the camp were rising, fires were lit, and the sounds of a new day drifted through the morning air.

"I suppose so." Polly sighed and sat up. "I had best see to fixing breakfast for the boys."

They stood and gathered the blanket and started for the wagons, hand in hand. Gunfire erupted and they ran.

Chapter Thirty-One

John Lee and several militia members crouched behind clusters of boulders on the hillside overlooking the wagon camp. A faint streak of gray crowned the mountains to the east. "What the hell is going on down there?" he whispered to the man beside him. "Why haven't they attacked?" He fussed and fidgeted as day broke and the camp slowly came to life. The plan had been for the Paiute and militia fighters assigned to assault the camp to attack before dawn, rushing the sleeping emigrants, catching them unawares and dispatching them before they could arm themselves and retaliate.

The attackers had spent hours in the night getting close to the camp, concealing themselves in the ravine and following the creek bed until they were but yards from the wagons. Once in position, they waited. And waited. Whether frozen by fear or uncertainty, or held back by leaders who wanted more visible targets, they delayed the charge and held their fire.

Impatient, Lee fumed. When, finally, a shot rang out, he cursed. "What the hell is that?"

The shot came not from the direction of the camp, but farther away, where the cattle grazed. With the report, and those that followed, Arkansawyers rolled out of their blankets, crawled out of bedrolls, and emerged from tents. Bullets cut through the camp from the gully as the men concealed there cut loose. A child fell, struck in the head. Captain Baker took a slug in the ribs. Lead ripped through Colonel Fancher's neck. More than a dozen emigrants fell in the first volley, half of them dead and others dying.

At the opposite end of the camp from the attack, a young couple ran away from the ravine, holding hands and dragging a blanket. Bullets tore at the ground around them and whistled through the air. Tom fell when struck in the thigh, but rose and, pulled along by Polly, limped into the camp.

Soon after, the drovers rushed in, whipping their horses through a fusillade of bullets. Skidding to a halt, the men swung to the ground and joined the emigrants squatting behind the wagons and whatever other cover they could find, returning fire. Three of the drovers' horses were shot dead and others wounded and all that were able stormed out of the camp. Men, and a few women wielding the arms of fallen husbands or brothers, took aim at fleeting targets in the ravine, and at sharpshooters concealed in the boulders and brush on the hillside beyond.

"What the hell's goin' on?" Howard said through heavy breathing.

Tom, propped against a wagon wheel, grimacing as Polly tended to his wound, said, "I don't know. They snuck up on us in the night—come up that gully—and just started shootin'. Indians, I guess."

Howard snorted. "Indians, hell. Some of 'em is, but there's white men out there, too. They stampeded the herd and shot one of us—I think it might've been Billy Brown they got."

The battle continued for some time. When the emigrants had opportunity to count the dead, they numbered sixteen—among them women and children. Nearly two dozen others carried wounds, some that would result in death. In the ravine, the two Paiute leaders, Big Bill and Moquetas, were wounded, each with bone-shattered legs. Others among their men were shot and killed. No one of the Mormon militia had died or been wounded. John Lee, flitting about from hide to hide on the hillside, had taken fire and his hat sported a bullet hole, and the sleeve of his jacket was ripped by a passing ball.

The firing faded as the attackers abandoned the assault and scurried back down the ravine, realizing their numbers were insufficient to overwhelm the camp. Lee delegated a few of the most accurate shooters to stay hidden on the hillside and keep the emigrants pinned down until further plans could be laid, then went off to rendezvous with the attackers.

In the wagon camp, all was chaos. With both leaders down, men argued, children cried, women rushed about caring for the wounded. Not until Jim Fancher, a nephew of the colonel, stepped up and assumed responsibility, did any sense of order prevail. Even then, some voiced disagreement with his orders. Most, however, pitched in, in fear for their lives.

Dodging the occasional bullet, the men dragged, humped, pushed, and pulled the wagons together and tightened the circle. With picks, shovels, pots, and pans they dug holes and rolled the outside wheels into them, lowering the wagon beds near to the ground. They heaped dirt into the gaps and in and under the wagons, and into the boxes to absorb bullets. Within the confines of the tight circle, others dug graves, trenches for cover, and slit trenches for toilets.

Jim Fancher gathered the leaders of the family groups. "How're you-all fixed for ammunition?"

The reports were not hopeful. Most of the emigrants had packed only enough for hunting on the trail with some allowance for skirmishes with Indians along the way, but had not anticipated a pitched battle. Others had wasted powder and ball in shooting contests and target shooting along the way.

"We'd be a hell of a lot better off if the colonel hadn't traded away all them rifles and powder and lead to them damn Indians back yonder," one man said. "I thought it was a damn foolish thing to do at the time."

Another said, "I ain't noticed your displeasure keepin' you and yours from eatin' the corn it got us."

The men squabbled for a time until Fancher quieted them. "The way I see it, other than powder and ball, our biggest problem is water. That spring ain't a hundred yards away, and the creek a few rods, but long as them shooters is up there on that hill, that water might as well be miles away."

"Way I see it," someone suggested, "we ain't got no choice but to hold out till dark and send parties out with buckets to fetch in water."

Another man pointed out that would only work if the Indians did not come back, or post guards at the spring.

"Be that as it may," Fancher said, "I don't see there's any other way. We'll go in teams—an armed man and a man haulin' buckets." He asked Abe Baker about the herd.

"Far as I know, there ain't no herd no more. They shot Billy Brown and stampeded the cows. Wasn't anything we could do but get out of the way. Other'n Brown, we all got back. He's layin' out there dead, far as I know."

"Some of you-all that was out there said there was white men in amongst the Indians. That so?"

"Damn right. Unless these Paiutes around here has got yellow hair. I saw one like that. And there was others with light hair and clothes that didn't look too Indian. All their faces was painted or smeared with dirt, but some of 'em looked mighty pale underneath."

A man sniffed. "Sounds like if you-all had paid more attention to the cows and not so much to them that was drivin' 'em off we'd have beef to eat. As it is, it's goin' to be rabbits and lizards—if we can catch 'em."

"Well, we weren't out there," Fancher said. "Far as I know, the drovers did what they could. And they didn't do no worse out there than what we done here. We lost a lot of good men—

men we'll need if the Indians—or Mormons, or whoever the hell they are—come back."

"I don't think there's any 'if' to it," someone said. "You think they're goin' to let us go after what they done? They'll be back, all right."

"I fear you're right," Fancher said. "There ain't nothin' we can do about it but be ready for 'em. I hope to hell it'll be enough."

Conditions were no less chaotic at the militia camp at Pinto. The Paiutes were near mutiny, angered at the death of some of their fighters, the wounding of Moquetas and Big Bill and several others, and that a fight the Mormons assured them would be easy turned out to be anything but.

That the attack on the camp had been delayed, and failed because of it, angered John Lee. The dispatch of the emigrants had turned into quicksand, and he knew not how to extract himself, or the Saints as a whole, come to that, from the mire.

Some of the Paiutes had already left for home, driving cattle ahead of them. Others wanted to do the same. Lee apportioned the herd as best he could, saving back a few head for camp meat, and a share of the herd to take back to Cedar City. He called out two militiamen who had come out from Cedar City and sent them back to town with a message for Haight, telling of the failure of the attack and of the situation at hand, and a request for further instructions or, better still, official orders from the militia and reinforcements. Along the way, the messengers stopped at a spring to rest and water their horses.

"Who the hell is that?" one said, eying the approach of two mounted men driving some ten head of cattle.

The drovers reined up at the same time. "Who the hell is that?" Skeets said.

"Don't know," Charlie said.

Skeets thought for a minute. "I guess there ain't nothin' to do but go find out."

They pushed the cattle ahead to the springs and stood by as they drank. The messengers rode up to them. "Good day," one said.

"Same to you-all," Skeets said with a nod.

"Those your critters?"

"Yeah. They wandered off from the herd and we come back to find 'em."

"Oh? And which herd would that be?"

"Not that it's any of you-all's business, but these cows, most of 'em, belongs to Captain Baker of Carroll County, Arkansas, soon to be of California. The rest of 'em, and that there bull, belongs to Colonel Fancher, bound for California from Benton County, Arkansas. Not that it's any of my business, but what are you-all doin' out here?"

"We're ridin' in to Cedar City. Got some business there."

The Mormon who had not spoken turned to Charlie, who also had not spoken. "Say, I see you got a tin cup tied on to your saddle there. Mind if I have the borrow of it? I'd like to step down and get me a drink."

"Sure," Charlie said.

He turned in the saddle and reached back to untie the saddle string. Before he could loosen the knot, his head burst in a red fog as a bullet from the man's pistol punched a hole in one side and blew a chunk out of the other.

The report of the pistol upset the horses, and their pitching and milling saved Skeets. Before the riders could bring arms to bear on him, he put the spurs to his horse and raced away, bullets buzzing past him as he went.

"Shit!" one of the Mormons said. "That fixes it! Them Arkansawyers'll sure as hell know we're in on it now. We had best get on and let Haight know."

Bullets would fly again as Skeets neared the camp in the

Meadows and the sharpshooters unleashed on him, but he would run the gantlet without injury.

The already bad news in Cedar City became worse with word of the shooting at the springs. It had Isaac Haight in a swivet, and turned Cedar City as chaotic as the emigrant wagon camp at Mountain Meadows and the militia bivouac at Pinto. Haight called meetings and councils to seek advice. Some demanded the fighting stop and the emigrants be allowed to go their way. Others advised against it, as the emigrants would carry word of the attack with them, further enflaming dislike of the Mormons and providing fodder for action against them. The lack of consensus, to Haight's way of thinking, leaned toward other opinions voiced in the discussions: finish the job—wipe out the emigrants and lay the blame on the Paiutes.

Over the next few days, as Mormon leaders waffled over how to proceed, more people died at Mountain Meadows. The sharpshooters kept up fire at any emigrant who ventured out of the camp. Bands of Paiutes and Mormons attempted to storm the wagons from time to time, losing blood of their own and drawing blood among the emigrants. The camp still lacked water, and soon firewood became scarce. Children were hungry. There was food, but with no water and no fires, cooking was all but impossible.

As casualties piled up with each attack, the Paiutes grew increasingly aggravated at the Mormons. Some left in anger, others arrived to demand a share of future spoils, but wanted no part in the fighting. Word of the siege at the Meadows spread from village to village as Paiute messengers came and went, their reports making their way from Mormon town to town.

Mormons also came and went, carrying messages of their own. Word reached militia commander Bill Dame in Parowan, but the reports were unofficial and did not come through militia channels, so he did not know how accurate they were or how to interpret them.

Haight decided things could only get worse if left to linger, so he, with a few other religious, civic, and military leaders—often the same people—from Cedar City drove north to Parowan to seek an audience with the militia commander.

Dame convened a council with militia leaders from communities under his command and listened to reports of the bad-and-getting-worse conditions at Mountain Meadows. As was the case in Cedar City, some favored doing nothing other than recalling the militia fighters, sending the Indians home, and simply letting the emigrants go their way. Some lobbied for a show of coming to the aid of the wagon train and laying blame for the attacks on the Paiutes. Still others could see no way out other than exterminating the Arkansawyers one and all.

It came to a vote. The resolution that passed ordered a militia company from Parowan to march to the Meadows, call the Indians off, help the emigrants gather what was left of their stock, and let them leave the territory in peace.

The decision did not sit well with Haight. Among those present, he believed that he alone understood the situation, and could foresee the result of the order. As the council disbanded and the members went their way or arranged accommodations at the Dame household or elsewhere in the town, he buttonholed the militia commander and demanded a private audience.

"Brother Haight, we have acted. The decision has been made."

"I know that, Colonel Dame. But, please, there are things you should know. Things I did not see fit to relate to the council. Things I will reveal to you, and you alone, in private."

Dame relented, and led Haight away from the house and into the barnyard where the men found seats on a stack of cedar posts.

"We can't let them go, Bill."

"But we have already determined to do so."

"Damn it all, Colonel, listen to me." Haight outlined the now familiar litany of complaints against the emigrants and their supposed sins against the Saints of Cedar City. He reminded Dame of the approaching army, and the possibility of the emigrants bearing testimony against the Mormons, should they be released.

Dame listened to it all, and said the council had weighed all that in making the decision.

"Fine, Bill. Fine. But those lily-livered council members do not know what those evil Gentiles out there on the Meadows know."

"Oh? And what do they know?"

"They know it wasn't just Indians that attacked them. They know white men were involved. Not only at the Meadows. One of our men shot down one of theirs at a watering hole. There were two herders from the wagon train sent out to bring in lost stock—they were sent out before the attack, see. They were coming back with a few cows when they met two of our men at the watering hole—two men I sent out to the Meadows to see what the hell was going on. They were on their way back to report. They shot one of those boys down. The other one got away."

Dame sighed and dropped his head into his hands. After a time, he shook his head, then raised it to stare at Haight in the moonlight. He sighed again. "And what about the attack on the wagons—you said the emigrants knew white men were involved. How?"

Haight admitted that he did not know that for sure, but knew from reports that the disguises of some militia members were not all that convincing. Despite orders to overrun the camp before dawn, the attackers had waited till daylight, and had likely been seen by the emigrants. Some of the snipers shooting from the hillside were not disguised at all, and may have been seen from a distance as they shifted positions seeking a better line of fire. And John Lee was fairly sure he had been seen by whoever fired the bullets that had pierced his clothing, if not by others as well.

"So you see, Colonel, it ain't as simple as just calling off the Indians and waving goodbye to the emigrants. If you think we're in trouble with the American government now, what do you think will happen when these damn heathen Gentiles tell them the Mormons are murdering emigrants on the road, and have the wounds to prove it? There won't a one of us be safe, not from Brigham Young on down."

Dame sat for long minutes, waiting for an answer to come to him. When it did not, he decided the decision, bad as it may be, had already been made by Isaac Haight.

On the ride home to Cedar City in the dark, Haight told the men with him that Colonel William Dame, commander of the militia, had given the order to call up the troops and destroy the emigrant company.

CHAPTER THIRTY-TWO

Tom slouched, his back resting against a wagon wheel. Polly sat beside him, mopping the sweat beading his forehead with an already damp handkerchief. Dried blood stiffened his pants leg, the fabric gaping open where slit to dress the wound.

"How do you feel, Tom?"

His head lolled as he turned to look at her. "I'm all right. That bullet didn't do nothin' but dig a little ditch in my leg. Ain't nothin' broke."

"But you are feverish. And I fear the wound is getting infected."

"Don't worry about it. Once we get some water to clean it good, it'll be fine."

"If ever we get water," Polly said with a sigh.

"No need to worry about that, either. Sooner or later, folks back in those towns will hear what's happened to us and come out to help us fight off these Indians."

A tear cut a trail through the dust on Polly's face. "But Tom, they are saying that some of those attacking us are white men. They must have come from the towns we have passed through—where else could they come from?"

Tom swallowed hard, his dry throat straining at the effort. "I don't know, Polly. But it can't be them. They're stirred up just now, but they're good folks. Good church-goin' folks."

"I don't know either, Tom. I just don't know. But I fear something bad is going to happen."

Lifting an arm, Tom wrapped it around her and pulled her close. "Like I said, don't worry." He pulled her closer. "I'll tell you what. When help comes, we'll go on back to Cedar City and I'll find a judge or someone to marry us. If that don't happen, we'll jump that broomstick you was talkin' about. I reckon I could do that, even with this bum leg of mine."

My Tom is in a bad way. He has been shot in the leg by Indians who attacked our camp and I fear it is infected. He is burning up with fever but is trying to be brave. We have been trapped here for three days without water except what little we can sneak into the camp at night but the Indians post guards to keep us from getting even that.

Tom says I should not worry as the Mormons will rescue us but many here are saying that there are white men dressed as Indians who are fighting us, at least some of them. It is my fear that if that is so then it is the very Mormons Tom expects to save us who are killing us.

Many from our company are dead and buried right here in the camp as we can not bury them elsewhere and the stink is awful. My friend Sarah is among them. There is also the constant smell of rotten blood and putrefying flesh of those who are dying but not yet dead. And of course the flies are bothersome. Both to the wounded and those of us so far untouched by the bullets of our attackers, whoever they are.

If as Tom hopes we are rescued he promises to take me back to a town and find someone in authority to declare us man and wife. But I have come to believe even more what I have written before—that we are as the star crossed lovers in the story and our union is not to be.

★ ★ ★ ★ ★

The militia assembled in the Cedar City town square. They were a disparate assemblage, from boys on the verge of manhood to men of long years. Firearms were equally diverse: muskets and rifles, carbines and shotguns. Despite being drilled in obedience by militia officers and religious leaders alike, not all had responded to the call to arms. Some found pressing business out of town, others hid out in barns and corn cribs and root cellars. Most who reported for duty knew what they were about, but not all. One man arrived armed with nothing more than a shovel.

Major Isaac Haight pulled him out of the line of men formed in a hollow square. "What the hell are you about? Do you intend to fight with that spade?"

The man stammered and stuttered, shuffled and scuffed. "But President Haight . . . we . . . we was told we was goin' out to the Meadows to bury the dead . . ."

"You damn fool! We cannot bury the dead until first we make them dead. Take that damn shovel and go home."

Haight stepped into the center of the square to address the troops. Once again, he rehearsed his now-familiar diatribe against the emigrants, their threats and bad behavior in the towns, the dangerous state of affairs in a territory under attack by the United States Army, and the possibility—certainty, to his way of thinking—that the Arkansawyers would somehow aid and assist the government soldiers in destroying the Saints.

"Those wicked, abominable evildoers are even now still in our midst—forted up at Mountain Meadows, awaiting their rendezvous with the army. Some of your brethren, in aid of the Paiutes hereabouts, have tried thrice to overrun their camp. But the Gentiles, armed with their Kentucky rifles, are better fighters than anyone imagined and have thus far repelled the attacks. This cannot be allowed to stand.

"John Lee is in command at the Meadows. Bishop Klingensmith and John Higbee will lead you as officers in the militia. They and Major Lee will devise a scheme to lay waste to the enemy and send them one and all to the grave, and on to the eternity in hell they so richly deserve!"

Haight's oratory raised the temperature of the blood of some. The air went out of others, but dutifulness and deference to authority kept most of them in line. One old man stepped out of the ranks and approached his commanding officer with pointed finger, staying the waggling digit mere inches from the major's face. "You can go to hell your own self, Isaac Haight! I'll be damned if I'll go out there and do your dirty work!" No one followed the old man when he broke through the ranks to go home, but some with similar sentiments slipped away as the militia set out for Mountain Meadows and the emigrants waiting there.

Higbee carried with him orders from militia commanders Dame and Haight that the emigrant company was to be "decoyed out and destroyed with the exception of small children too young to tell tales."

Friday morning, the eleventh day of September in the year of our Lord eighteen and fifty-seven, dawned clear and warm. The disheartened Arkansawyers lazed about in the confines of the circled wagons, awaiting whatever change the day would bring.

"Look sharp!" a sentry hollered. "There's somethin' happenin' out yonder!"

The armed men took up positions and leveled rifles at a few mounted men with a large, disordered group of men afoot following them, and two wagons drawn by teams of horses bringing up the rear.

"I make it to be near fifty of 'em," the sentry said. "Who are they? And what the hell do they want?"

"Can't say," Jim Fancher said. "Hold your fire till we find out."

The men stopped at the edge of the effective firing range of the emigrants' long rifles and stood watching the wagon camp. One of the mounted men hoisted a white banner affixed to the barrel of his rifle.

"What do you think, Jim?" someone said.

"Damned if I know. I guess they want to talk, whoever they are."

"What should we do?"

Fancher stepped back and addressed the camp. "I'm goin' out there to see who it is and what they want. You-all stay steady. If anything untoward happens, shoot the sonsabitches."

Finding a hank of white cloth, Fancher affixed it to a stick, climbed through the barricade and walked out. The mounted man with the flag rode forward to meet him.

John Higbee reined up his horse and studied the young man standing before him. "Who might you be?"

"Jim Fancher."

"Fancher, you say? Where's the old man called Fancher?"

"Colonel Fancher. Alexander. He's dead. Our other wagon master, John Baker, might as well be. Took a bullet to the ribs. Who are you-all?"

"We come out from Cedar City. Heard word that you folks was in trouble out here and called up the militia to come to your aid." Haight reined his horse around to stand sideways and pointed with his chin toward the militia troops. "You see that man on the gray horse?"

Fancher nodded.

"That man is John Lee. He's a militia officer. He's also something of an Indian agent. Knows most of the Paiutes around here, and they know him. And trust him. He's got the Paiutes settled down some, and moved them out of the way."

He nodded toward the south. "They're yonder, down the creek a ways. They're none too happy about it, but they've agreed to hold off attackin' you anymore. For now."

Fancher waited for more.

"John Lee wants to come in and talk to you. Tell you what he's worked out with the Paiutes to save your skins."

Fancher thought for a moment then agreed to listen to what Lee had to say. "Send him on. I'll wait for him inside the wagon camp. Just in case." He turned and walked back through the barricade and ordered the men to shovel the dirt away from one of the wagons and shift it out of the way to allow entry into the camp.

"You're a fool, Fancher," Howard said.

"What do you mean?"

"That feller you was talkin' to out there. He's that sonofabitch lawman what tried to arrest me back in that town."

"So?"

"So, you saw the way them Mormons in that town treated us."

"Well, Howard, I can't see as there's anything else we can do but hear what he has to say."

"I say we start shootin' and don't stop till every one of 'em is dead."

Others in the camp disagreed, believing that the Mormons were the only hope of survival they had. Some sided with Howard, supposing that some of the men out there may have been among those aiding the Indians in their attacks on the wagon camp. One man swore up and down that the man on the gray horse—the one Higbee had identified as John Lee—had been seen, by himself and by others, around the Meadows since the first attack.

In the end, the emigrants agreed to listen to what Lee had to say, and voiced their inclination to accept whatever relief he had to offer.

Tom, leaning for support against Polly, his arm around her shoulder and hers around his waist, leaned down to whisper. "See, Polly! I said they wouldn't leave us out here to die. I told you they'd come for us."

Polly did not answer. Tom wondered if joy, or maybe relief, prompted her tears. It was neither.

A steady stream of emigrants flowed from the camp to the creek, hauling back bucket after bucket of water, young and old alike gulping down the sustenance and refreshment denied them for days. By the time Lee arrived at the camp, bringing the two Mormon wagons with him, all the emigrants had drunk, and gathered round to hear what he had to say.

He told them he had persuaded the Paiutes to give up the fight for now, but they were not pacified and waited nearby to renew their attacks if the emigrants resisted their demands or failed to follow Lee's directives.

First, the emigrants must give up their arms and ammunition.

Second, they must abandon their wagons and worldly goods to repay the Paiutes for the deaths of their people killed in the fighting.

Third, they must follow the Mormons out of the Meadows back to Cedar City, and promise to leave the Paiute homelands forever. The women and children would go first, the men later.

Howard was the first to react. "Bullshit! I ain't doin' none of that. I ain't got but a pistol, but they damn sure ain't gettin' it. And I sure as hell ain't goin' back to that town!"

"Shut up, Howard," Abe Baker said. "You ain't got no say in the matter."

"Like hell I don't! What are you, Abe, some kind of a damn coward? Them Indians killed your old man—leastways he's as good as dead. And you, Fancher! They killed the colonel. I say we stay here and fight. If the goddamn Mormons won't help us, we'll fight them, too!"

John Lee looked on but said nothing, believing it best to let the emigrants come to their own realization that they had no choice but to do as he said. It took some time, and considerable argument, before those who did not agree with the course of action before them succumbed to the inevitable—the inevitable, in their eyes if not those of others, being certain death.

Downhearted and desultory, the Arkansawyer men carried their arms to the lead wagon and dumped them in the bed. Lee oversaw their concealment under blankets gathered from the camp. The wounded, including the unconscious Captain Baker, barely clinging to life, were laid out in the wagons. Small children, some only infants, filled the remaining space in the wagons. Some stood at the sideboards, arms reaching out for the people abandoning them, their crying further upsetting the parents and brothers and sisters who could do nothing to comfort the children, or themselves.

The wagons pulled out, the women and older children ordered to follow.

"Tom, I cannot leave you. Tom!" Polly sobbed, clinging to Tom, her face pressed to his chest, her tears dampening his shirtfront.

He held her tight, willing to let her go with his words but not his body. "You got to go, Polly. You got to."

"I can't. I won't."

Tom pressed the palms of his hands to her waist and pushed her away with gentle pressure. "C'mon, Polly. They're goin'. You got to go with them. Don't worry. I'll catch you up. And when we get to Cedar City, we'll get married, just like I promised."

Her face washed with tears, Polly pulled Tom's head down and pressed her lips to his. She clung to him, holding the kiss, until John Lee pulled her away.

"Miss—you have to go now." They caught up to the wagons, Polly taking her place among the walking women and children. She did not look back. Lee untied his horse from the back of the lead wagon and mounted up to ride between the wagons. Some of the militiamen followed the wagons but most stayed behind to escort the men.

The women and children were well out of sight when the Mormons ordered the emigrant men out of the camp to walk in single file. As they went, an armed militiaman fell in step beside each Arkansawyer.

Though the pace of the march was slow, Tom struggled to keep up, limping along on his wounded leg. He turned to his escort, a young man not much older than he was. His face was pale and the white-knuckled hands grasping the rifle trembled.

"How're you doin'?"

"Shut up. I ain't talkin' to no damn Gentile."

"But I ain't. I'm a Mormon, just like you."

The man looked at him.

"It's true. I come from up in Springville. My father—stepfather, anyway—is the bishop up there."

The man looked away. "Don't matter. You've thrown in with these wicked sonsabitches so you might as well be one of them. You made your bed and now you're goin' to lay in it."

Up ahead, Polly walked along, lifting the hem of her dress clear of the dust and dirt. She wondered why they traveled through the brush rather than following the nearby road. She still felt, or imagined, the imprint of Tom's kiss on her lips.

Floating on the gentle breeze wafting out of the meadow came the sound of gunfire as the men fell, shot down by their escorts.

She heard war whoops as Indians stormed out of the brush, the bedlam snarling with the savage yells of the Mormon guards as they fell upon the screaming women and children.

And then she heard no more.

AUTHOR'S NOTE

The murder of some 120 innocent men, women, and children at Mountain Meadows in Utah Territory on September 11, 1857, is a fact of history. While based on that tragedy and events leading up to it, *With a Kiss I Die* is fiction. It includes the names and actions of many real people, but those are used fictionally and the acts of some are sometimes assigned to other characters, whether historical or imagined. Many details of known history are altered or left out altogether for purposes of simplicity and storytelling.

While there were investigations, court trials, and the eventual execution of John D. Lee, retribution for the massacre was delayed, drawn out, incomplete, and insufficient. For the better part of a century, the massacre was covered up and concealed from Utah history. If mentioned at all, it was in whispers. The first meaningful light was shed on the crime with the release in 1950 of *The Mountain Meadows Massacre* by Juanita Brooks. Much has been written on the subject since. To my mind, *Blood of the Prophets: Brigham Young and the Mountain Meadows Massacre* by Will Bagley (University of Oklahoma Press, 2002), and *Massacre at Mountain Meadows* by Ronald W. Walker, Richard E. Turley, Jr., and Glen M. Leonard (Oxford University Press, 2008) are the most reliably researched and well written. Both of those books were invaluable resources in the writing of this novel. Casual discussions over the years about the massacre with my friends Will Bagley and Richard Turley also colored my understanding. But deficiencies in telling the story are mine.

The inspiration for *With a Kiss I Die* goes back many years. At a Western Writers of America Convention in Helena, Montana, the already legendary Western author Dusty Richards approached me, a writer of comparably little experience, with an idea to tell a story of a young couple, one an Arkansas emigrant and the other a Mormon settler, who fall in love and find themselves at Mountain Meadows on the fateful day of the massacre where, as Dusty put it, we would "drop the curtain." He would tell the Arkansas story and I would write the Mormon perspective and we would have a book.

Well, Dusty Richards always had more ideas than he had time, and the project never got off the ground. When we lost Dusty to a car accident in 2018, I toyed with the idea of writing both sides of the book myself. After much thought and considerable research, the story more or less told itself. *With a Kiss I Die* is the result.

ABOUT THE AUTHOR

Winner of four Western Writers of America Spur Awards and a Spur Award finalist on six other occasions, and winner of two Western Fictioneers Peacemaker Awards, **Rod Miller** writes fiction, poetry, and history about the American West.

A lifelong Westerner raised in a cowboy family, Miller is a former rodeo contestant, worked in radio and television production, and is a retired advertising agency copywriter and creative director.

Miller's award-winning poetry and short stories have appeared in numerous anthologies, and several magazines have carried his byline.

Find the author online at writerRodMiller.com, writerRodMiller.blogspot.com, and RawhideRobinson.com.

The employees of Five Star Publishing hope you have enjoyed this book.

Our Five Star novels explore little-known chapters from America's history, stories told from unique perspectives that will entertain a broad range of readers.

Other Five Star books are available at your local library, bookstore, all major book distributors, and directly from Five Star/Gale.

Connect with Five Star Publishing

Website:
gale.com/five-star

Facebook:
facebook.com/FiveStarCengage

Twitter:
twitter.com/FiveStarCengage

Email:
FiveStar@cengage.com

For information about titles and placing orders:
(800) 223-1244
gale.orders@cengage.com

To share your comments, write to us:
Five Star Publishing
Attn: Publisher
10 Water St., Suite 310
Waterville, ME 04901